THE CASTLE — DIARY OF A LOST WOMAN

*A modern gothic story of
myth and misadventure*

R A Wodecki

RAW Books (Rosalie A. Wodecki)

For Victor.

*In memory of those we lost. And for those that
live, especially the ones with a love of words.*

"I passed a night of unmingled wretchedness."

MARY WOLLSTONECRAFT SHELLEY,
FRANKENSTEIN

CONTENTS

CHAPTER ONE

The castle loomed overhead.

Anna stood on a road at the foot of the mountain. Looking up, she could only see mountain and castle. The castle soared above her and erupted out of the earth, a mass of spires, turrets and looming, crumbling walls. Tendrils of ancient stone cascaded down every crevice.

'I have to say, this seems like a bad idea.'

Anna rolled her eyes and said, 'It was your idea to come with me. This is about my family, not yours'.

'It might be about the Harker family, but it's my family's country. I wasn't about to let you go off alone on a strange quest to the middle of Transylvania,' said Catalina.

'Oh, come on. You know it's not called that anymore. You're just being a jerk,' said Anna.

'Romania, then. *Romania* sounded like a wonderful idea. Bucharest is beautiful and so are the people. But this place? There's nothing here. Not even a decent restaurant.'

'We'll find one later. Promise.'

'It will need to be a good one,' said Catalina.

'Since it's *your* family's country, I thought you'd be a bit more keen to be here. Doesn't the thought of being here excite you? I thought you had respect for tradition and all that.'

'Tradition, yes. Remote, barren mountains not quite so much.'

'You just don't trust anyone do you? There's a serious character flaw in you.' Anna looked Catalina up and down. She had to look a long way up. 'Is it the blonde hair? Does the bleach affect your brain?'

Grinning, Catalina punched Anna on the arm. 'Seriously, Anna. You can't tell me you believed that story. I give it one day, two at most, before they're asking you for money.'

Rubbing her arm, Anna said, 'They can ask all they want. After paying for the flight here, I don't have much left. I had to know. The curiosity would have killed me. I always thought the family name was no more than a silly story'.

'I still think it is.'

'But how cool would it be if it were true?'

'Oh, yes. *My Great-great-great Grandpappa was a vampire hunter you know.*' Catalina snorted. 'You do realise vampires aren't real.'

Anna kicked some pebbles along the ground. 'Oh, come on. You know I don't believe that. That doesn't mean that *he* didn't believe it.'

'And if turns out not to be true?'

'At least we came. We've been here and seen it,' said Anna. 'It'll be a good story to tell dad later.'

'Seen what? This? You travelled halfway

around the world to see this?' Catalina gestured at the valley of rubble and decaying castle above her. 'What a place.' As she spoke, lightning cracked overhead. Moments later the thunder boomed, drowning out her voice.

Anna pulled her jacket tight around her shoulders. 'Just remember. It was your choice to come with me. Your choice. That's all I'm saying.'

'My choice, yes. But it's your sense of adventure that got us here.' Catalina said, 'All I can promise is to try and make the best of it'.

Anna smiled. 'That right there? That's why I brought you. Your uncontrolled enthusiasm.'

Catalina smiled back. 'Well, then, my friend,' she said as she pointed, 'How do we get up there?'

Both women stared up at the castle again. It didn't merely dominate the sky; it was the sky. Clouds obscured the upper reaches, drifting in and out of the near-ruined crenellations.

Rolling down the slope, rivulets of bricks and mortar merged with the countryside. It was impossible to see where the castle stopped and the mountain started. It was a towering wreck, carving its way slowly out of the earth. It seemed to stretch as wide as it did high. Before they had come to the foot of the valley, the castle had looked like a curious old relic in the distance. Now it was their whole world.

Anna felt that if she looked behind her she would no longer see the beautiful, rolling hills they had been walking along. She turned back, half expecting to see yet more castle, and was relieved to still see a long, winding path. It disappeared into the gap at the entrance to the valley, but it was still there. Feeling a little embarrassed, Anna turned to Catalina and said, 'Doesn't exactly look inviting, does it'.

'I don't think I will live long enough to discover the right words to describe how this place looks. I'm sure, though, that 'inviting 'won't be one of them.'

Anna checked her phone. 'Still no signal,' she said, shoving it back in her jacket pocket. 'You?'

'No. I thought I saw a blip an hour or so ago, but it was only a mixture of hope and imagination. I've turned it off.' She shrugged. 'Might as well save the battery.'

Anna looked up at the valley of sharp, jagged features. 'Maybe we should we go back.'

Catalina groaned. 'It took us so long to walk here from the village. We may as well keep going.'

'I can't believe there weren't any buses. It's like we've travelled back in time,' said Anna.

'Yes, a good hundred years or so. I can still see the look on the taxi driver's face when we asked him to bring us here.'

'I know. It was like we'd offered to buy his first born. Anyway, that doesn't change anything. What's your preference? A long hike up or a long walk back?' said Anna.

'Up. If worst comes to worst, we can camp out for the night. Turning back seems—' Catalina cut herself short.

'Appealing?' Anna said, staring at black crevices, and dark and lengthening shadows.

Catalina leaned against a tall, sharp, jagged rock and sighed. 'A little, yes.'

'Let's push on. I know it got dark early, but there's a lot of moonlight about. At least we can see where we're going. 'As Anna spoke, rolling, black clouds covered over the harvest moon. 'Oh, very funny.' She could still see Catalina, but only just. 'The email did say someone would meet us here. I thought they meant down here, but maybe it's up at the castle.'

Catalina said, 'If it's down here, I wish they would make their presence known'.

'Can I help you?' came a voice out of the darkness.

Anna yelped and both women jolted at the sound. Catalina tripped over backwards, landing on top of her backpack. The contents clattered as they fell out.

A cold breath pricked the skin on the back of Anna's neck.

A torch flared in the darkness and, this time, both women screamed.

The face that appeared before Anna was aged, scarred and bent with time. The pockmarks and scars were made worse by the flickering shadows of the torchlight. Tendons stood out in his neck and the scars traversed over and down towards his shoulders.

'We await you, Mistress. I apologise for my lateness. I was expecting only one. I am Igor. At your service.'

Anna, off-balance, managed to pull herself together enough to say, 'Uh, yes. Sorry, I guess that's my fault. I should've let you know. This is my friend, Catalina Dalca.'

'Your name is Igor? *'Igor?'* Catalina's face was a mixture of shock and stunned amusement.

Igor ignored Catalina's question and said, 'You are Romanian?'

'Sort of, but not exactly,' said Catalina. 'My family came from here a couple of generations ago.'

'Victima sau lider, doamna mea ...?' said Igor, bowing.

'Sorry, I'm not sure I quite understood you,' said Catalina. 'I don't really know enough words. I'm a little rusty.'

Igor stared at Catalina for a moment, then looked away, seeming to dismiss her. He looked at Anna, his gaze intense and studious. 'Mistress Harker, you do not have many belongings for such a long stay.'

'We're staying one night. Two at the most. We've got accommodation down in the village and our friends are expecting us back first thing in the morning.'

'I see' said Igor.

'I'm sorry,' said Anna. 'We'll definitely try and make a second trip up while we're here.'

'No need.' He glanced over at Catalina and said

to Anna 'Mistress Harker, we only have transport for you'. As he spoke, a horse moved into the torchlight, whinnying as it came close to the torch's flames. 'We will need to return for your friend. I was expecting one.'

'You are not splitting us up,' said Catalina.

'No way, Igor. Together or not at all.'

'Of course,' he said. 'We shall walk.'

The lightning bolt that struck lit up the entire sky, the mountainous castle and rolling hills below. The horse reared, turned and bolted.

'Follow me.'

Tired and faced with a choice of bad or worse, Anna and Catalina did as they were told. And followed.

As Igor walked on ahead, Anna thought she heard him say once more, 'I was expecting only one.'

✳ ✳ ✳

Halfway up the mountain, the lightning had started again. It lit the night sky above and the valley below. The rolling, green hills were still visible, but only in the distance. Most of the view was filled with long fingers of slate and tumbling piles of boulders and rubble.

Anna and Catalina stood and watched the lightning play over the ancient scenery below. Anna was grateful for the light show as it had given them a chance to rest. They were both out of breath and struggling to keep their footing.

'I'm not saying it's worth the view, but it's a close thing,'said Anna.

In the darkness, almost unseen to Anna, Catalina nodded.

'I wish it was daytime. The scenery must be unbelievable. This is more like watching a strobe light show.'

Another bolt lit up the valley, illuminating a series of half-dissolved shapes in the limestone mountainside. The cavities of dark rock seemed to shimmer in its wake.

'We'll see it on the way back in the morning, at least,'said Catalina.

'I'm not sure we'll even make it to the top before morning,' said Anna.

'Mistress, we must carry on.'

Anna shivered. She'd sort of forgotten Igor was there. All the way up, Anna could hear Catalina's breathing and her weary steps. She could hear nothing from Igor.

She sighed and started to climb again.

❊ ❊ ❊

Anna and Catalina were perched on the edge of an uncomfortable rock. Anna leaned against Catalina for support, and Catalina leaned back. Even in the darkness, the rock seemed to have its own light. As Anna tilted her head back and forth, the surface of the rock glittered.

'Down there, this looked like a long way. I

had no idea. It's not a long way. It's a seriously ridiculously bloody long way. What were we thinking?'

'I'm not sure thinking came into it, on either side of this little party,' said Catalina.

'Can't argue with you there.' Anna threw a small stone and listened to it tumble down the valley. 'How long do you think we've been climbing?'

'Too long.'

'I meant in hours. I've completely lost track of time. 'As she spoke, Anna looked towards the sky, seeking the stars. There were none in sight. One part of the sky was occluded by the decrepit castle. The rest of the sky was full of rolling clouds, backlit by the moon; a thousand shades of grey. The lightning had eased off and a miserable drizzle had taken its place. What had already been a treacherous and exhausting climb had become next to impossible.

'Hours, fearless leader? It feels more like days.' Catalina looked up at the castle. 'It does seem to be getting a little closer.'

Anna stood up and offered Catalina her hand. 'Let's go.'

And they climbed.

* * *

The castle filled the sky.

Anna was too tired to take in the sheer size of the ruins and the castle. All she knew was that they were almost there. She shook her head. She was pretty sure she'd had the exact same thought more than an hour ago.

Both women had long since stopped watching the view. The sky, the castle and the valley below had vanished from Anna's mind. After each step her only thought was for the next one.

CHAPTER TWO

At last they stood before the castle doors.

Anna had seen pictures of castles before, but this was something else. It loomed and it had presence. It looked fully capable of consuming her.

As they arrived, Igor had disappeared again. Anna hadn't noticed him leave, but it wouldn't have been hard. Everything ached. Her legs, her back. The only thing keeping her eyes open was a trembling low-level fear. Catalina looked about as bad as she felt.

'Where did Igor go?' said Catalina, leaning against the stone walls of the castle.

'I don't know. Maybe he's just the collector.'

'Not a good choice of words, Anna.'

'Sorry. You know what I mean. Maybe there's a butler behind those doors.'

'Doors? Again, your vocabulary falls short'.

'Portals of doom?' Anna tried to laugh. It started as a joke, but her words were swallowed up by the presence of the doors. It was like calling into a dense forest.

Both women looked up at the entrance. Up, and up. Anna wasn't even sure the doors were made of wood. They seemed too alive for that. The whorls and knots were intricate and detailed. They appeared to shift under her gaze. As she stared, the doors began to open, the heavy iron hinges creaking and protesting.

Without thinking, Anna sought out Catalina's hand and they both began to back away. As they were about to turn and run, the doors swung inwards and Igor said, '*Vă rog.* Please. Mistress, come in'.

'What? How did you …?' asked Anna.

'Mistress, yes?'

Anna's hand trembled. She couldn't tell if the shaking was coming from her hand or from Catalina's. She looked at her friend; her face seemed to mirror her own thoughts. They had made it all the way up here and now all she wanted to do was run. It was a long way back, but it was all downhill. Anna stepped back, stumbling at the edge of the castle's foreground.

Igor beckoned her forward. 'Mistress.'

'I think we're having a change of plans, Igor.'

Igor looked confused and said, 'But the storm, Mistress. It does not worry you?'

The storm had eased as they approached the castle, but as Anna turned to look over her shoulder, the sky broke open and great sheets of rain thundered down. As the rain came roaring in, all Anna could do was stare.

'I have never, ever seen rain like that,' said Catalina.

'Mistress?'

Anna hesitated. She didn't know what to do, but she knew that nothing felt right. Her heart beat louder than the thundering rain behind her. She couldn't hear herself think. At last, she managed to say, 'No, Igor, we'll take our chances, I think ...'

The end of Anna's sentence was drowned out by the sound of crashing hail.

Anna and Catalina stood and watched the treacherous valley behind them. The winding pathways and ravines were already flooding with water. Every crevice and scallop of grey-slated rock soon filled with icy pools of hail.

They turned to face Igor.

'I guess we haven't got a choice,' said Anna.

'None at all,' said Catalina.

'The castle. She awaits you, Mistress.' Igor bowed and shuffled out of the way.

❋ ❋ ❋

'Your castle,' said Igor as he swept his stumpy arm behind him. The gesture attempted to encompass the cavernous room before them.

Before she came, Anna had thought – or hoped – the castle would be slightly modern inside. An old, quirky place, but somehow familiar and welcoming.

Instead there was wrought iron, cold tiles and guttering torches. Anna stared into a space that resembled the inside of a volcano. There were windows, of a sort, but not made of glass. Mere slits in the stone, carved at odd angles, rose high above her head. Deep red velvet draped most of the walls and much of the furniture. Where the walls were not covered with velvet, there were streaming white ribbons of silk. They swayed back and forth, in silence.

Along with the blackened torches high on the walls, candles lay everywhere. Lumpy, fat white blocks on iron stands covered every bare surface. Wax trickled down edges and cornices, eventually piling on the tiled floor. The flames were still, but a filthy smoke billowed from them, thickening the air and obscuring the uncertain light.

Anna's gaze rested once again on the silk as it pushed back and forth. There was no breeze. At least, nothing she could feel. Mesmerised by their haunting movements, she couldn't stop staring. They seemed to be moving with care. With consideration.

'Mistress Harker. You will eat?' said Igor, interrupting her thoughts.

Anna wasn't sure it was a question, but she was starved. She could have eaten anything. 'Sure. We both will.'

'Oh, Mistress. I was expecting only one. I have set for one.'

'We'll share, it's okay.'

Igor stared at her.

Anna stared back. 'I said, "We'll share".'

'Mistress. As you will.'

'Okay, then,' said Anna turning back to the

curtains, but instead meeting Catalina's stare. 'Cat, you sure know how to wield an eyebrow.'

'Enjoying being the "Mistress" are we?'

Anna ignored her and moved back towards the curtains.

'I have prepared your room. I will take your belongings.'

'No, thank you, Igor. We'll hold on to them for now,' said Catalina. 'We'll put them in our rooms later.'

'Mistress?' said Igor to Anna.

'You heard her, Igor,' said Anna without turning around.

'Very well, Mistress. I will prepare a second room. First, you will eat.' Igor nodded and was gone.

'Well, he is more than a little ... Interesting,' said Catalina.

'You might've been right. This is getting pretty weird. Weird as in "not safe".'

'This is beyond even what I imagined.' As they spoke, Catalina began digging around in her backpack. 'Oh, no. Please no.'

'What's the matter?'

'Some things fell out when I tripped. Important things. Like our flashlights.'

'Damn,' said Anna. 'Still, as long as it wasn't—'

Catalina held up her hand to cut her off. 'The pepper spray canisters. They're gone.'

Anna tried to shrug it off. 'You can't honestly think we'll need them.'

'Look around you, Anna. Look closely.'

Catalina gestured at the floor.

Anna looked at the tiles at her feet. The coldness of the ceramic had seeped in through her thick-soled hiking boots, chilling her from the ground up.

The tiles were not lain like anything she had ever seen before. They were set into a series of crisscrossed iron bars. The iron made a giant latticework that spanned the entire floor. Each tile was as broad as her shoulders and held a different, but similar, pattern.

From a distance, the tiles bore patterns and nothing more. On closer inspection, Anna realised they were painted with scenes. Of people and animals. Of battles. Of war, death and destruction. They showed chaos and a sort of descent into hell. Over and over again.

Anna looked back to Catalina. The flickering candlelight danced across her features, casting dark shadows under eyes. In the shifting light, she was barely recognisable. Anna couldn't stop staring at her. She had become as strange and wild as the rest of the room.

'Anna?'

Anna rubbed her eyes. 'Maybe we should go. Just turn around and leave. It's not too late. 'Outside, the hail that had previously been a steady sound grew louder again and pelted insistently against the stone walls.

'It appears we won't be leaving quite yet,' said Catalina.

'Mistress?' Igor's voice echoed from down a stony hallway 'This way, Mistress.'

As Anna and Catalina walked towards Igor's voice, the silk curtains swept up and snaked across the room. They settled and fell over the women's shoulders, brushing against their arms and faces.

'This is getting quite ridiculous,' said Catalina. She bunched up the silk and shoved it aside.

Anna said nothing. The silk had purpose. It wrapped itself firmly around her shoulders, caressing her, and travelled towards her breasts.

'Anna?' said Catalina.

Anna felt ridiculous. She couldn't move. The silk was suffocating her. And it was touching her. Where it shouldn't be. She could hear her own blood pulsing, roaring. She whispered 'Why is it doing this to me? Why me?'

'Anna. What is it?' asked Catalina as she batted the last of the silk out of her face.

Anna didn't respond.

Catalina grabbed Anna by the arm. 'Anna, talk to me.'

The spell broken, Anna shuddered and looked at her friend. 'I don't like it here.'

'Come on. We'll eat and put our feet up for a while. It will help.' Catalina walked on, leading Anna behind her.

In the invisible breeze, the curtains swayed and trailed after Anna, trying to follow in her footsteps.

❋ ❋ ❋

Anna looked down the hallway that led away from the front of the castle. She could see a little way in. There were torches, but set far apart. There were circles of light, but mostly there was darkness. A painting hung under each of the torches, blackened and formless from the smoke.

Having seen what lay on the castle floor, Anna was relieved she would not be able to see any of the images in the paintings. However, as she walked along, coming into the circle of light, the black smoke seemed to clear and the intimate details in the painting were revealed. Anna gasped. It was not what she expected.

'What is it, Anna?' said Catalina, looking back.

'My dad,' said Anna, pointing at the painting. 'It's a painting of Dad.'

Catalina came into the circle of light. 'It does look a little like him, I suppose.'

'A little?' said Anna. 'Come on. It's him. Down to the last wrinkle.'

Catalina paused for a moment before saying, 'Anna, isn't this a good thing? He must be a relative of yours. It's what you came to find. Though why a painting of an Englishman hangs from these walls, I don't know.'

'You're right. It's … I don't know. I don't like it.' She shrugged. 'It feels like a threat.'

'Oh, Anna.' Catalina shook her head. 'You need

to rest. We both do.'

'Can't you feel it? It's like the castle is talking to me. It's either a threat or a warning.'

'I'm not sure about that, but we'll take it that way,' said Catalina looking between Anna and the painting. 'We can rest, eat some food and leave. Okay?'

Anna nodded. As they walked on, Anna kept glancing back to the painting behind her. She shook her head and tried to shift her thinking. She was being ridiculous. Cat was right. It's exactly why she came she'd always been curious about this old relative of hers. She'd come back later and take a photo of her 'Dad'. Maybe bring a bit more light somehow. Anna smiled. She could imagine her dad's reaction, and the thought of it cheered her a little. As she turned to move on, Anna noticed something metallic on the ground. Suspicious, she moved closer, but with careful and deliberate steps. She stooped low to inspect it, being careful not to touch it.

It was a coin. An ordinary coin. For purchasing things. Old, and that was all.

'What is it?' asked Catalina, standing back a little.

'A coin. An ordinary old coin,' said Anna, picking it up. She snorted. 'I'm being an idiot, aren't I.'

'No comment,' said Catalina, smiling. 'You never know, with your eagle eyes we might get lucky and find a little silver or gold. Are you coming?'

Anna smiled and popped the coin in her back pocket. 'With you all the way.'

Outside, the hail continued to beat against the castle walls.

CHAPTER THREE

Anna walked around a tight corner of the long, curving hallway. And found Igor waiting for her.

'Mistresses, please.' He gestured towards the door.

The room beyond the door was the size of an auditorium. It was a dining room, but it was vast. To call it a room was to belittle it.

Three of the walls were hung with delicate paintings, all with themes of food, seasons and harvest. They hung on a soft, yellow wall that reached up to wooden carvings that spidered out from each corner.

The fourth wall was mostly absent. A connecting set of carved archways lined a balcony. The ranges of the neighbouring mountains were visible through the archways. The ranges seemed to go on forever, curving around the earth's surface before, at last, falling from view. Below, manicured gardens merged with a nearby ancient forest.

The archways themselves were ancient and beautiful. They were crafted and carved, but weather and time had also left their mark. Rounded and sandblasted, hundreds of tiny lines revealed the path of the centuries. Each line eddied around the columns. They were the wind itself. Solid and monstrous in size, they were, all the same, a picture of frozen movement.

The women stood together, speechless and unmoving, taking in the view.

'It's ...,' Anna cut herself off. 'Amazing.'

Catalina said, 'Like a monument to time'.

Instead of one long dining table, the space was filled with a number of small wrought iron tables and chairs. Some round, some square. Each set had its own design and peculiarity. Beyond the magnificence of the balcony, each one was a small masterpiece.

Some were so intricate or outlandish that Anna thought they would be impossible to use. One table was made from lengths of iron so thin that it more closely resembled a spun spiderweb than a construction. Another set of chairs had four different types of antlers, each one made from bone entwined with wrought iron—the largest chair held antlers from some sort of huge beast, like a buffalo or auroch. The biggest table resembled a small organ, with pipes jutting up from the backs of the chairs. As the wind picked up, haunting melodies were carried along with the breeze.

Anna couldn't decide where to look next. After glancing from table to table, she realised that only one setting was ready for use. Here, the iron chairs had been rendered with long, tall stalks, curving at the top like lilies. There were two places set.

Igor stood by the table and said, 'Mistress'.

Catalina and Anna walked forward, their eyes still darting around the room, desperate to try and drink in all of the details.

The palatial beauty and splendour of the room was a slight shock to Anna. She had been forced through a small nightmare, only to find a welcoming hand at the other end. In a daze, she moved towards the table.

At one end of the hall, a tremendous fireplace roared. It was almost as wide as the wall itself. Two scaly, thin, serpentine forms with wolverine heads were carved into each side of the marble fireplace. The heads of the twin beasts reached up towards the ceiling and at the top, metal tongues leaped from their sharp marble teeth. With the wind and the haunting tunes, Anna felt that the beasts might, at any time, come alive and jump from the walls.

Igor noticed Anna studying the fireplace. '*Draco*.'

'I'm sorry?' Igor had startled her once again.

'The beasts, Mistress. *Draco*.'

'It's like they're watching us,' said Anna.

Igor nodded. 'They watch, they guard. They protect us.'

'*Dacian Draco*?' said Catalina.

'This is one tale, yes.' Igor said turning to look at Catalina. 'You know of it.'

'Not much more than a name, but yes. I've heard it before.'

Igor, for once, gestured to both women. 'Please, sit.'

Catalina and Anna took their places.

After she was seated, Anna looked around for Igor. He was nowhere to be seen. She grimaced. One minute he was there, the next gone.

'He's quite the magician,' said Catalina. 'A little too good at it, too.'

'Way too good at it.'

There was cutlery, but it was battered and old. The knife looked to be better suited to carving, not cutting. Anna picked up the fork. It had two long prongs and a stubby bone-coloured handle. There were tiny, intricate carvings in the fork's handle. She ran her fingers over the surface. It appeared to be a coat of arms.

'A beautiful little thing.'

Anna smiled. 'Do you think he'd notice if I stole it?'

'Almost certainly, yes.'

Outside, the wind howled. It carried the sounds of baying dogs.

Anna didn't jump, but it took some effort. She tightened her fists and sighed. Her nerves were frayed. She felt as if she were hardwired to the sounds of the castle. Catalina had jumped at the sound, but didn't seem as bothered. 'This place …,' began Anna, rolling her eyes.

'I know. But we shouldn't let it get to us.' As Catalina spoke, her hand ran along an edge of one of the iron lilies in her chair.

'It's a bit more atmosphere than I'm used to.'

'It's what you came here for though, isn't it?'

'Sure. But, come on. This is like some weird nightmare.'

'Eldritch.'

'Okay. If that's how you want to put it. As long as you end with "nightmare",' said Anna.

'There is beauty here too,' said Catalina, gesturing at the room and the balcony.

'You're such a …'

'Aesthete?' said Catalina.

'I was going for snob, but okay,' laughed Anna. 'Aesthete. But you're easily swayed.'

Catalina inclined her head, but said nothing.

'I'm hoping that's wine,' said Anna surveying the table. A flagon and two pewter goblets sat in the centre. The goblets were more filigree than metal. Inside the delicate metalwork were small beechwood cups. The flagon bore a coat of arms upon a delicate array of ivy and hanging vines.

Anna reached out to grasp the flagon, and Catalina put out a hand to stop her. 'Should we? Can we trust that strange little man?'

'Are you going to eat whatever food he brings us?'

'Yes,' said Catalina after a moment's thought. 'I'm ravenous. It was a long walk. And I suspect our camping food won't go as far as we'd hoped.'

'Okay. So, why no to the wine? What's the big deal?'

Catalina was silent as she pondered her next

words. 'None, I suppose. He's got me on edge.' She shrugged. 'Go ahead. Eat, drink.'

'Be merry?'

'You are quite ridiculous, even when you're right. You *are* right though.'

'Everyone needs a chance to shine now and then.'

'Now and then? That's a little modest for you.'

'Come on. I'm not that bad. Am I?'

Catalina raised a silent eyebrow.

'Okay, okay. Huzzah! May I present The Great Anna Harker. Better?'

Catalina ignored her. Glaring at the flagon, she said, 'We should have brought more food with us. Real food'.

'We planned to be here the one night. No one packs a three-course meal for an overnight stay.'

'We should have realised how long that hike would be,' continued Catalina.

'How could we have known? We couldn't find this place online, only the village.' Anna shifted in her seat. 'We could only guess.'

'That's precisely my point. Not knowing how far it would be meant we should have planned for the worst.' Catalina shook her head. 'I've been too rash.'

'Oh, come on, Cat. We're here looking for adventure. This might not be the sort of adventure I was after, but we've got one all the same. So we didn't bring enough food. We're here now and might as well try and make the best of it.'

'I think we have little to no alternative.'

'Settle there, Cat. You were bordering on the positive, 'said Anna. 'Okay. So, now what?'

Catalina gestured at the flagon and said, 'Is it wine?'

Anna smiled and picked up the flagon. Peering inside she said, 'Looks and smells like it'. She held it up with a flourish and said, 'Madame? May I?'

Catalina nodded, grinned and said, 'If you would be so kind'.

* * *

'Only one,' said Igor to a small, empty room. Igor looked at the excessive array of food before him. Great stacks of fruits, vegetables, meats lay on platters. At the ends of the table lay dishes of tiny, succulent delicacies and sweetmeats. His fingers drummed on the table. 'Only one.'

Igor sighed and picked up an empty wooden platter. He turned it around and around in his hands. Without putting the platter down, he moved to a small window carved into the immense castle wall. The storm continued to rage outside, but only the roaring wind came through. The sounds of baying dogs could be heard here too.

Igor nodded to himself. He looked away from the window, towards a nearby chair. A stark, elegant piece, altar-like in its simplicity. Igor studied it for a moment, before appearing to come to a decision. He sat down, still holding the single, empty platter on his lap.

Igor leaned back in the chair. And waited.

* * *

The storm had picked up outside. The sound of the distant dogs had died away. Only the roar of the wind could be heard.

Catalina and Anna had moved their chairs over to the balcony. The wind whipped at their hair. Catalina had tied her long, blonde hair into a loose plait behind her.

Anna let her bob do what it wanted. She knew it would anyway. It played havoc with her view, but she loved the feel of it as it lashed against her flushed cheeks. Watching the storm, Anna's fingers traced the rim of a pewter goblet, smiling as she discovered each new ridge and bump.

The wind dropped away. And in the sudden quiet the sound of a raven cawing rung out above the storm. The women sat up and looked out the over the balcony.

The raven cawed three times, short and clear. And stopped.

The howling winds returned. Anna looked at Catalina. She was sitting forward in her chair, ear turned to the storm. There was no doubt. She'd heard it too. Without warning, a long and lengthening streak of darkness rushed past the balcony. As fast as it was going, it took several seconds to move beyond their view.

'O-kay,' said Anna. 'What was that?'

'We heard a raven, I think,' Catalina began.

'A raven.' Anna tilted her head to look at her. 'Are you trying to tell me *that* was a raven?'

'What else could it be?' Catalina shifted in her chair.

After a moment's silence, Anna whispered 'It looked like the wind.'

Catalina ignored her.

Without speaking, both women picked up their chairs and moved away from the balcony, leaving behind the view of a tumultuous sky.

❋ ❋ ❋

A long, dark, undulating streak rushed towards the window.

'*Vântoase*,' whispered Igor.

As it drew closer, the streak changed shape. It thickened and splintered, as if striking an invisible wall.

Time compressed. In the next frame, the dark streak had transformed, and a large raven flew across the last couple of feet. It came rushing through the window and landed, with brutal force, on the back of Igor's chair.

Igor stood up, twitching with nervous energy. The small platter dropped to the stone floor, clattering as it fell. He turned to look at the raven —an avian picture of beauty and grace. As it settled on the back of the chair, its black feathers shone with iridescence under the subtle light of the moon – sometimes purple, sometimes blue.

'*Vântoase cetăţilor.*' His lips stretched thin. 'Welcome, protector.'

Igor hurried over to pick up a large platter of meat. As he brought the platter close, the raven launched towards Igor and the meat he carried, landing on Igor's forearm. The great bird's fearsome claws drew blood, but Igor did not seem to mind. He set the platter down on the chair, and the bird with it. The raven ate, but with one eye on Igor the whole time.

Holding his wounded arm, Igor smiled, a smile that wrestled its way from the corners of his mouth to his eyes. Keeping a watch on the bird, he rambled across to a set of oversized, wooden shelves at the back of the serving room.

Igor picked out two clean, small, wooden platters. And began serving the food.

For two.

* * *

Igor returned carrying platters overflowing with food: two giant stacks of cheese, breads and pickled everything. With great ceremony, he set the platters down in front of Catalina and Anna.

Anna looked over the offerings and realised that most of the food was fresh. For a moment she was relieved, thinking that if they stayed away from cooked food, they would both be fine. Anna shook her head and glanced up at Igor. One minute she felt she could trust him, the next she wanted to get the hell out of there. It was like being on the world's most ancient roller coaster.

'Mistress?' said Igor uncertainly.

'Sorry, Igor,' said Anna. 'The food looks great.'

'There's so much of everything,' said Catalina. 'It looks divine. How do you get the food up here and have it stay so fresh?'

'We have our ways,' he said. 'Everything you see is from here.'

'You grow it yourself?' said Anna.

'Mistress, please. This matters not. Enjoy.' Igor bowed and left the room.

Catalina stared at the door after he left. 'He is …,' she shrugged. 'I can't even think of the right word.'

'Cat, when he speaks in Romanian can you understand what he's saying?'

'It's difficult,' she said, shrugging. 'His accent is like nothing I've ever heard.'

'But you seemed to get what the villagers were saying earlier—,' began Anna.

'Yes, but it was a quite limited conversation. And even then, they were speaking slowly. I imagine it was because they know we're tourists. They didn't need to be told.' She looked at Anna. 'You don't exactly fit in.'

Without realising what she was doing, Anna rested her slight fingers against her freckled cheek. She ignored Catalina's comment and said, 'But if

Igor made an effort you might be able to understand him?'

'Not necessarily.' Catalina looked at the imposing, antiquated room. 'Look at this place. It's from another time altogether. I think his language is too. The villagers speak about modern things and use modern words.'

'But you understand your grandmother okay,' said Anna. 'Don't you?'

'It's not the same. If something happened and you found you couldn't speak English, I would still understand much of what you were trying to convey. You and I, my grandmother, *Bunică*, and I, we can communicate without words. We have a shared life and a background.' Catalina stared at her hands in silence for a moment. She said, 'If I'm honest, I feel a little embarrassed by it. Especially as we're here, in my *Bunică*'s home country. A small part of me feels drawn here and at home. The rest of me feels out of place. I feel like a stranger in a foreign land. And I want to feel like I belong'.

When Anna was about to reply, the storm rose in ferocity once again, drowning out any possibility of conversation. Anna found that the hail and wind never quite went away, but ebbed and flowed. The storm was as unpredictable as it was dangerous.

Catalina seemed to read her thoughts. 'Even if the storm stopped, we can't know when it would start up again. We might find ourselves halfway down the mountain trapped by a torrential downpour or murderous hail. It was so treacherous on the way up. Imagine us now, exhausted and slipping and sliding.'

'I know.'

For a short while, neither Catalina nor Anna said anything.

Anna didn't want to say it and she didn't want to hear Catalina say it. She said it all the same. 'I think we're stuck here. At least for the night. Like it or not.'

Catalina looked at Anna. She nodded. 'You're right. I don't like it, but you are right.'

'This is one time I'd love to be wrong.' Anna shrugged. 'But at least we're decided. One night's stay.'

Catalina turned to look out over the balcony again. She made an expression somewhere between a grimace and a smile. 'This doesn't feel like a decision.'

'We'd always planned to stay a night or two.'

'No,' said Catalina. 'We had planned to stay *no more* than a night or two. This isn't part of our plan. To stay, despite feeling unsafe. We're staying, but only because it's unsafe to go.'

'Come on. It's only one night, Cat. I'm sure the storm will break by morning.'

'You're right, I'm an over-worrier,' said Catalina. 'I'm sure we'll be fine.'

Even to Anna's hopeful ears, it didn't sound convincing.

Outside the balcony, a thick rod of bright white lightning lit the sky. Electricity arced and bounced back and forth between the different archways. An ear-splitting thunder followed, and reverberated around the room. Anna was struck blind and almost deaf.

After a time, the ghost images dispersed and the echoes died away. Anna realised she could see again. She tried to collect her thoughts. To pull herself together. It wasn't easy. 'Uh-huh. *Fine.* We'll be fine.'

* * *

When Igor returned, neither of the women were talking. They sat, not looking at each other, fiddling with their empty plates.

'Mistress, is something amiss?'

Anna looked at Igor's troubled face. 'No. Everything's fine. Really.'

There was an extended silence as Igor hovered nearby.

Anna tried to ignore him for a while, but his presence was difficult to ignore. Exasperated, Anna said, 'What is it, Igor? What do you want?'

Igor stared at her. He seemed to be incapable of speaking.

Catalina tilted her head and said, 'Igor? I hate to be rude, but could I ask if there's any more food? I'm still a little hungry.'

Igor's face split into an almost maniacal grin. 'Mistress, yes!' He scuttled away.

Anna watched Igor leave and turned to

Catalina, not even sure which question she wanted to ask. 'Still hungry? You're seriously still hungry? After all of that?'

'Yes, Anna. He was clearly troubled. Besides 'all of that 'was only one course.' Catalina shrugged. 'People like to see you eat. It might be a good idea to befriend Igor. At least a little.'

'Maybe. I don't know. He seems so unpredictable.' She looked at Catalina. 'Making friends with the hermit guy next door isn't something you would normally do.'

'We're in uncharted waters.' Catalina shrugged again. 'I honestly have no idea what the right thing is anymore.'

'You and me both.'

* * *

Some time later, Igor returned again, this time carrying a large wooden tray full of small plates, each one bearing a succulent, syrupy dessert.

'Igor, don't say you made these as well,' said Catalina. 'They're so delicate.'

'Mistress. 'Igor bowed.

Anna said, 'Is that a 'yes' or a 'no', Igor?'

'Mistress, I took some part in this.'

'There are more people in the castle?' said Anna.

'There have always been so.'

'I was beginning to think it was only you and the raven. When will we meet the others?' said

35

Anna.

Igor stepped back a little. 'You saw the raven?'

'Yes,' said Anna. 'It flew right up and sat on the balcony. 'It was clear to Anna that Igor was unnerved. She wanted to see how much more she could rattle him.

'Mistress, when?'

'Only a little while ago,' said Anna.

Igor's brow furrowed. 'It was here? In this room?'

Catalina interrupted and said, 'It didn't come in. We heard it'.

Igor smiled and stepped back to the table. 'Mistress.' He nodded at Catalina. 'I see you speak the truth.' He glared at Anna, who shifted under his gaze.

'Saw, heard – what's the difference?'

'The difference is the truth, Mistress. That is enough.' He gestured at the food on the table and said, 'Please'. Before either of the women could speak, Igor turned and stalked out of the room.

Looking at the food, Anna realised she'd been diverted from her question. Who made the damn desserts? Igor was harder to pin down than a butterfly in the sun. Not expecting an answer, she asked Catalina, 'So, where are all these other people?'

'People, I don't know.' Catalina held up a square, butter-coloured sweet. 'Halva, I do.'

Despite herself, Anna smiled. 'Hopeless. You're hopeless.'

❋ ❋ ❋

Catalina and Anna leaned back in their chairs.

Anna was so full, she almost felt sick. The waistband of her jeans was taught against her stomach. By comparison, Catalina looked comfortable and content. 'Happy?' asked Anna.

'Deliciously so.' Catalina stretched and yawned.

'What happened to staying on our toes? You don't exactly look alert.'

Catalina shrugged. 'Perhaps I was wrong. It's a strange, unsettling place, at first glance. As is Igor. Given time, they might even grow on you a little. Anyway, what is it that you want? An adventure or a safe holiday? This was your idea. Your adventure. And here we are. As requested.'

Anna said nothing. She knew Catalina was right – there was nothing she could say that would sound reasonable. It was her adventure, but the whole place jarred with her; plucked at her nerves. Whatever it was, good or bad, it invaded her. She was beginning to feel like she was a specimen ready for dissection.

❋ ❋ ❋

Igor returned once more, this time holding a small wooden box.

'No, no, no.' Anna held up her hand in protest. 'Seriously, no more. Igor, we couldn't. Not even a crumb.'

'Mistresses. These are gifts. Ceremony. To welcome.'

Surprised, Anna leaned forward to look. The box was simple and undecorated, and lined with padded black silk. On the silk lay two intricate and quite different carvings.

The first was carved from wood. It showed a number of tiny flowers poking up from flowing blades of wooden grass and cut wheat. The tiny, nodular flowers were painted a pale yellow. The blades of grass and wheat swayed and wound around each other. The carving as a whole was of movement, like wind in the grass.

The second was carved from bone and depicted a kind of many-headed dragon. It was yellowing, dirty and old. Ancient.

Fascinated, Anna leaned forward to inspect the dragon in more detail. It was impossible to count with any accuracy, but she thought there were as many as twelve serpentine heads. The tiny body was covered with scales and the tail curved up so much that it folded over the top of its own head. Its eyes glowed and shone. They appeared to be made from deep dark-red rubies.

Each gift was beautiful in its own way. Anna smiled and looked up at Catalina. Catalina was pushing backwards in her chair. Her lips were tight and she had turned pale. 'Cat? What's wrong?'

Catalina turned on Igor. 'Why would you do this?'

Igor said nothing, but instead started to back away.

'Cat, what is it? They're just little carvings. They're harmless enough.'

Catalina stood up. 'Igor. Do *you* think these are harmless carvings? Both of them?'

Igor held out his hands in a gesture of mollification. 'Mistress. I do not understand.'

'Oh, is that so?' Catalina pushed her chair back and moved towards Igor. 'The dragon, Igor. Would you prefer that I name it?'

Igor glanced sideways to the exit from the room.

'Cat, stop it. What's going on?'

Catalina spun to Anna. 'This,' she said pointing at the dragon. 'This is an omen. It isn't something you would give in a warm and welcoming way.'

'An omen? This? I thought you were 'Little Miss Logical 'Of all the things we've seen today, this is what freaks you out?'

'Yes.'

Out of Catalina's view, Igor started to walk back towards the door.

'It's only a little dragon,' said Anna. 'Aren't they sometimes benevolent? In myths, I mean.'

She shook her head, once. 'Not this one.'

Before Catalina could stop her, Anna picked up the carving of the dragon. 'It's only a carving. Some gems and an old bone. Isn't it?'

Lurking by the door, Igor grimaced. 'A carving. Yes.'

'What have you done?' said Catalina.

Igor scuttled from the room.

*　*　*

Flames roared.

Igor sat at a table by the fireplace. Two leather-bound books at rest before him. Each cover bore careful, detailed engravings. One book was deep green and marked with simple sine waves that wrapped from front to back. The other was old and decaying; and the original colour had faded long ago. Under the word *Balaur*, there was a subtle, embossed image of a dragon.

Igor opened the dark, green book and picked up a nearby quill. On the inside cover he wrote the words "Catalina Dalca". Shutting the book, he turned to face the roaring flames behind him. At first, he flinched and shrunk away.

He sat and contemplated both books. After a few minutes, he reached out to the book of the dragon, his fingers hovering over the cover. He grabbed at it. He held the book tight, his knuckles turning white.

More time passed.

He whispered, 'No. I will not.' He put down the quill. And he threw the book into the fire.

The flames roared higher again, for a second,

then died down.

After a time, the flames died out. On the top of the glowing embers, the book was blackened, but remained otherwise untouched and intact.

At the desk, Igor buried his head in his gnarled hands.

❋ ❋ ❋

The weather had changed once again. Rain poured from the sky, the view all but obscured. Both women stood against the archways in the balcony, each one in her own little alcove.

Catalina was the first to speak. 'I'm sorry. I overreacted.'

Anna stuck her head around the balcony. 'I'm sorry too. It bothered you. That should've been enough for me. I shouldn't have picked it up.' Anna walked around and came close enough to let her fingertips rest on her friend's wrist. 'This is going to sound silly, but …' Anna faltered and stopped mid-sentence.

'What is it?'

'We could make a pact. To not have to say sorry. Not while we're here. We can make up for it once we're back.'

'You're right. It *does* sound silly. What was the name of those books you used to love?'

'My Mum's books?' Anna's cheeks flushed. 'The Nancy Drew Mysteries.'

'Yes.' Catalina raised her eyebrows. 'We are not

inside one of those stories.'

'Way to state the obvious, Cat. I wish we were.'

'Of course you do,' said Catalina, grinning.

'Okay, okay, the idea is silly, but the sentiment isn't. Come on.'

'You want to do this?'

Anna nodded. 'Please?'

Catalina shrugged. 'Okay'. She looked out over the balcony.

A corner of Anna's mouth turned up. She knew she shouldn't do what she was about to do, but she also knew that sometimes she was her own worst enemy. She tapped Catalina on the shoulder. As she turned around, Anna thrust out her hand and said, 'Spit on it?'

Catalina laughed. She grabbed Anna by the arm and reeled her in. Instead of closing the deal, she held her close. Anna, weary and happy for comfort, fell into her arms.

❋ ❋ ❋

Catalina and Anna stood apart, watching the storm transform before them.

Anna said, 'We haven't heard from Igor for a while.'

'I suppose that means dinner is over'.

'No coffee?' said Anna.

'No coffee.'

'That is seriously not okay.'

'I know. Barbarians.'

Igor poked his head around the corner. 'Mistress? Mistresses, it is time to move on.'

'Okay. We're coming, Igor,' said Anna just as he vanished. To Catalina, she said, 'Anything to get this adventure done and dusted.'

'I'm sorry to leave this room though.' Catalina ran her hands over the worn stone of the balcony. 'It has a certain presence and grace. A soul.'

Anna raised her eyebrows in surprise. 'What happened to your so-called scientific mind?'

Catalina rolled her eyes and said, 'Very funny. You know what I mean'.

After a moment's pause, Anna decided to say nothing more, even though she hadn't been joking. The one thing she had always been able to rely on was Catalina's sense of reason and logic. 'Come on, we don't want to upset dear Igor.'

They followed Igor's fading voice back into the depths of the castle.

CHAPTER FOUR

As they walked along another winding, stony hallway, a painting of an elegant man came into view. When they walked out of the circle of torchlight and on to another, Anna recalled an earlier corridor and a different painting.

'Igor?'

'Mistress? 'he said, scuttling back to her, his face bright in the light of the torch he held.

'When we first arrived, I saw a painting of a man that looked like my father. Do you know anything about him?'

Igor nodded at the painting. 'He is a distant relative of yours.'

Anna stood stunned. She didn't know where to start, so instead allowed the first question that came to mind to stumble out. 'Was his name Jonathan?'

Igor glared at her. 'That name is myth. A little child's tale.'

'You know—'

Igor thrust up a gnarled, open-fingered hand.

Anna looked at Catalina, who shrugged. She tried a different tack. 'So, he was my father's, father's uncle or …?'

'It is not clear, Mistress. But the name is shared and there is a bloodline. We are sure of that.'

'Okay, so what's with the painting?' said Anna.

'He convinced many people in the village that he had become the owner of this castle,' he said.

'He owned the castle?' asked Catalina.

'Mistress, no. He did not.' Igor's brow furrowed. He seemed to be struggling to find the right words. 'He was able to convince many people of many things.'

'I still don't get it. If he didn't own it … why the painting?,' said Anna.

'He did not own the castle, Mistress, but he resided here. For a time. The villagers had respect for him.'

'Why did the Romanians respect him? Was he a missionary?' said Catalina.

'Transylvanians, Mistress. This was long ago,' said Igor.

'Of course,' she said, with a bow of her head. 'This used to be the border of Transylvania and Moldova, yes?'

'Yes,' said Igor.

'So, what had he done that earned the respect of the Transylvanians?'

'Good question. Igor?'

'The details are lost to history. This is all I can tell you. 'His lips had become a thin, tight line.

Anna couldn't hide her disappointment. After coming all this way, she couldn't believe that was all he knew. She wasn't sure what she'd hoped to find, but she sure as heck wanted more than this. Something more substantial. Something she could take home with her. An adventure she could tell from beginning to end.

To Anna's surprise, Catalina said, 'Igor, I would be a little surprised if that's all you know. I suspect that's all you're willing to tell us'.

Igor cringed and looked away.

'It's okay, Igor. Come on. Tell us what's going on,' said Anna reaching out towards him.

Igor only cowered more.

Anna had never seen anyone look more pathetic. With her softest voice, she said, 'I'm sorry, Igor. It's okay, really. Maybe we'll be able to discover some things on our own'.

Igor stood straight. His face broke into a crooked smile as he said, 'I have a surprise for the Mistresses'.

✱ ✱ ✱

'Please, Mistresses. This way. You will like this. You are tired. You are both tired. It will bring you comfort.'

Anna's legs buckled on hearing even the suggestion of rest. Her body knew what was needed. She knew she was overreacting to everything. Once she'd had a decent lie down she would be able to think straight again. 'You're right, Igor. I can't believe how tired I am.'

He nodded. 'I exist only to serve you, Mistress.'

Anna couldn't think of anything to say.

Catalina stepped forward and said, 'I hope not, Igor. If so, you would vanish when Anna leaves'.

Igor smile's was fleeting, but it too soon vanished. He opened the door, stepping aside to allow the women in.

The room was opulence itself.

The tall interior stretched overhead, seemingly endless. In truth it rose as high as a two-storey house. Slender and narrow, the roof curved in steeply, creating the feeling of a cocoon, despite the height. The ceiling was an octagon of curving, white concrete buttresses. Between each curve of concrete, swoops of deep-blue silk fell in folds across the ceiling.

Stained glass windows, beautiful, tall and thin, rose on each side. They began just above the ground and soared far overhead. Each window held a different scene of the seasons, wrought in iron and coloured glass. Early winter, a swirl of blues, washing down like the coming rain. Late spring, a riot of colours, bedded on rolling hills of green. Summer, a gold and burning glow of sun and red-hued lands. Autumn, a mosaic of leaves, of oranges, tans and browns.

Light spilled through the windows from the outside; wan, moonlit hues sprawling into the room. The colours fell across the floor, tinting the floor's small, grey and white tiles. A padded circular lounge filled the centre of the room, its surface strewn with luxurious furs, silks and finery. Where the rest of the castle was power and force, this room shone bright and intense. It overwhelmed with a strident beauty.

'This is extraordinary,' Catalina smiled. 'So intricate. So beautiful. It almost makes this trip worthwhile.'

Anna's heartbeat had slowed the moment she stepped into the room. It was too comforting. Not comforting; blanketing. Cloying. Like a dream or a trance. Overwhelmed, she watched Catalina walk around the room. Smiling and bright-eyed, she seemed unaffected. Anna's head spun. She swayed and shut her eyes.

'Anna?'

Anna opened her eyes. 'I want to go.'

'What happened? Did you see something? You're white as a ghost.'

'I want to go.'

'I think that's a good idea. I don't quite know what's going on, but I don't want you to rest here.' She held Anna's face up, so that their eyes met. 'We're leaving. Yes?'

'Leaving?' whispered Anna.

'Yes.'

'Mistress, please,' said Igor. 'This room is a sanctuary. It is for you.'

'We're leaving, Igor,' said Catalina, not shifting her gaze from Anna's face. She put her arm around Anna's shoulder and guided her towards the door.

Igor stood at the doorway, unmoving, his face

torn by indecision.

'You heard me, Igor,' said Catalina. 'We will rest, but not here.'

'Yes, Mistress,' said Igor. 'As is your will.' He lowered his head and stormed out of the room.

❧ ❧ ❧

Igor marched ahead of the women away and down the corridor. After a while, he could only be seen as a tiny, flickering point of light in the distance.

'I think we've upset him.' Anna peered into the darkness. 'He seems so far away. This hall must go on for miles.'

'It smells mouldy too. Perhaps this part of the castle is underground,' said Catalina.

'But we haven't gone downstairs,' said Anna. 'Have we?'

'It's a little hard to think clearly, but we must have,' said Catalina. 'Look at the walls next time we get under torchlight. The stones are more moss than rock.'

'I hadn't noticed,' said Anna, her fingertips brushing against the wall. She could see, barely, that it was mouldy. But under her fingertips it was soft, warm and inviting. Pliant. She paused for a while and allowed the sensation to seep in. Her fingers pulsed. Rhythmic and hypnotic. She thought she could stay there for eternity. From behind, Catalina nudged her along.

'We need to walk faster if we want to catch up

to Igor.'

'Okay,' said Anna, 'But look, do we even want to stay close?'

'I might not trust him entirely, but I don't want to lose sight of him. I'm already turned about in this labyrinthian castle. I'm not even sure I could find my way back out. We've already been in so many tunnels that I've lost count.' Catalina paused. 'I even wonder if he's trying to lose us.'

As they moved on, both women fell silent.

Every now and then Anna would catch sight of Catalina as she came into the next circle of torchlight. Her face was unreadable. When the distance between the torches stretched even further apart, she couldn't help but feel a sort of relief. The featureless darkness was a welcome void.

'He's even further away. Is it possible he's trying to lose us?' Catalina picked up her pace. 'Hurry up, Anna. I don't want him to get away from us.'

The floor changed. The stonework crumbled away to tightly-packed dirt. The slight incline deepened. Catalina said, 'I'm pretty sure we're going downhill now.'

Anna didn't reply.

'Anna?' said Catalina.

There was still no reply. 'Anna?' she shouted 'Anna, where are you?' Her voice echoed up and down the long, curving hallway.

Catalina turned around and headed back up, moving one careful step at a time. Her arms stretched out towards each side of the dank hallway.

Anna crouched on the floor in the dark, leaning against a wall.

'What are you doing?' said Catalina.

'I was tired. I needed to rest.'

'This is no place to rest. You're only a little tired. You need to get up.'

Anna didn't stand, but Catalina pulled her to her feet. 'I'm so tired.' said Anna. 'It was so comfortable.'

'You should have told me you'd stopped. What if I'd lost you?'

Anna's fingers rested on the soft, spongy moss of the stones. She smiled to herself. Catalina's concern was so silly. There was no safer place than right here. This was home. Funny, sweet Catalina. 'I wasn't lost. I was fine.' She pressed the side of her face against the castle wall.

'Fine?' Catalina looked Anna up and down. 'You are not the picture of "fine". Anyway, that's not the point. We need to stay together. If you want to rest again, you only need to tell me.'

'Yes, Cat.' Anna hadn't moved.

Catalina was silent for a moment. Finally, she said,' We should go.'

'Can't I have one more minute,' said Anna.

'You can rest later. We are going. Now.' Catalina dragged Anna away from the wall.

'Yes, Cat,' said Anna as she started to stumble forward.

Catalina let out a long breath. 'I know you're

tired. You can do this. Pick up one foot and place it in front of the other.'

Anna did as she was told. One foot, then the other. Catalina stayed close behind her. As she walked, Anna's fingers sought out the castle wall.

* * *

They had lost sight of Igor. And it had been a long time since they had seen any torchlights. There appeared to be a dull, dim glow emanating from the moss on the castle stones.

Anna said, 'I'm tired. Can't we rest now?'

'No,' said Catalina

'Come on. Please?'

Catalina stopped. 'I don't know what's going on, but you're not right. Not at all. I realise how tired you are, but I'm not going to let you rest here. I want to find Igor. Or a way out. 'She peered into the darkness and tried to look around. 'It looks more like a tunnel or a dungeon now.'

The hallway had deteriorated rapidly in the last few hundred feet. 'It's not a dungeon. It's a catacomb.'

'Catacomb? Why would you say that?' said Catalina.

'Can't you feel it? Them?'

'Stop being ridiculous,' said Catalina, her words rushed and short.

But Anna could feel it. She was sure Catalina could sense something too. It didn't matter. *She* knew they weren't alone.

* * *

Now that Anna's eyes had adjusted to the dark, the walls seemed to glow all the more.

The moss had changed colour and thickened as they walked lower and left behind any trace of torchlight. Snaking down from the ceiling, it smothered the corners and crevices in the wall. Wherever the moss appeared it brought with it a soft, luminescent glow. It traversed part-way across the floor, suffusing their feet and legs with a pale green light.

The moss also climbed under and over a series of gnarled tree roots. If the moss had not provided the slim light it did, they would have had to turn back. Anna laughed to herself. She wasn't even sure where 'back 'was.

'Look at this, Anna. You were right.' Catalina stood in front of a small alcove in the wall. It was full of bones. There was a skull in the centre and row after row of slender white rods. Stacked with the bulbous joints pointing out, they lay bundled together in a repeating series of eight.

Anna said, 'It's beautiful.'

To Anna's slight surprise, Catalina said 'Yes, beautiful.'

'That's not the sort of thing you'd normally say.'

'It's not the mysticism, Anna. It's the history.

A way to connect to people hundreds of years after their death.'

'That's an elegant way to put it. I wouldn't have even thought to say it like that. I guess it's a sort of connection. 'Anna didn't say the rest of what she was thinking. She had known these people were here long before she saw their bones. They spoke to her. Not in whispered voices; nothing that weird. But they had made their presence felt. She knew what Catalina would say, so she kept her thoughts to herself.

'Yes. It's a tangible connection to my family's past, I suppose. I wonder if we'll see any others.'

'Yeah. We will,' said Anna. And then added quickly, 'Where there's one alcove, there's going to be more.'

Catalina allowed an eyebrow to lift. 'Yes.' She reached out, her fingers moving towards the bones.

'No!' said Anna.

Catalina turned to her. 'I wasn't going to touch the bones.'

'It didn't look that way.'

'No, honestly. Look closely, Anna. There's an inscription underneath.'

'You're right,' said Anna peering at the engraving in the darkness.

Catalina reached forward again and ran her hand over the words. 'Maybe I can read it.' Her fingers traced the corners and curves of each letter, slowing as they discovered little lumps of tunnel moss.

'Any luck?'

'There's something, but it's hard to make out and even harder to understand.' She paused before going on. 'It's something like "unnatural death".'

As Catalina turned, her face was lit by the dim and eerie glow of the moss. Anna's words were quick and to the point. 'Time to move on, I think.'

'Move on? Or go back?'

Anna was struck by indecision. She didn't know what she wanted, never mind what was best. 'Oh, come on. Who are you kidding? You seriously think we could retrace our steps?'

'I don't know. I've lost all sense of direction. But I'm not enjoying just forging on like this. You?'

'I guess I'd still like to try and find Igor.' Anna shrugged. 'Maybe?'

'We'll never get out of here if we stand around talking all night.' Catalina shook her head. 'I don't like either choice.'

'That's because neither choice is good,' said Anna, hooking her hands in her back pockets. Her thumb touched on the coin she'd found earlier. She pulled it out. 'Let's toss on it. 'Anna spun the coin in the air. 'Heads: forward. Tails: back.' She clamped her hand down on the coin as it landed. 'Heads.'

'Forward it is. Let's go.'

* * *

The alcoves in the walls were increasing in frequency. Each alcove a different shape: some square, some curved, and all of the bones stacked in different patterns. Sometimes one skull, sometimes two, often many more.

'I think we have to face it,' said Anna as they passed a wooden-framed alcove covered with intricate carvings. She had never seen anything so old. And yet, she was getting used to seeing it. They swung around yet another corner to find a relatively empty corridor.

'Face what?' said Catalina, peering into the ever-dimming darkness.

'Not only have we lost Igor, but we're lost as well. Dead lost. Come on, Cat. Wouldn't he have come back by now if he was going to?'

'True. I thought if we kept moving forward we'd meet him coming back the other way. Perhaps he was trying to lose us. Or maybe we missed a turn or a stairwell—' Catalina's words were interrupted by the sounds of scurrying feet.

Anna and Catalina stopped cold.

The sounds were coming closer, scurrying back and forth, as if in a sweeping movement.

'What do we do?' whispered Anna.

'We have nowhere to run,' whispered Catalina. 'We may as well wait. It could be Igor.'

'You don't believe that,' said Anna.

'No. I do not.'

For the longest moment, they waited.

The scurrying sounds grew louder. And louder again. At last, Anna thought she could see movement. At first she thought it might be a dog or even some sort of oversized cat.

Catalina and Anna both stood breathless. Catalina said two words. But they were two words that Anna would never forget. 'A ... rat?'

'It can't be. It's too big,' whispered Anna. 'Surely, it's too big?'

And too big it was.

Anna could make out fur, claws and tail. The thing moved forward in terrifying sweeping movements, back and forth, left and right. It seemed to be looking for something. It came just close enough for Anna to see its eyes.

Anna heard Catalina draw in a sharp breath. Her own mouth dropped open and bile rose in her throat.

There was not one set of eyes in the darkness, but many pairs of beady red dots. A tight-packed cluster of filthy black entities had stirred. As one entity, it started to scurry down the tunnel towards them. Swaying and moving as one. A single metamorphous beast, but one that moved like a tangled wave of creatures, each scuttling over the other.

Anna and Catalina scrambled backwards, and tried to climb the walls in a senseless effort at escape. Anna wanted most of all to get her feet off the ground. She had a gory vision of being trapped here for aeons, the gruesome beast gnawing away at her feet and toes. She forced her fingers deep into the cracks and crevices on the wall. She managed to half-hang, her feet not quite scraping the ground.

At the sound of its scrapes and scrambles, the seething rat-mass stopped scurrying and sniffing. The king-rat stilled and the eyes, as one, monitored Anna's and Catalina's every move. For a moment, the creature appeared startled by their presence.

Anna stared into the collective mass. Dozens of eyes stared at her. There was intelligence there, real intelligence. Not merely staring at her in fear. It was studying her.

'We can't hang up here forever,' said Catalina, her voice hoarse. She had also managed to half-climb the stone wall.

'It looks like it's inspecting us,' said Anna. 'Judging us. Like some sort of royal rat monster.'

'I don't wish to be found suitable,' said Catalina, clinging desperately to both the wall and her sense of humour.

The king-rat made a series of soft, clicking sounds as it studied them. Its tails – long, tangled, thick and gnarled, like skinned tree roots – twined into the mass. The tails at the back of the king-rat-pack twitched and skittered, seeking out gaps and bumps on the floor. Many of the tails knotted and matted together.

A number of the front rats sniffed at the air. Many heads tilted and the bulk of the bodies snaked from side to side. And the entirety of it stood upright. They again moved to create a single swarming mass. The clicking noises stopped.

The king-rat appeared to have reached a decision. It moved. Towards them. En masse.

In a blind panic, both women jumped from the wall and ran. Anna didn't care where she was running, just so long as it was away.

* * *

The women did not stop when they had lost the enormous king-rat, but instead kept running. They came to an exhausted halt in a curving corner of the tunnel. Together they collapsed against the wall.

Anna had never known such primal fear. She knew she wouldn't ever forget the sensation of being watched. The sound of scrabbling over the ground behind her – the clicking, snuffling and squeaking – would forever haunt her dreams. She shuddered. To try and calm herself, she took in one deep breath after another. As she leaned against the wall, Anna relaxed, comforted by its presence. She allowed her shoulder to sink against the stone. Her skin pricked wherever it came in touch with the stone or moss of the castle. With each breath, her thoughts settled.

'No one will ever believe us,' whispered Catalina. She sat with her head buried in her hands. Her whole body shook.

'Come on. Are you seriously going to tell anyone about that? The Giant Rat Ball of the Catacombs,' said Anna, trying hard to smile. If not for her own sake, then for Catalina's.

Catalina glanced up. 'I suppose not.' She smiled, her lips closed and tight. 'It was almost more surreal than it was terrifying. Almost.'

'Almost. Have you even heard of something like that before? What the hell was it? Are they mutants? It moved like it was one creature.'

'I'm not sure,' said Catalina. 'I vaguely recall a myth. From when I was little. The name şobolan seems familiar. But it was no more than a child's tale. It was about giant rats. A bedtime story to scare me.'

'That was no bedtime story,' said Anna.

'No. And I might be mistaken. The tale might have been about a real creature. All the stories – real, ancient, make-believe – they sometimes get mixed up in my head. They blend together. There were so many stories.' Catalina shrugged and rubbed at her eyes. 'It doesn't matter. Whatever it was, it was real. It was terrifying, but it was no monster. Rats, tangled or not, are just that. Rats.'

'Cat, come on. That wasn't just a big tangle of rats. It moved like one horrid thing. A monstrous beast tracking our every move. A King of Rats.'

Catalina watched Anna for a long moment. 'You're enjoying this, aren't you?'

'No, of course not! I was terrified.'

'I'm not so sure.'

Anna ignored her and said, 'There's one thing *I* know for sure; we need to get out of here. And we need to go up, not down. If I was a mountain climber, maybe we'd have been okay. It looked like they couldn't climb.' She shuddered. 'At least not all of it.'

'That's not going to help,' said Catalina as she pointed to a large, untidy pile of rubble down at the end of the tunnel.

'A dead end?' Anna sighed and ran her fingers through her hair. 'Of course.'

'I do not wish to be trapped in a dead end with a creeping, colluding mass of intelligent rats on my trail.'

'There's got be another way,' said Anna looking around.

'I am beginning to fear we may never find a way out.'

As Catalina spoke, Anna heard the very faint, soft echo of thunder. Even down here, it seemed it would never let them be.

* * *

There was a rapid movement at the end of the tunnel.

'Did you see that?' said Anna.

'Yes,' said Catalina.

'It looked like a man,' said Anna, her brow furrowing. 'It was very quick, but I don't think it was Igor.'

'I'm not certain it was Igor,' said Catalina.

'At least it was a man, not a pack of rats.'

'And how is that better exactly? You're always a little too trusting, Anna.'

'A man I can reason with.'

Catalina half-smiled and half-grimaced. She

shook her head. 'Well, here we are again. Will we go the way he went? Or try and backtrack?'

'I honestly don't think I could find my way back. I was lost before. Now I don't even know how to describe it. This place is a whacked-out maze.' Anna shrugged and said, 'We don't have much of a choice. Besides, I've got no other plans'. As she stood, her hand slid along the castle wall. She held out her other hand to Catalina to help her stand up. 'You?'

Catalina took Anna's hand, stood, and walked over to the pile of rubble. 'There's something here.'

'That's not what I'd call inviting,' said Anna, looking over her shoulder. A small dark hole was visible in the wall behind one of the boulders. It was big enough to fit a man, but only just. And a slender man at that.

'Let me look inside.' Catalina hunkered down and peered up into the crawl space. She felt around before poking her head and shoulders, into the small, dark space.

'What can you see?' asked Anna.

'Nothing.' Catalina's reply was an indistinct echo. As she stood up, dust and tiny pebbles fell from her shoulders. Her hair was plastered with cobwebs.

'Wonderful,' said Anna, trying hard not to roll her eyes.

'It's so dark.' She shook some of the dust out of her hair. 'I could feel metal rungs, like steps on a ladder. There's just enough space to fit us and our backpacks. It's not what I'd call roomy, but we could do it. The rungs felt a bit loose and rusty,' said

Catalina. 'It's fairly unstable. But someone else has climbed it recently, so we should be okay.'

'So you think the man came this way too,' said Anna.

Catalina raised an eyebrow, but remained silent. 'Look at us,' she said. 'We're exhausted, lost, pushed beyond belief. I don't know what I think.'

'I don't think say we can't trust our senses,' said Anna, slumped against the wall. She looked up and said, 'But the other options don't look good, do they?'

'Maybe we should backtrack a little and use the ladder if it's absolutely necessary,' said Catalina, stepping back from the hole. 'I hate small spaces.'

'Shh,' said Anna, interrupting. 'Can you hear that?'

For a moment, there was the gentle but insistent sound of clicking.

Anna and Catalina froze.

Anna held her breath. It had started again. It had found them and was getting closer.

The women looked sideways at each other.

Anna made a slight gesture towards the uninviting, dark hole in the wall.

Catalina nodded carefully.

Anna watched Catalina forced herself up into the crawl space, squirming to squeeze herself in. It was slow-motion torture. Looking back, Anna could again see the swarthy tangle of rats. It seemed even bigger than before. The rat-pack was making its slow, inexorable path towards her. Sweeping left, sweeping right. *Click, click, click.* Anna stood near-hypnotised by its movement.

She looked back again to see that Catalina's body had all but disappeared up and into the tunnel. She was still moving slower than an iceberg. Anna whispered, 'Please, Cat. I can see it. It's getting closer. Hurry!' Anna's voice crept higher with each word.

'I'm trying, I'm trying!'

Anna heard Catalina yelp.

'My backpack. It's caught!', said Catalina.

'Cat! Come on!'

Behind Anna, the scurrying continued. Anna swore to herself.

She heard Catalina's cry.

'Got it!'

Anna watched as Catalina's legs rushed up and into the crawlspace.

It was now or never, thought Anna. She took a deep breath and dived into the crawl space. In one awkward and rushed movement, she made it most of the way in, leaving her legs showing, from the knees down. Anna scrambled blindly, grabbing at the bars to pull herself up.

A series of tiny, sharp pains stabbed into her calf. Something, many somethings, had gripped her and pierced her flesh. Her leg was alive with pain. Almost blind with terror, she shook and flailed. She slammed her leg wildly. Again and again.

The knot of rats tumbled down onto the tunnel floor.

When the pressure released, she yanked

herself up into the crawl space.

She scrambled up the ladder until she hit Catalina's legs. She wound her arms around and clung on tight.

Catalina screamed.

'It's me, Cat. It's just me!' said Anna. Her breathing was ragged, she was bleeding, and she was exhausted, but she pummelled her fists on Catalina's legs, desperate to stop her screams. 'Me. Just me.' She wrapped her arms around Catalina's legs again.

'Oh, Anna. Anna, are you alright?' Catalina's voice choked as she held back tears.

'I'm okay. The rat-thing had me, but I shook it loose. Eventually. I'm okay. We're both okay.' She wasn't sure if she was trying to calm herself or Catalina. Or both.

'It had you? Are you hurt?' asked Catalina.

'Yes, but I'm okay. I can keep going,' said Anna, as Catalina's fingertips reached her own. 'Come on, really. I'm okay.'

Below them, the furious sound of clicking and huffing did not die away.

Without speaking, Anna and Catalina scurried on up the ladder.

* * *

Igor stood before a mirror.

It was a strange mirror, convex in parts, concave in others. Made with polished metal, it had been long since broken up by streaks of rust. The refracting, distorted image appeared to make Igor younger.

'It is not necessary,' said Igor.

He turned away from the mirror. A younger voice, much like Igor's, said 'Perhaps not for the fair, young Englishwoman. The other one? It is necessary.'

Igor said, 'She is logical. We like her.'

'She is too strong.'

'The castle is enough. It will take them both. It will overwhelm them,' said Igor.

'She is cunning. It will not be enough.'

'The castle is all that is required,' said Igor. He turned his back on the mirror. He walked over to a table brimming with beakers, old-fashioned burners, and bubbling liquids. An alchemist's delight.

Igor picked up a small, round black bottle. The liquid inside spat and bubbled.

'I will not do this,' said Igor. 'We have been alone too long.'

Silence.

After a moment, Igor continued. 'The Mistresses have their senses, their wits. The castle will test them. It is enough.'

'It is not right!'

Igor returned to the mirror. 'No, it is only right. It is only fair,' he whispered. 'They must have a chance.'

'Then you must watch them. Follow them, monitor them.'

Igor flinched at the command. He looked away from the distorted image of his younger self in the mirror.

'Can I not leave them be? Let them wander alone?'

For the briefest moment, no voices could be heard. But then: 'Do you wish them to become like *you*?' the voice sneered.

* * *

Anna had long since lost track of time.

At first it had been strangely satisfying to be climbing. Hands, feet. Hands, feet. Hands. Feet. But after an interminable length of time, it became a blur. Anna thought they were high enough now that a fall would kill them. But she wasn't sure. The sheer physical effort of the climb had caused her to lose her sense of scale. Her hands ached. Covered with tiny cuts and scratches, they'd blistered but were now numb. Her feet weren't so bad. She'd never been so grateful for her old hiking boots. Her right leg was sticky with blood from the bites on her calf and ankle, but the boot had held and she was able to keep moving. She decided that her boots were her new best friend.

Her hands came up against Catalina's feet. 'Cat?' There was no reply. No movement. 'Hey, what's wrong? Talk to me.'

Catalina's voice was a thin whisper. 'There's something on my neck.'

Anna turned cold with fear. She tried not to let it show in her voice. 'Well, brush it off.'

'What if it's a spider?' said Catalina.

'You still need to brush it off,' said Anna.

'What if it falls on your head?'

Anna was silent. She hated this place. Before she could speak, Catalina said, 'It's on my face now.'

'Brush it off.' Anna tried again to sound calm. It wasn't easy. It was next to impossible.

'It's near my eyes,' said Catalina, her voice rising. 'My eyes. Oh, please, no. Not my eyes.'

'Stay calm, Cat. You're the sensible one. Deal with it. Whatever it is, brush it away.'

'No, no, no. My nostrils!' Catalina clawed at her nose, coughing and spitting.

Anna reached up to hold Catalina by the leg. It was a strange feeling. It was difficult to console someone by holding their calf, but she tried. 'It's okay, Cat. Brush it off. Scare it away.'

'I can't see. It's too dark. I can't breathe.' Catalina's words spilled out so fast, she'd was barely coherent. 'I need to get out of here!' She burst out. And then nothing.

'Cat?'

Catalina let loose a terrible and sickening scream. Her fingernails raked at her face and thin streaks of blood began to appear.

As Anna stared up at Catalina's face, she could at last see the spider. It was huge and trailing a web. Unspeakable, hairy and huge. She shook her head. It didn't matter. She knew if Catalina let go, she'd take both of them with her when she fell. Anna climbed halfway up over Catalina's body and wrapped her arms around her midriff, clinging to the rungs of the ladder, squeezing the two of them together and wedging them in place. She reached up and flicked – more pushed – the spider from Catalina's face. She crawled further and managed to rest her face against Catalina's shoulders. She spoke to her in the most comforting voice she could manage. 'It's okay, Cat. I've got you. I'll hold onto you. Forever.' She held her tight and whispered, 'You're safe. I won't leave you. You're not alone'.

Catalina stopped panicking. Surrounded by Anna's warmth and soothing words, her breathing returned to normal.

'Is it gone?' said Catalina, wiping sweat, blood and silken threads from her face. 'It's not gone, is it!' Catalina's voice had risen again.

'It's gone. Fucked off out of here.'

'Don't swear at me!'

'Well, hello,' said Anna. 'That sounded more like you.'

'Gone. It's gone.' Catalina shook her head. 'I hate spiders.'

'I know, Cat. I remember'.

'I would have been lost without you,' she said, leaning into Anna's arms.

'It's okay.' Catalina's chest rose and fell in time with Anna's own breathing. 'I promise you're okay.'

'I could have killed both of us,' said Catalina.

'I wouldn't have let you do that. Your

grandmother would have killed me,' said Anna.

Despite everything, Catalina managed a slight smile. Anna couldn't see it, but she could feel the tension ease from her friend's body.

After a few quiet minutes, Anna said, 'Come on. Let's keep moving. The only way out of here is up.' She pushed Catalina with an energy she didn't feel herself. 'Upwards and onwards.'

'Onwards and upwards.' Catalina began to extricate herself from Anna's hold.

And they climbed on.

* * *

'I don't think I can keep going. This is a joke. My body's a sick joke and I ache everywhere, 'said Anna.

'We have to keep moving. It can't be much higher. There's only a little more. Anyway, going down would be worse than going up,' said Catalina. 'The rats ...'

'The spiders ...'

'So ...'

'Okay, okay.' She knew Catalina was right. She didn't care. She only wanted to hear herself complain. 'I've got blisters. On everything. Even my feet now.' She hated her boots. They had betrayed her. 'Bilious boots,' she muttered.

'Wait. I can see a light. I think we're getting close.'

Anna groaned. Her movements had become agonising and slow. For the next few rungs, she tried to pull herself up using her arms, to rest her aching legs. She was too weak. She'd abused her body too much. Anna braced her arms and pulled, at the same time pushing up with her legs. Shove, instead of step. And again.

'A little more. Almost there.'

Anna was amazed. Her friend was nothing if not robust. She sighed and managed to pull and shove herself up another rung.

Then another.

And another.

And on.

* * *

Catalina clambered up and out of the filthy crawl space. She turned and reached down towards Anna. Anna, seeing Catalina's arms, grabbed hold was dragged up the last few steps.

Once up, Anna curled into Catalina's arms, and then both women crumbled to the floor. Anna lay on her back, the hard tiles cold and soothing, even through the thick layers of her clothes.

Eyes shut, the women's breathing slowed and shallowed until, exhausted, they fell asleep.

On the far side of the room, a tall, slender figure slipped through a doorway and let the door close behind him. Without trace or sound, both he and the door vanished into the wall.

* * *

An ornate, heavy black cloth draped over the rusty, polished mirror.

At the sound of a caw, Igor turned to the window.

The raven once more sat on the windowsill. It surveyed the room. Spying the covered mirror, it tilted its head and looked at Igor. It cawed a second time.

Igor, working at a bench nearby, did not lift his head. He only said, 'I know'.

The raven jumped down and pecked and jabbed at the cover. It grasped a corner and flew into the air, dragging the heavy cloth behind it.

Igor struck at the bird in mid-flight. The raven dropped the cloth and flew away, back onto the windowsill. 'I have pushed him away. I will not allow him to return.'

The raven launched at his arm. Its beak pierced the wiry flesh of Igor's wrist.

'No!' Igor shook the bird free. It flapped around the room, circling and cawing, swooping in great, mad arcs. At last, it calmed down and settled on the windowsill. Black, glistening feathers floated down from the ceiling.

'This will not be.' Igor had ignored the bird's frenzied flapping and had already returned to his work at the bench. He picked up a bottle and tipped it sideways. Black ichor seeped over its lip. Igor waited, still and patient, as the liquid oozed away. He held up the bottle for inspection. It was not quite empty.

Igor walked over to a nearby basket full of old metal implements. He picked out different implements – a slender metal tong, an intricate bronze spoon, a curling strip of wire – and compared each one to the mouth of the bottle. He whistled as he worked. When he found the right tool for the neck of the black bottle, he smiled. He scraped out the last of the tincture, allowing it to dribble down into the depths of a garderobe. Igor's face twitched each time the ichorous fluid made a noise as it landed on the bottom of the odorous pit below.

The raven had been quiet as Igor worked. As he finished, it came closer and gave Igor a curious look.

'It *can* be done another way.'

The raven's caw was loud, like angry laughter. It launched itself from the chair and leaped out the window. Its flight was so fluid, so graceful, that it was as if a waterfall flowed but in reverse. It let loose a final raucous caw. As it flew up and away, the grey, rolling clouds followed on its tail.

As the great bird departed, Igor said, 'I will protect you, Mistresses. I promise you. I will watch over you and protect you'.

CHAPTER FIVE

Anna woke up first.

The vision overhead took Anna's breath away. A painting covered the ceiling, seemingly unending. It spanned the breadth of the room, only interrupted by arched wooden beams that crisscrossed the roof. Even there, the painting worked with the wood and told a story in scenes. The first image held a young girl picking up flowers in the heart of a valley. The flowers swept under the next arch to a man and woman captured mid-stride, holding hands and walking towards the next wooden arch.

Anna, fascinated, allowed her gaze to wander across the ceiling. Each scene wove into the next. A young boy playing a drum walked past an older man beating sticks together; he leaned against vines that wrapped around the arch and into the next scene. An elderly woman held her head high and sang to the sun-filled sky; the clouds in the sky skittered across and under the wooden beam. Two young girls ran hand-in-hand, trailing long ribbons behind them; the ribbons combined and crossed under the arch, exploding in colour on the scene next door.

It was a festival. A musical event. It held

everything. It had energy, but was peaceful. Anna stared, mesmerised. Her gaze gradually found its way back down and settled on Catalina. Starting with guilt, she took in her friend's sprawled form, her head on the harsh tiled floor. She took off her jacket, folded it up and, gently pushing the blonde plait aside, slipped it underneath. Catalina muttered in her sleep, but didn't wake.

Anna stood up. Her muscles burned, the bites on her leg throbbed, and her feet and hands stung from far too many blisters. Ignoring the pain, she took in the rest of the room. It overflowed with musical instruments. Every niche had something new. A harp in this corner, a pianola against that wall. A great hanging wall of chimes that stirred from an unseen breeze. Brass and strings; a trumpet, a violin, a viola. Most of the instruments Anna recognised, but a few she had never seen before. Each alcove displayed its own unique set of instruments and chairs.

Anna paused in front of one alcove and ran her hands over the wooden back of a chair; made up of a myriad slivers of wood in beige, black and shades of brown. Up close, the parquetry was a wonder in detailed and dedicated handiwork. Pulled back, the mosaic became a scene of a winter forest. Each chair in the alcove depicted an unparalleled scene. The scene on one chair looked, when viewed from far enough back, like a castle and a valley.

'It's a masterpiece. A wonder,' said Catalina.

Anna turned. Catalina had woken up and was

lying staring at the ceiling. Rather than go to her, she let her be. There was no rush. She felt safe here. She didn't understand why, but she felt welcomed and at home.

She hobbled around the room. A nearby alcove lined with more parquetry seating and woodwind instruments filled her with a kind delight. Its neighbour had a number of beautiful padded, covered chairs; some in shades of blue, some green. In the middle, a hefty low chair made out of black marble loomed, seemingly climbing out of the floor. Its luxuriousness peaked with a seat covered by a deep-red silk cushion, trimmed in gold brocade, and a coat of arms atop. Its neighbouring alcove bore an elegant harp. Anna had no idea how to play one, but couldn't help let her fingers caress its strings.

'Anna? Is that you?'

'Yep, it's me. I thought you could do with a rest.' Anna walked over and looked down. 'Sorry. The harp was too tempting.'

'A harp?' asked Catalina, as she sat up. 'That was truly a harp?'

'It really was. Looks like we found ourselves a music room.' Anna smiled as she watched Catalina take in the rest of the room.

'Oh, my. It's almost too lovely.'

'No kidding.'

Catalina tried to stand up, but flinched and sat back down.

Anna winced in sympathy. 'I think it's time for a bit of repair work. At least the first aid stuff is in my backpack.' Anna looked over Catalina, frowned and said, 'I don't even know where to start'.

Catalina pointed over to the spreading, bloody stain on Anna's jeans. 'I think you start there.'

* * *

Igor gazed out the window. The storm twisted and rolled. The clouds moved at high speed and split as they neared the castle. The rain continued, relentless. Igor's fingers drummed on the balcony. He glanced over at the covered mirror from time to time.

On the back wall of the alchemist's room, a wide shelf bowed under the weight of stacks of stained, torn old books. He picked one up. It fit neatly in the palm of his hand. The words engraved on the cover read *'Hora Unirii'*.

Igor read a passage out loud. As he read, he stood tall and his voice sung out, booming out of the room and across the sky. The thunder echoed his words. If Igor's stage was the castle, his audience was the weather and the world.

Măi muntene, măi vecine
Vino să te prinzi cu mine
Şi la viaţă cu unire
Şi la moarte cu-nfrăţire!

'I will watch over them. Keep them safe.' Igor opened the voluminous folds of his cloak and tucked the musty book inside, pressing it against his chest.

* * *

Bandages spilled across the floor.

Anna and Catalina each sat on an amber-coloured damask chaise longue. Anna's jeans were rolled up and her right leg neatly bandaged. Catalina's face was a network of disinfectant-tinted scrapes. Both women had their boots off; their feet and hands neatly wrapped in a range of big and small bandages.

Catalina said, 'All we need now is a decent cup of coffee and some cake'.

'Make mine a good stiff drink, thanks,' said Anna.

Catalina leaned into the soft cushion behind her and relaxed her shoulders. 'Honestly, I'm happy enough with a little sit down for now. Anything else would be an extravagance.'

Looking around, Anna said, 'Mum would love this room'. She recalled her mother sitting at the tiny electric piano in their lounge room. Her Dad stood nearby, singing off-key. No one had ever looked so happy. Her parents weren't meant for their own era – they were far better suited to the 1930s or '40s. Or something. As a young teenager, she'd always been deeply embarrassed by them. It pained her to think about it. Now they were still embarrassing, but they were her kind of embarrassing. A lot of her favourite songs were all but unknown to most of her friends. Anna started to hum to herself.

Catalina started humming a song. A song about storms. *'Don't know why.'*

Anna smiled. It took so little to get them both started. A sunless night sky full of storm and weather was more than enough. *'There's no sun up in the sky.'*

They joined voices and sang together. Everyone has a favourite storm song. This was theirs. Full of yearning and loss.

Anna strolled around as they continued to sing. They just about made it to the end of the song, but when Catalina gestured to the gloomy sky through the window, Anna stopped, overcome by a fit of giggles.

Anna laughed until her ribs ached. 'I used to love that song. Here was me thinking it was about the end of a relationship. Turns out it's yet another tale of "dark and stormy nights".'

Catalina grinned, 'I'll never listen to that song quite the same way again'.

Thunder boomed and white light flooded a tall arched window at the other end of the room.

Anna stared vacantly at the window as her eyes recovered. 'Every time I feel low, this place seems to pick me back up again. It's like something's playing with me.'

Catalina said nothing and gazed out of the window.

'How does he do it?' asked Anna.

'Who? Igor?' asked Catalina.

'Yeah. I mean, look at this place.' She gestured at some of the polished furniture and immaculate instruments in the room. 'Maintaining this alone could keep him busy for a month.'

'He must have help.' Catalina shrugged.

Anna looked at her. 'The man!'

They both did a double-take, glancing around the room.

'But there's no other way out. We were climbing forever, 'said Anna. 'I mean, come on, he could hardly have gone out over the window.'

Anna and Catalina went over and looked out at the view. Under the moonlight, the valley below shimmered black and silver. Even though Anna had walked up that same valley, she couldn't recognise any landmarks. It was all too small. Like looking at a plastic model of the valley. She knew the village was down there somewhere, but hidden from view.

'Clearly he didn't go that way.'

'We did see him,' said Anna. 'Didn't we?'

'I was going to say, "Of course we did", but how can we be certain of anything here?'

'I know it was only a second, but I swear, it was one of the most real things I've seen since we've been here,' said Anna.

Catalina looked thoughtful for a moment. 'You're right. This,' she said tapping the heavy stones of the castle wall behind her, 'sounds real and feels real, but there's so much intensity, such grandeur, that it seems to demand us to consider it unreal. He was only a man. An ordinary man.'

'Yup. And so our problem is …'

'Where is he?'

'There's got to be another way out. We've got to find it.'

Anna and Catalina set about searching the room.

* * *

'This is ridiculous.'

Catalina ignored her and concentrated on running her fingers along seams in the wooden archways.

'We'll never find it,' said Anna.

Catalina turned to her and said, 'Finish packing up. If we find it, I'd like to be ready to go'.

'Sure thing, boss.'

'Shh.' Catalina stared at a blank section of wall. 'There must be a way to solve this. We have to be a little logical.'

Anna smiled as she packed away the first aid gear. 'I thought *I* was the Nancy Drew fan.'

Catalina ignored her.

'Okay, okay. Shutting up.' Their gear packed, Anna sat on an oversized, smooth marble chair and began lacing up her hiking boots. As good as they were, she was still hating the idea of putting her feet back inside them. She grumbled to herself as she went. Leaning down to thread a frayed end through an eyelet of her boot, Anna noticed a slight depression in one corner of the marble base. Anna glanced at the other corners and said, 'I think I've got something'.

Catalina turned, her eyes bright. 'What have you found, *Nancy*?'

* * *

'Well, I wasn't expecting that,' said Anna.

Anna and Catalina stared into the wide, open, well-lit tunnel. A few feet long, another room was visible at the other end.

'So many, many books,' breathed Catalina.

'They're probably all in Romanian,' said Anna.

'Or Transylvanian or Moldovan.'

'What are we waiting for?' asked Anna.

'I don't trust it,' said Catalina.

'Oh, come on. It's hardly a mirage.'

They stared again through the tunnel. Row after row of books beckoned them forth.

* * *

Igor stood in an alcove of a dim, dark corridor, his ear to the wall.

The wall of the alcove, unlike the rest of the corridor, was smooth and papery. Igor pressed his head closer to the wall.

After a little while, he smiled to himself and whispered, 'My Mistresses. You will be safe'.

* * *

'What are you even saying? It must be a trap because it's too beautiful? Come on. Books? Books are a trap?' Anna couldn't believe it. 'Let's check it out. It's got to be a library. An ancient library. Lie-brair-ree. Cat! Are you even hearing me?.'

Catalina put one strong hand on Anna's shoulder. 'No, please, Anna. We've been pushed along at every stage. We should wait and think about this. Let's take it slow. Just this once, let's look around first.'

'But the books …' said Anna, her voice flat and low. 'I'll go through on my own and have a quick look.'

'And leave me behind? No. Definitely not.'

Anna sighed and released her pressure on the square of marble. The entrance to the tunnel swung shut again. 'Okay, so we'll look around some more first. But I don't have to like it.'

'Clearly, you don't.'

* * *

'I've never seen so many books,' said Anna. 'Come on, Cat. Imagine how many are in there.'

'Yes, Anna,' said Catalina, as she continued her search. She kneeled on the ground, feeling the floor around the base of a harp. She ran her fingers over the delicate, blue-shaded tiles that covered a small rectangular dais.

Anna looked behind a diminutive pipe organ. Peering into a thin, narrow strip of darkness, she said, 'Each one looked like a treasure, you know'.

'Anna, we weren't even close enough to see.' Catalina looked at a corner tile on the harp's dais. Each corner tile displayed a different emblem of the four seasons. Catalina poked at one. It slid sideways. Catalina tried pressing each corner in turn. They all moved. She tried different sequences, then two at a time. She called out to Anna, 'I could use a little help here'.

Anna trundled over, muttering about books under breath. She looked at the intricate designs on the polished blue tiles. Beautiful. One of citrus trees, one of flower buds, one of autumnal leaves, and one of blues and whites and snow. 'They're lovely,' whispered Anna.

Catalina stage whispered back, 'Why are we whispering?'

Anna shrugged and said, 'It seemed like a good idea?'

Catalina smiled and continued in a hushed tone. 'The tiles move. Slightly, but they move. I've tried a few things, but not all four at once. They're set too far apart.'

Anna grinned. 'This is so cool.'

Catalina rolled her eyes. It was slight, but Anna noticed. 'Want my help or not?'

'If you would be so kind, Nancy.'

Anna poked out her tongue, but kneeled down anyway.

They positioned themselves at either end of the harp's dais. As their palms pressed down, the little tiles all slipped forward, twisting slightly. A thin, papery door opened across the other side of the room.

In the gloom of the now open doorway stood Igor. On seeing them he started and stood straight.

'Igor!' said Catalina.

'Were you spying on us?' said Anna.

Igor's mouth dropped open. He glanced sideways and dodged out of sight.

Speechless, Anna and Catalina looked at each other.

'Um …' said Anna.

'Igor? Are you still there?' called out Catalina.

There was no reply.

Anna tapped Catalina on the shoulder and said, 'Gloom of night or library of light?'

'I want to know why Igor is spying on us. I want him to get us out of here.'

They stood up, releasing the pressure on the tiles. The door slammed shut.

Catalina sighed. 'I'm a little tired of being pushed around.'

Anna eyes lit up as she said, 'Pushed around, you say?'

* * *

Anna pushed the last chair into place and, with a gentle hush of air, the door swung open. She grinned at Catalina. Four chairs stood in a neat square, each one with a single chair leg on the corner tiles. 'Ready?' said Anna.

'Please, after you,' said Catalina with a slight bow.

Anna stuck her head into the near lightless corridor. There were no torches, the only light coming from behind them in the music room. Beyond the first few feet of its warm, yellow glow, nothing could be seen.

'That's more than a little disappointing,' said Catalina, looking over Anna's shoulder.

Anna walked forward a couple of steps, allowing her fingers to traverse the stones that were the heart of the castle. She sighed to herself.

'Anything unusual?' asked Catalina, keeping back to make sure the door stayed open.

'The same stony wall. The same dank corridors.'

'No Igor?'

'No Igor, 'said Anna.

'That decides it for me. I'm not going back into the darkness.'

'I guess so,' said Anna as she walked back, her fingers trailing against the stones. 'The library it is.'

CHAPTER SIX

Anna walked into her own personal daydream.

The library was sprawling and majestic. Every space covered with books. Stacks of ancient tomes soared on towering shelves. Anna didn't know where to start. The books were only the beginning. The room was no mere library. It was an archive. A haven of repair and restoration, and a place for the soul of an old-style artisan. For a fleeting moment, Anna wished she were a hundred years older. She stared in quiet awe.

Near the outer walls of the library, waxed wooden tablets covered a series of thin trestles. Each tablet showed a different story through a mixture of pictograms and old intricate scripts.

The outer walls held purpose-built alcoves every few feet. A collection of different tools and a bundle of broken and new wooden spools stood near a stack of undamaged parchments. On a little shelf there lay chunks of wax and an assortment of carving tools. In another alcove, a collection of inks huddled up next to a stylus in an elaborate cut glass pot.

Walking to the centre of the room, Anna

found a monolithic desk covered with untidy piles of crumbling parchments. Some were laid flat, open to the ravages of time, but others were stacks of tied scrolls. The desk had eight sides and eight hefty chairs. One chair was pushed out a little, as if someone had been interrupted in their research yesterday. But at the same time, yesterday seemed like it might have happened hundreds of years ago.

Feeling giddy, Anna sat in the chair and looked around her. 'Too much. It's too much.'

Curved shelves lined the inside of the room, and smaller and smaller sets of shelves carved their way towards the centre.

Nearby, Catalina stared wide-eyed at a packed set of shelves. She picked out a book at random. The cover – a series of beautiful engravings – like many of its neighbours, had no title.

Anna sat back and watched Catalina. She had seen books like this before; they both had. But those books reminded her of trapped butterflies. Held under lock and key, in low light and encased in wood and glass, they were the wordy prisoners of museum curators and musty librarians. Beauties to be worshipped from a distance, but never touched. This was something else. She got up and wandered over to the nearest shelf and reached out, letting her fingertips rest on the spine of a great, deep-blue book. It was warm to the touch and Anna flinched her hand back. The air in the room was crisp and cold. Anna stepped away from the book.

'Please. Give me a moments peace,' she

whispered. Hearing her own words, she felt stupid. It was as if the castle was watching her, even as she mocked herself for thinking it. She knew she couldn't share her thoughts with Catalina. She could imagine the humiliating and all too logical response. She moved along the shelf, touching books at random. Every now and then, a book would seem to speak to her and invite her touch. It was these that felt different; warm and pleasurable. She shivered with delight.

'Look at this,' said Catalina, bent over a massive tome.

Anna walked over to Catalina and looked over her shoulder. The script on the pages was extraordinary. The beginning letter on each page was a singular work of art. 'Can you read it?'

'No,' Catalina said, shaking her head. 'It's beautiful, but it's ancient. There really is very little I understand.'

'I feel a bit like a naughty kid might if left alone in a library. The librarian could wander in at any moment. And you know you'll be in trouble if she does.'

'I think you mean "he".' No doubt the librarian is Igor. 'Catalina stood and positioned the book back in its proper place on the shelf.

Anna's brow creased. 'Igor?' She felt a little disappointed as she'd been enjoying imagining a mysterious elderly woman taking care of the even more ancient books. 'I guess you're right.'

'I can picture him here, working and reading.'

Catalina looked about the room and added quietly, to herself, 'I begin to understand why he lives here. With a room like this, would you want to leave?'

* * *

'I wish I was a better at this. I'm yet to find a book I can properly understand,' said Catalina.

'I *know* there's nothing for me. It seems so cruel. A room full of books and nothing to read.' Anna ran her hands along the row of books until she found another tome that was warm to the touch. Its spine was covered with coloured, engraved curlicues and whorls. As she pulled it down from its shelf, she had the pleasurable shock of seeing that the cover was comprised of a trio of ivory carvings.

Three different ivory panels covered the book, each with a different image. The first seemed to depict the sun, but diminished and darkened in some way. An engraving of the moon filled the central panel, but it was an unhealthy moon, one that bled and seeped into the landscape far below. The final scene in the triptych showed a night sky full of falling stars. The deftness of touch, the beauty, was stunning to behold, but at the same time it was a nightmare in white. Anna couldn't look away. After a time, she opened the book to the frontispiece. Inside was a drawing of a simple windswept valley with a brief inscription underneath: *Moroidava cetate.*

Anna realised that Catalina had been talking

to her.

'Anna?'

'Mm?' said Anna without looking up.

'I asked you if you'd found something.'

Anna dragged herself back to the here and now. 'I don't know. It's this book. There's something about it,' she said turning the page. The script on the pages was beautiful, but not old. Anna could recognise most of the individual letters. 'I can't read it, but it looks sort of familiar.'

'Were you intending to share it with me?' said Catalina.

Anna sat the open book down next to Catalina.

Catalina glanced over the words.

'Anything?'

'Yes. It's old, but it at least resembles a language I can almost read. A language I *should* be able to understand.' Catalina groaned. 'What a pity Bunică isn't here. She'd enjoy my suffering immensely.'

'Also, she could read the book,' said Anna.

'Ow! Thank you for that.'

'Come on, you know I'm kidding.' Anna squeezed her friend's shoulder. 'We're not doing research here. It's not an exam. It's an adventure. If you find something intriguing, good. If not, it doesn't matter.' She smiled and said, 'You're not on trial'.

Catalina looked around the ancient book-filled room. Every curved surface, every shelf, overflowed with antiquities and records of the past. 'It doesn't exactly feel that way.' But she smiled all the same. She selected a couple of thicker pages in the centre of the tome. As the pages fell open, Anna drew in a sharp breath.

The image was of a beautiful, rolling scene in grey. Every line and curve of the drawing was a minor masterpiece. The sky full of rolling storm clouds. The landscape made of dangerous and unscalable rocks. The scene was unmistakable. It was the valley. And the castle.

Anna and Catalina looked at each other.

'This place just loves coincidences, doesn't it.'

Thunder rolled.

* * *

The women stared at the image of the towering castle.

Catalina said, 'See what else you can find. I'll try my best to read some of this'. She took a deep breath and turned the pages until she was back at the beginning of the book. She lowered her head, already lost in translation, lost in words.

Anna let her be and wandered off among the papery shelves.

* * *

Anna followed the circles of shelving until she

reached an outer wall of the library.

Walking around a corner, Anna discovered an alcove that contained a tiny window.

Anna stood on tiptoes and leaned against the castle's ancient wall so she could look through the gap. Tension drained from her body as she felt the comforting touch of the stones. Eerie and illogical though it might be, she had sort of come to expect it now. The castle – the true castle – knew her and welcomed her. It warmed, comforted and caressed her. The longer she spent in contact with it, the more intimate the connection became.

Anna's breathing slowed as she peered through the tiny window. She allowed her gaze to rest on a small, enclosed space, lit by walls covered with tiers of narrow candles. The little square contained a verdant, manicured garden.

Peering through the tiny gap, she could see a trickle of a creek that split up the lush greenery on the dirt-packed floor. On either side of the garden there were white-painted wrought iron benches. Both had rusted through long ago. The paint peeled and crumbled to the ground.

Anna didn't know how a garden could be grown in such a space, who maintained the candles or even how she could get in, but she wanted with all her heart to get in. She had never seen anything so heartbreakingly beautiful. She knew that if she could get in, she would live out the rest of her days in the little garden, listening to the sounds of trickling water, breathing in the heady fragrance of the wildflowers. Her fingers and feet prickled at the thought it.

Trying to push her head further through the small window, she scraped her face against the stonework. Her face flushed with the warmth of it. Peering up through the gap, she couldn't see the top of the garden, but she watched the long trailing vines vanish out of sight. Spiderwebs connected the flowering vines, their gossamer threads shimmering in the candlelight.

The garden's presence was as exquisite as it was inexplicable and she longed to be a part of it. She pressed her whole body against the wall. Every touch sent fire through her body and set her senses alight. She knew it could consume her, body and soul. She knew it and she wanted it, like she had never wanted anything before.

* * *

At the desk, Catalina sat up straight and pushed the book away from her. With great care, she closed the book.

Running her fingers across the front of the cover, she said, 'What is this place? Where are we?'

She looked around the room for Anna. 'Damn her.'

* * *

'What on earth are you doing?' said Catalina.

Anna, her head stuck halfway in a tiny stone window, didn't respond.

'What's wrong with you?' With still no response, Catalina tapped Anna on the shoulder. 'I've been looking for you everywhere.'

Anna made no movement at all.

Catalina tried to pull Anna back. Anna ignored her and burrowed her face deeper into the window, her body closer to the wall. Catalina grabbed Anna by the shoulders and dragged her away.

'What are you doing? Leave me alone!' Anna's eyes were dark and unfocussed.

'What happened to you? Surely you haven't been here the whole time?' said Catalina.

'The garden,' said Anna.

Catalina glanced over Anna's shoulder. 'Yes, it's a garden.'

'The garden.' Anna swayed backwards.

Catalina slapped Anna hard on the face. In the quiet of the room, the sound of the slap rung out.

Anna blinked and held her hands to her cheeks. Looking up, she said 'What the hell! Why did you do that?'

'Oh, Anna, Anna.' Catalina pulled her close and held her. Anna, dazed and confused, allowed herself to be engulfed in her embrace.

Pulling back, Catalina grasped Anna by the hand and dragged her back towards the centre of the room.

Anna walked in silence, unable to take her

eyes away from the little window of heaven.

* * *

'Are you feeling a little better?' said Catalina.

'Yeah. I don't get what happened, but … I'm okay, I guess.'

'I don't know. But no more gardens for you. And no more wandering off on your own.'

Anna nodded. The fog in her head hadn't quite cleared. She knew she'd been looking at a garden but she couldn't remember very much. Except that it felt good. She flushed hot at the memory of it and shook her head. She'd also managed to make Catalina angry. For now, that was all that mattered. Anna opened her to mouth to apologise but decided against it. She said, 'Was I gone long?'

Catalina shrugged. 'Only a little while, in truth.'

'Thanks for coming to get me, anyway, 'said Anna. She wasn't sure why, but she didn't feel particularly grateful.

'Forget it,' said Catalina. She hadn't taken her eyes off Anna for a moment. 'If you're thinking clearly, I can tell you what I found out.'

'You found something? What did you find? A clue?'

'I thought that might get your attention,' said Catalina.

* * *

'It's very unclear. There are some words that I'm able to translate, but too much of it means nothing to me.'

'But you still discovered something?' said Anna looking at the book.

'Something small, but, yes, I think so.' Catalina flipped to the frontispiece again. 'These words appear again and again throughout the text,' she said, tracing her finger along the letters *Moroidava cetate.* 'I think, given the way it's been used, it's the name of the castle.'

Anna shook her head. 'Nope, I was told this is the castle *Gheorgheni.*'

'Yes, but how do you know. You couldn't find anything online about it.' Catalina looked at Anna. 'Who told you that name? Was it Igor?'

Anna was half listening to Catalina. She couldn't forget how good the garden had felt. She longed to be near it. To feel its warmth. She shifted in her seat and tried to let herself drift away, but Catalina's drumming fingertips dragged her back again. She said, 'What difference does it make?'

'Perhaps Igor lied to you. Or you misinterpreted something he said.'

'No way.' Anna gestured the notion away with her hand. She was bored with the conversation. She wanted to be back by the garden. 'Besides, I had an interpreter.'

Catalina said nothing for a moment. 'An interpreter?'

'Yes,' said Anna, gazing at her fingernails.

'Why would you need an interpreter? Igor speaks great English.'

Anna let slip a harsh, short laugh. 'Sure. But do you see any computers here? Any internet? How did you think he reached me?'

'How?' said Catalina.

'Like I said. An interpreter. A guy from the village spoke to him, took notes and then put it all together in an email to me.'

'You weren't communicating directly with Igor or anyone who lived here?' Catalina stopped drumming her fingers. 'Every time he spoke to you it was via someone else?'

'Yes,' she said. 'Good grief, Cat, why do you think it took so long for him to get back to me?'

'You didn't tell me there were delays,' said Catalina.

'Geez. I thought you knew. I mean any "big old castle" is hardly going to have all the latest and greatest tech,' said Anna, fidgeting with the edge of the table.

'Some castles do. Many castles only exist now for tourists.'

'What can I say. This one's different.'

'Wait,' said Catalina holding up her hands. 'You knew. You knew this place wasn't modern. That there were no computers, no access to anything. You knew we wouldn't have any direct contact with the outside world. You *knew*?'

Anna looked up at Catalina. 'I guess so, yes.' Catalina's anger had at last gotten through to her fog-filled mind. Her cheeks burning red, she said, 'I'm s—'

Catalina cut her off. 'Don't say it. Do not even think about saying it.' She stood and walked away.

After a moment's indecision, Anna went after her.

* * *

'Wait up. Please, Cat, hang on.'

Even at walking pace, Catalina's long legs meant she was always able to outpace her. Anna sometimes thought she had spent her whole life chasing after her. She caught up with her just as they approached an entrance to a small, golden-hued stairwell.

She held Catalina's elbow. 'Come on. I know what we said about not apologising. This is different. It was before we came. I'm sorry. I guess I thought it didn't matter.'

Catalina pulled her arm free, but turned to face Anna. 'You lied to me.'

'Not on purpose. I wasn't thinking. I was too excited. I should have told you. Come on, Cat. At least let's stick close.'

Some of the tension fell from Catalina's face. 'You're right. We should stay together. It isn't safe to split up. I certainly can't trust you to be on your own.'

Anna said nothing. She didn't agree with the sentiment, but knew it would be best to let her have things her own way for a while. She decided to try and distract her, instead of letting the conversation get any worse. Pointing at the stairwell behind Catalina, she said, 'What's through there?'

'I have no idea,' said Catalina looking at the entry to the stairwell.

'Come on, let's find out.'

* * *

The stairwell glowed a pale gold and the stairs unfolded above them. Wooden banisters curved gracefully overhead, obscuring the view.

On each side, the walls were lined with thin paper, decorated with repeating patterns of elaborate webs of gold.

Walking up, Anna tried her best to put the garden out of her mind. It was, she realised, only a distraction. But it felt real. A deliberate temptation from the castle. It didn't matter. Even if she wanted to succumb, she had to put Catalina first. Or at least try.

Ahead of her, Catalina climbed methodically. She hadn't said a word since they left the library.

Without noticing, Anna slowed her steps as she tried to think of a way to break the tension. Glancing around, she recognised a pattern in the decorations on the wall. 'Hey, Cat, Look at this.'

'More scenes of torture?' said Catalina without looking back.

'Constellations, actually.'

Catalina stopped mid-step and peered at the detailed line drawings. 'Oh, my.'

Each microscopic pattern was a part of the night sky. The constellations were unfamiliar to Anna, but she knew them to be exactly that. Next to each constellation was a small, thin wire frame diagram of their namesake. It was the bear that had caught Anna's attention.

Catalina moved closer to look where Anna looked. Next to the first big bear, there was a smaller, younger bear. 'Ursa Minor,' said Catalina.

'Worth stopping?'

Catalina allowed a smile to escape before turning away.

As they continued up, both women stopped now and then to look at unusual configurations or streaming comet tails. The steps narrowed and the corners of the stairwell tightened.

Looking up, Anna said, 'I wonder where they keep the shrinking potion.'

Catalina, hunched over, twisted around and said, 'No potions. No mysteries. No creatures of the night. Not even a raven, if you would be so kind'.

'Oh, you.' Anna made pacifying motions with her hands. 'Okay, okay. No boogly-woogly. It'll be dull as dishwater.'

'Good. I've had my fill of interesting today,' she said turning away.

Unseen, Anna rolled her eyes.

* * *

Catalina pushed open the compact wooden door, ducked down and scrambled through.

Beyond, there was no ceiling. There was only sky.

Catalina stood at the top of a turret, the wind catching her loosely plaited hair. She turned to help Anna through the small door, holding her as they fought to stand upright in the gusty winds.

An intricate, angled wrought iron frame stood in the centre of the turret.

Anna's first thought was that she was standing in front of a giant, oversized crossbow. After a moment studying it, Anna realised what they were looking at. 'Is that what I think it is?'

'Yes,' breathed Catalina. Her hair streamed out behind her, breaking loose of its plait; a river flowing around a stone.

'What do you call it? Like ... what? An observatory? Or is there another word?'

Catalina whispered her response. 'A sextant. A framed sextant. For observing the stars.'

Anna delighted in watching the expressions on Catalina's face. Her eyes sparkled. 'It's beautiful.'

'It's heavenly.' Catalina gestured at the dark, rolling clouds in the sky above. In one corner of the sky, the moon shone through a gap in the wall of the storm. It cast a long, silvery shadow across the turret. 'It can measure the *heavens*.'

'Are they usually outside like this? It looks a bit,' Anna wiggled her fingers, 'fussy?'

Without taking her eyes off the sextant,

Catalina said 'I honestly don't know. I've never seen one outside of a museum.'

'This whole place is a museum.'

Catalina moved closer and inspected the sextant. 'As delicate as the ironwork looks, it is solid. It looks like it was built to withstand the elements.'

Above them, a gap in the perpetual storm opened up, freeing the moon from its cloak. Moonlight shone down on a cosy scene in the distant horizon. Silver washed across the rooftops of a faraway village.

Anna walked over to one of the crumbling balustrades. 'Look at that. We can't have walked all that way. It must be another village.'

Catalina looked where Anna was pointing. 'No, I think that's the right direction.'

Both women stood looking at the distant dwellings below.

As quaint and oddball as it had been when they first arrived, Anna now couldn't imagine any place more familiar and comforting. Her heart ached for the ordinary. For her family, for her mother and father. For everything that she didn't have here. For home.

In a voice no more than a whisper, she said, 'I want to go home'.

* * *

'We shouldn't have let them go.'

The residents of the village had gathered at

the local inn.

A tall, domineering grey-haired man stood by the open fireplace. 'What would you have had us do, Petre?'

'Anything. Not this,' said the young, slender man.

'We couldn't have stopped them. They wouldn't have believed us, no matter what we said.'

'But to just stand around and let it happen ...'

There were murmurs among the small crowd. Many there were young. It was the youngest that complained the loudest.

'You are too young to remember,' said the grey-haired man.

The young man, Petre, spoke again. 'True. But it's the same for you.'

'Yes, but I remember the fear. My great-grandfather was brave. He fought when we needed to fight. He worked when we needed the workers.' He turned to the fire, holding his hands to the flames. 'This, though, this was different. My father made me promise to never ask him about it a second time. He did not need to ask. I never wanted to see or hear his fear again. The stories were malevolent and terrible.'

'Can't you hear yourself? "The stories". What were we thinking? We should have stopped them. The valley alone could kill them. It isn't right to have allowed innocent women to walk into a storm like that, alone and unguarded.'

The grey-haired man turned back. 'You know

they aren't alone.' He stood taller than before, his shadow flickering long and dark into the room. 'My son—'.

'Your son isn't the problem, Nikolai,' said another voice.

Another voice spoke up. An old woman. 'Hush, both of you.' Turning to the younger man, she said, 'He speaks the truth. They would not have believed us. It would not matter what we said or how we said it. We are not even certain of the truth ourselves. How could we have convinced them?'

'All the same—' Petre began.

'Enough. Mihai will watch out for them. He will make sure no harm comes to any of them.'

CHAPTER SEVEN

The clouds raced across the sky. The harvest moon was once again lost from sight.

Anna watched the clouds build. They piled one upon another, grey knots tangling together to form a solid wall.

The temperature plummeted and Anna thought she could see hail in the distance. 'We have to go.' There was no reply. Catalina was no longer at her side. She looked around. Catalina was on her knees, inspecting the sextant.

The wind roared. Anna's hair whipped at her face. She said, 'Come on Cat, we have to go'.

Catalina looked up and shook her head. She mouthed the words 'One more minute'.

Anna looked at the dark, malevolent sky behind her. She grabbed Catalina by the arm and dragged her towards the door. The storm raged around as they ran. Hail hammered down from the sky.

* * *

Catalina was shivering and her teeth chattered. The cold and lashing rain had blasted them both, but it seemed to have hit Catalina harder.

Anna held her close.

They sat at the top of the stairwell, not talking. Resting.

Once Catalina had warmed up enough to stop shivering, Anna said 'Now what?'

Catalina shrugged. 'I don't know. I want to rest. I don't want to risk going to sleep. I want to find Igor. I would be happy never to see Igor again. I want to go home.' She gestured towards the library at the bottom of the stairwell. 'I don't know what I want.'

Anna looked at her friend. 'If a helicopter flew in now to pick us up, are you saying you wouldn't leave?'

'Of course I would leave,' she said as she held Anna's gaze. 'Would you?'

Anna decided that a partial truth was good enough. 'Of course I would. I just want to go home.'

Catalina raised an eyebrow. 'No more garden? No more library? No solved mysteries?'

Anna looked away and said, 'We need to find somewhere to rest. I can't go on like this'.

'I thought we said that hours ago.'

The unmistakable cacophony of a pile of books falling over rang out. It was loud, muffled and nearby.

Catalina said, 'Do you think it's Igor?'

'I hope so. Strange as he is, he's all we've got.'

'Time to find out,' said Catalina. Exhausted,

they took their time and trod down the stairwell.

In the middle of the library, a large stack of books lay sprawled across the floor.

Beyond the books, there were no signs of living people.

Anna and Catalina walked the circle of the library, searching, but found no one.

'You know this room is perfectly designed for hiding out in. If you're not in the central corridor, you can't see anything but the shelf in front of you.'

Catalina paused and looked around. 'You're right. They could still be here.'

Anna's voice dropped low. 'So, instead of hunting, we should be waiting?'

Catalina matched her voice to Anna's. 'Waiting. Hunting. You label it however, you see fit.'

'I like your thinking.' She grinned. 'Time for some table turning.'

They settled on the floor and leaned against a shelf. The hunters waited.

*   *   *

A confident young man strolled around the curving bookshelf and nearly tripped over Catalina and Anna's legs.

The women sat up. Anna hadn't expected it to work and they had both begun to doze off. She blinked at the man standing before her.

He stared at them both for a minute before turning away to make a break for it.

'Hey! You!' Anna yelled after him.

Catalina stood and said, 'We want to talk to you'.

To Anna's complete surprise he stopped, turned back and said, 'Yes?'

* * *

Anna ran her eyes over the young man before her. He was a medium build, not too tall and olive-skinned. If it wasn't for the dark hair and even darker eyes, he would have been exactly her sort. She tried not to let herself smile. She could make do.

'Well?' he said. 'What do you want?'

Catalina spoke before Anna could jump in, 'Have you been following us?'

'Yes.' And crossed his arms over his chest.

Catalina looked at Anna. Anna shrugged and said 'Okay. Honest. I like that. Why?'

'This is how my parents raised me, yes?'

'What?' said Anna in confusion.

He looked at Anna with a mischievous smile. 'This is why I am honest.'

'I can see you're going to be a mess of trouble.'

He grinned.

'Why are you following us?'

'Good. This is a better and more useful question. However, the answer is longer. Shall we find somewhere comfortable to sit and make introductions?'

Anna nodded and jumped to her feet.

Catalina pursed her lips before saying, 'If this is the only way to make you talk, we'll sit'. She got up and walked off to the centre of the library.

He nodded in Catalina's direction and said, 'She must be fun at parties'.

'She is actually. She just takes a bit of getting used to.'

'I will take your word for it.'

Anna laughed. 'Come on. Let's go. No point making her wait.'

* * *

'Glad to see you could make it. Finished flirting have you?'

'Cat!'

Catalina rolled her eyes. 'Oh, sit down.'

Anna sat down. The young man leaned against a chair, grinning at Anna.

Catalina glanced at his stance, shrugged and said, 'Let's start with your name'.

He stopped smiling at Anna, half-bowed at Catalina and said 'Mihai. Mihai Troester. And I have the pleasure of meeting?'

The two women tried to speak at the same time, but Catalina's attempt of *'That's none of your business'* was overrun by Anna who said, 'I'm Anna Harker and this is my friend Catalina Dalca. Cat, for short'.

'Oh, very well done,' said Catalina.

'There's no harm in that. What's the harm in

that?'

'Anna, we know nothing about this man and he has been following us.' Catalina paused and said again, 'Following. Us'.

'Sure, but that's what we're here to find out. Why hide who we are?'

'Because I wanted to find out what he already knows.'

'Good grief.'

Mihai moved away from his chair.

'Where are you going?' said Catalina

'I thought you wouldn't mind if I left. Your conversation was going so good without me.'

'We'd rather you didn't go quite yet. Sit back down.'

'Please,' said Anna.

'Yes, *Doamna* Dalca.' Mihai saluted Catalina and sat back down.

Catalina looked at Mihai. He smiled at her and gave her a silly thumbs up. She smiled back, shaking her head. 'I'm sorry. Anna is probably right. My name is Catalina. Or, Cat, if you like.'

'It is quite okay. I would wonder about me too. You are probably right to be concerned.'

Anna studied the young man in more detail. He was dressed in quite ordinary clothes. Rough, but the sort of thing that you'd feel comfortable hiking in. However his shoes were brand-new. Big, sensible boots, but shiny and new.

Mihai noticed Anna looking at his shoes. 'They are good, yes? I got them recently. I should probably not have worn them on the trek up here.' He shrugged. 'Docs. Everyone gets a little excited, yes?'

Anna smiled at him. She realised he was not much older than Catalina, and not so different from either of them. 'I love my Docs too.'

He looked down at her feet, his brow creasing.

'Oh, no. I left them at home. These are my hiking boots. Boots for every season, that's me.'

'Still, they are good.'

'Could we talk about something other than boots?'

'Sorry, Cat.' Anna tried to sound a little shamefaced.

Mihai smiled.

'Why are you following us?'

'I apologise. I thought you did not know I was here. I am here to watch over you. To be your overseer. Or is a better word protector?'

Catalina snorted.

Mihai looked confused. 'That is the right word, yes?' he asked Anna.

'Yes, you're okay. She's just being mean.'

'Mean?' Catalina sounded confused. 'How was I mean?'

'Clearly you're implying Mihai here isn't up to the job of protecting us.'

Catalina shook her head. 'No, I wasn't. I didn't believe him when he said he was here to protect us. He looks perfectly capable,' she said glancing at Mihai. 'I think it was you who was being mean. I was being suspicious.'

'I wasn't the one who snorted!' said Anna.

Mihai stretched and leaned back in his chair, the picture of insouciance.

'So,' said Catalina, switching her attention back to Mihai. 'You say you're here to protect us. Why? Who sent you? What are you protecting us from?'

Mihai said, 'Ah, well. There is the problem. I can tell you who sent me. I can tell you a sort of why. But who or what I am protecting you from – I am not entirely sure'.

Anna and Catalina looked at each other.

Catalina raised her eyebrows. 'Go on.'

* * *

'It is not only that I was sent. My family sent me. No. Some of them. Yes? Our whole village were a party to it. My father thinks I was unwise to have come, you see?'

Catalina nodded and listened, her eyes never leaving his face.

Anna tried hard to listen, but found it difficult to pay attention. She felt far from the heart of the castle. She knew she should be interested in what he was saying, and he was definitely someone she could enjoy keeping an eye on, but he wasn't the castle. She listened to the storm outside as it picked up in ferocity. It sounded to her as if the storm were trying to find a way inside. She realised he was still talking and she tried to tune back in.

'No one was sure what I would find up here. We live in the village and try to keep to ourselves. We leave the castle and the valley alone.'

'Why?' asked Catalina.

'This is how we have always lived. Our grandparents, our parents too, to some degree, are very superstitious. Especially when it comes to the valley. The castle.'

'Yes, they didn't appear delighted when we said we were coming up here.'

'Not to the valley, they said, but to the castle, no?'

Outside the thunder boomed loud enough to break through to the centre of the library.

Anna waited for the noise to die down before she said, 'Yes, Cat thought she had given one man a small heart attack'.

Mihai smiled. 'I can imagination this, yes.'

'You, on the other hand, seem very relaxed about it all.'

'It's always here. The old myths, the terrible stories. You shouldn't ever take it all too seriously. You would never sleep. You shouldn't ignore it, no?' He nodded to himself and shrugged. 'We have to live our lives.'

'Yet, here you are, just in the nick of time, come to save us,' Anna said.

'Not to save you, no. You are not in peril. It is merely that I will be here if you need me.' He glanced around the room. 'Here or somewhere nearby.'

'But now we know you're here, you'll stay with us, right?'

Mihai hesitated before nodding. 'For a small while, at least. I am not sure I should stay with you the whole night. I must be careful. I have absolutely promised to be careful.'

'To your family?' asked Anna.

Mihai spread his hands before him.

'Why can't you stay? Why would your family ask you to stay hidden from us?' asked Catalina.

'I do not hide from you. I hide from the keeper.'

'Igor?'

'I promised to try and stay unseen. He should not know I am here.'

A thunderous noise rolled and cracked with such force that for a moment no one could speak. The echoes of the thunderclap bounced around the room.

'I'm sort of afraid to ask,' Anna said at last. 'Why can't Igor know?'

Mihai said nothing for a moment and shifted in his seat. 'This is another thing I cannot explain easily to you. For whatever I think of my family, I must keep my word, you understand?'

'Not really,' said Anna.

Catalina nodded. 'Your word is your word. It is though, as you say, best not to allow tradition be your entire world. 'A smile flicked across her face. 'Right now, *we* are your entire world.'

'I have made a promise,' said Mihai. 'What I

can say is that no one in my family wants to see either of you hurt. This is the truth.'

'And so they've sent us you.'

Mihai smiled and bowed.

'Lucky us 'said Anna as she smiled warmly.

'Are there more questions or can we move on?'

'Where to?' asked Catalina.

'I don't know about you, but I would like a rest, or at least something to restore me. I know that I would give a million lives for a cup of coffee, yes? Many castles have similar layouts. We will find a way.'

'Coffee? Oh, mercy, yes,' said Anna.

'We'll move on,' said Catalina. 'But this isn't where our questions will end.'

Mihai nodded. 'I will answer whatever I can.'

* * *

Mihai scratched his head.

'This makes no sense.'

Anna shrugged. 'I told you.'

'But there should always be more than one way out.'

Catalina said 'There is. It's the tunnel that leads to the music room.'

Mihai shook his head. 'No, that is not really an entrance. It's secret, as is the room. There must be another way.'

'What about the garden, maybe there's a way out there?'

'No,' said Catalina. 'No gardens. Not for you.'

Mihai raised an eyebrow. 'It's good you have brought your mother on this perilous trip, Anna.'

Anna tried not to smirk. She was not quite successful. 'She's right. No garden for me.' She felt despondent at the mere thought of it, but carried on. 'We could go around a second time, I guess. But we went all the away round the outer perimeter. How could we have missed anything?'

'I suspect we're not thinking laterally enough,' said Catalina. 'One way out of here is up, to the observatory. Perhaps the library is in the attic and so the entrance is below?'

All three looked at the floor.

'A low door? A trapdoor in the floor?' Mihai looked at the polished wooden planks and said, 'It's possible'.

'I'm getting dizzy going around this library,' said Anna. 'I know that.'

'We would make better time if we split up, no?'

'No, no, and no.'

'Absolutely not. We're sticking together. That's that.'

'Very well then.' Mihai gestured first right, then left. 'Which way first?'

'Left,' said Anna. She knew it would draw her closer to the garden.

'Right,' said Catalina. 'We can go back to the centre and work our way out from there.'

'Fine,' said Anna. She never knew how her friend always knew what she was thinking, but she always did. This time she resented her for it.

* * *

'Well, there you go.'

The three stood around a metal ring in the middle of a floorboard. A long rectangular outline was visible, showing where the floorboards would lift up.

'It isn't even a secret door. It's just a door in the floor. I guess we didn't see it because we weren't looking for it.'

'Okay, we shall go, yes?' Mihai reached forward to grasp the metal ring.

'Wait,' said Anna.

Catalina and Mihai turned to her and waited.

Anna couldn't think of anything to say. She knew that once she left the library she would probably never see the garden again.

'Yes, Anna?' said Catalina.

'I want one last look at the library. It's so beautiful. Come on. When are we going to see something like this again?'

Catalina said nothing. But she looked up and around her.

Mihai turned to look around the room. 'You're right. It is remarkable.'

Looking around, the library now appeared to Anna more like the inside of a puzzle. Every shelf and every surface seemed interlocked with the other. Before, the beauty of the library had come from the ancient tomes and papers. Standing here, in the centre, the room itself became the focus. It was a globe and an arena. A bibliotic colosseum. Anna could well imagine that the castle had been designed down, not up. Drawn out from this room, this ancient treasure. It was beautiful and timeless.

After a gentle pause, Mihai said, 'We can always come back. We can see what we will see and we can always come back'.

Anna nodded sadly. She had no argument for staying. All the same, she wanted to stay.

Catalina had not stopped staring at the room. Anna realised that, in truth, neither of them wanted to leave. Not this room. Not yet.

Mihai hooked his fingers under the trapdoor's ring and pulled.

* * *

They peered down into the stairwell below. It wasn't dank, it wasn't foul. It wasn't spectacular. It was an ordinary set of wooden stairs.

'It's sort of disappointing, isn't it,' said Anna.

'It's a good sign,' said Mihai as he set off down the stairs.

'I'll catch up,' said Catalina. 'My shoelace is loose.'

As Anna went to move past, Catalina pulled her close and whispered, 'Is this your man? Is this your dear little email interpreter?'

'No. Or, at least, it's not the right name.

Besides, he doesn't know why we're here. He's surprised we're here at all. He doesn't even know we were invited.'

'True, but we'll keep that to ourselves for now,' said Catalina.

Anna half-shrugged before nodding her agreement.

'Ladies? You have changed your mind?' called Mihai from down the stairs.

'Okay, okay. We're coming,' said Anna, heading down. Catalina followed at her heels.

At the bottom of the first turn in the staircase, they found a simple wooden door to the left. The stairs kept going below, but no other exits could be seen.

'Should we really take the first door we find?' said Catalina. 'It seems a little unwise.'

Behind her, Anna said, 'It's a.functional door, not a thing of grace.' It's probably for a servant. It's fine.'

Mihai and Catalina both reached out to open the door. Their hands touched. Mihai allowed his hand to linger and smiled at Catalina. 'You would like the honour, yes?'

Catalina's face flushed and she hesitated before breaking contact. She stepped back. 'No, please, after you.'

Anna watched in silence. She was surprised to find herself feeling jealous. She looked away, unsure of exactly who her jealousy was aimed at.

❋ ❋ ❋

A small, tidy and jam-packed room showed through the doorway.

Wooden shelving covered one entire long wall, each shelf stuffed full of containers, sacks of legumes and so on. Rows and rows of cups and glasses hung from the ceiling, starting with tiny at front and large at the back. Stacks of plates and bowls lined the small, far wall. The other long wall in the room was an uninterrupted long bench, covered with a mystery of stains. One end of the bench, made of cast-iron, looked to be a small warming plate.

Catalina reached out her hand to the plate but yanked it back. 'It's still hot. Was someone else just here?'

Mihai said, 'I doubt it. Some castles have a sort of ancient heating. There are furnaces at the base, full of burning fires and stacks of hot coal. Over the coal are layers of great rocks that store a terrible heat'.

'Oh, come on,' said Anna.

'No, this is true, yes? I have seen other old castles that have heated floors.'

Catalina raised one eyebrow and said, 'I see. And where was this exactly?'

'In Poland. It was a castle of the Knights Templar. You won't know it, I know.'

'Hey! We've heard of them.'

'Yes,' Catalina agreed, 'but I hadn't heard that they liked to keep their feet warm.'

'It is a true fact. As true as the warmth on that plate, yes?'

Catalina shrugged. 'With no internet access, I guess we'll have to believe you.'

Anna sighed. 'I miss Google.'

'It is probably missing you also. So, coffee?'

'Really? You weren't kidding?'

'I don't think he was, Anna,' said Catalina as she pointed to an old metal cylindrical pot with a long wooden handle.

'Wonderful! Just like your grandmother's.'

'Yes,' said Catalina, her smile full of warmth.

'I see my coffee making skills are not needed, yes?'

'Oh, no. You offered. You're making.'

'I agree. If we can find coffee, you mister, are our personal barista.'

Mihai bowed. 'It will be absolutely my pleasure.'

* * *

As the coffee pot warmed on the hotplate, Mihai, Anna and Catalina gathered around it.

Anna was heartened by their company, the warmth of the plate and the heady, ordinary scent of coffee brewing. She breathed in the bitter, burned smell and sighed deeply. Since coming here, she hadn't felt so sane, or so settled. The last few hours were beginning to seem more and more like a hazy dream.

'Mihai, you seem like an okay guy. I don't get why you won't stay with us. Why do you think you need to hide?'

'I will answer that as well as you answer my next question, yes?'

Anna looked at Catalina, who nodded and shrugged.

'Why are you both still here? You were terrified when I first found you. Are you lost? Can't you find your way out? Have you even tried?'

Catalina pursed her lips and looked at her feet. Anna tried to step in, but couldn't think what to say. She couldn't explain it to herself.

'We've been pushed at every step. We aren't making rational choices,' said Catalina.

'We've tried to leave. The storm seems to … I don't know,' Anna shook her head, 'to get worse if we even talk about it.'

Mihai looked at Anna. 'The storm is listening to you?'

'No, that's not what I mean. It's not like that.'

'So, why have you not left?'

'It's not that easy,' said Anna.

'"*It's not that easy.*" Is this such a very good answer?'

'You're making us sound incompetent. We aren't. If we could go, we would,' said Catalina.

Anna said nothing. She wasn't sure how she felt about anything anymore. Her grip on reality seemed to waver from minute to minute.

'So, if I left, now, you would come with me, yes?'

Anna said, 'Oh, but we'd need to find Igor first. And we haven't found out anything yet. No, not yet, but …' Anna trailed off in the face of Catalina's glare.

Catalina looked at Mihai and said, 'Yes, we'd go with you. If you say you can find the way out and that we could safely return down the valley through the storm, we'd go'. She looked back at Anna and said, 'We'd both go.'

'Okay, okay,' said Anna. 'We'd both go.'

'Can you promise that?'

'A safe way back through a midnight storm?'

The thunder rolled in the distance. It was far away, but ever present.

'Yes.'

'No, this I can't promise you. It's a treacherous valley, even by day. At night in a storm? No. I would be telling you no more than a lie.'

'Yeah? So, how come you're asking us why we haven't left?' asked Anna.

'To see what your answer might be.' His glance shifted to Catalina and he said, 'Your Anna's answer was an interesting one, yes?'

Catalina said nothing and her face remained blank.

Anna began to speak, but the thunder boomed again so she stayed silent, allowing the noise to reverberate through her body. The storm did listen to her. She knew it. She was going to do her level best not to say anything about it from now on, but she couldn't ignore how she felt. It was seeking her, as was the castle, and that was that.

Mihai smiled. 'Let me pour the coffee, yes? We'll be better set for whatever happens next.'

* * *

Catalina sipped her coffee. She was already on her second cup.

Anna was halfway through her first cup. She was enjoying the familiar bitter rush and wanted to savour it. The caffeine seemed to soar in her blood. Thick, rich and obscenely good, it made her tongue cloy.

Since the coffee had been poured, no one had spoken. There'd been much sighing, but no actual words.

At length, Catalina spoke. 'Let me try again. Questioning you is like questioning a sphinx.'

Mihai laughed. 'You have met and questioned a sphinx?'

Catalina smiled. 'In my dreams, perhaps.'

'She dreams of sphinxes and antiquities your friend, yes?'

'Yep. Wonderful, isn't it?'

Catalina coughed. 'My question.'

'Please,' said Mihai. 'I promise that I will be worthy of the sphinx-dreamer.'

'You said the villagers live their own lives and have nothing to do with the castle.'

'Yes.'

'How did all this get here?' Catalina gestured at the food in the room. 'Was it the same person who was communicating with Anna?'

'You spoke the truth. You *have* met the sphinx.'

'And the answer?'

'Wait,' said Anna, holding up her hands. 'Let me guess, it goes something like this: "Oh, my dears, it's not straightforward. It's too complicated to explain." Well, how 'bout you give it a go anyway.'

'Let me start with the easier question. I don't know who was communicating with Anna. I didn't know anyone was. Wait,' he said. 'Does this mean that you were invited here?'

'Yes,' said Anna.

'No,' said Catalina.

Mihai looked at both Anna and Catalina in turn. 'Which is it?'

Anna allowed to Catalina to speak. 'We're the ones with questions. You'll have to wait your turn.'

Mihai nodded. 'The food. Yes. It comes from the village, but we do not come here, you see?'

'Igor comes down and gets it from you?' asked Catalina.

'It is readied and collected. I do not know the absolute details.'

'Yeah. Of course you don't,' said Anna.

'I can only share what I know. Beyond that it would be story. Imagination, yes?'

'Yes, very imaginative,' said Catalina.

Mihai was humourless as he said, 'Who invited you here?'

'It is a bit, uh, complicated.'

Catalina said to Anna, 'I thought it was straightforward.'

'Well, yes and no,' said Anna.

'What else haven't you told me?' demanded Catalina.

Mihai sipped his coffee and sighed as he leaned against the wall.

'Nothing important, Cat. It's … there was no name. I mean, uh, the person from the village, the person passing on the messages, had a first name. The messages in the emails were not signed by a person, they were signed from a place. 'She gestured and said, 'This place'.

Catalina rubbed at her temples. 'We came here because you responded to a message from a mysterious castle.'

'Yes.'

'A castle that emailed you?'

'Yeah. I guess so.'

'And that signed the email *The Castle.*'

'Um. Yup.'

Catalina stared at her. And rolled her eyes.

Mihai smiled. 'I begin to see why you have not left yet, yes?'

'What? Why?' said Anna.

'You are here for your bit of adventure and you have not had your fill yet, is that right?'

'No. It's not like that.'

'Yes, Anna, I think he's right. Exactly right' said Catalina.

'No, I'm here to find out about my family.'

Mihai tilted his head. 'You are not Romanian. Why would you come here?'

'I … It's …' said Anna.

'Time to tell the tale of the family vampire hunters?' said Catalina. 'Or are you feeling a little silly now?'

Anna's face felt hot as it flushed red with embarrassment. She put her cup down and left the room, slamming the door behind her.

✳ ✳ ✳

Catalina ran after Anna, calling her name. 'Anna, please come back. Don't leave us.'

Halfway down the next flight of stairs, Anna paused and looked up. 'Enough with the jokes about vampire hunters, okay?'

'Yes. Please come back.'

'I can see another door one flight down.'

'Come back. We can stock up with whatever edible food we can find before we go on.'

Anna nodded and with some reluctance made her way back up the stairs, one slow step at a time.

✳ ✳ ✳

Mihai, Anna and Catalina stood before another

simple wooden door. Straightforward, but locked and barred.

'Now what?'

Mihai and Catalina both tried the door. Mihai was able to remove the bar, but the lock stayed locked.

'We move on,' said Catalina.

'Let me have a go,' said Anna. She leaned against the comforting warmth of the stonework in the doorway. Keeping touch, she jiggled with the doorhandle until it clicked.

The door swung open.

Mihai stepped back. 'You.' He looked at Anna and said, 'How did you do that?'

'Lucky,' said Anna shrugging.

Mihai shook his head. 'That was not luck.'

'It doesn't matter how. Let's just have a look inside.'

He held up his hand. 'Not you. You wait here, please.' He pushed Anna aside and stepped through. There was another small room, similar in shape to the kitchen above, empty except for a few tools and implements. Stacks of large rakes and shovels piled against one wall.

Mihai looked in the corners and under the bench. There was nothing unusual to see.

'A storage room? That's strangely disappointing.'

Mihai looked up at the sound of Catalina's voice.

'Yes. How was Anna able to open the door?

Who is your friend?'

'What are you saying?'

'What are you hiding?'

'What are *we* hiding? What are you hiding, Mihai?'

Anna walked into the room and looked around. 'The stonework.' Her fingers drifted towards the walls. 'It's so lovely.'

'It's an empty storage room, Anna. You find beauty in the strangest of places.'

Anna blinked and smiled at both of them and allowed herself to rest her head against the stonework. She could hear it.

'Anna?' said Catalina.

The smile remained on Anna's face, but she did not respond.

Unspoken, Catalina and Mihai herded Anna out of the room.

Mihai barred the door behind him.

Catalina said, 'Anna, why don't you lead the way downstairs?'

Anna nodded. She didn't understand why they were always taking her away from the things she liked. It was such a gentle room. Full of voices and memories and castle. Dragging herself forward, she plodded down the stairs.

❉ ❉ ❉

As they walked down, Catalina asked Mihai 'How do you know Igor isn't watching us now? You might already have been observed. You know this place, or places like it. Won't you stay with us?'

'You think that he is watching us now?'Mihai glanced around.

Catalina shrugged. 'I know that I can never tell when he's right behind me.'

'I suppose I'll have to chance it. There were stories my father told me. Rooms to stay near and rooms to avoid. The library was a good place. It was not the keeper's domain. Or so they say, yes?'

Catalina seemed to consider this before saying, 'The library was not covered with dust and cobwebs. Are you sure that no one else lives here?'

'No. Only that no one from the village does.'

'Oh.'

'I will take my chance. Have my own little adventure, yes?'

'Yes, an adventure. No wonder Anna likes you.'

He smiled. 'I like her too. She is Western, but not too Western.'

'Yes,' Catalina smiled back at him. 'She is that.'

'She is also deaf, I think, yes?'

Ahead of them, Anna walked on in blissful ignorance of their conversation.

'Or something like that, yes.' Catalina called out, 'Anna?'

Anna did not reply.

'Anna?'

Anna slowed and turned around. She seemed to look right through them. There were dark circles under her eyes.

Mihai and Catalina stepped backwards.

Anna stood and stared.

CHAPTER EIGHT

'I think we should find young Anna a place to rest.'

'Yes. She's definitely more than a little ... uh,' Catalina glanced at Mihai, 'tired.' She held Anna by the arm and encouraged her on, prodding her every now and then.

'Yes. *Tired*,' said Mihai.

The stairwell broadened as they came to a junction. Mihai and Catalina watched Anna as she turned left towards the heart of the castle. Without thought. Without hesitation. Again unspoken, they steered her to the right.

'Why are we going right?'

'Why did you want to go left, Anna?'

Anna paused and leaned on the banister. 'I don't know. I feel dizzy.'

'We will find a resting place and you can eat again, okay, yes?'

'Okay.'

Several floors lower down, the stairs opened onto a small footing. An open doorway led into a beautiful, plush, red room. Lined with little shelves, small tables and a haphazard arrangement of lounges and chairs, it had an inviting feel. Most of the lounges were long, one-armed affairs. Many chairs were overstuffed and oversized, but one or two were high-backed, stiff and wooden.

'What sort of room is this? Is this where they keep all the spare furniture?'

'Not entirely, no 'said Mihai, 'but it does look disorganised. It's a drawing room. All the little things are here. It's just not as formal as the bigger rooms'.

'Yes.' Catalina was watching Mihai.

Mihai turned to her and said, 'Where do you live, Catalina? In a city, no? A modern, western city?'

'Yes,' she said, without offering any more details.

'Are there many ancient ruins or castles near your home?'

Catalina smiled. 'Of course not.'

'So, if you lived near a place like this, you would know about these things also.'

'Yes. I know what you're saying.'

'Too gracious. My friend, you are absolutely too gracious.'

They were interrupted by the sounds of gentle snoring.

Unwatched, Anna had slipped down onto the nearest lounge and fallen asleep, her limbs dangling over the edge. Catalina settled Anna more comfortably on the lounge, arranging her arms and legs until she was safely ensconced.

Mihai said, 'You're a good friend, Catalina'.

Catalina turned to Mihai and said, 'No'.

'No?'

'If I were a good friend, I would never have allowed her to come here.'

'Perhaps now is when you should tell me a little about this, yes?'

Catalina opened her mouth if to object, but instead slumped into the nearest chair. 'Yes.'

* * *

'I think you need to tell me who she is, yes?'

Catalina looked at Anna's sleeping form.

'Do you hear me, Catalina? Or should I call you Cat?'

Catalina turned to Mihai and said, 'What gives you the right to ask me anything? Who are you? Why are you here?'

'We have already discussed this Catalina.'

'Not true. I've tried to ask you questions. You've given me inadequate answers.'

Mihai sighed. 'You don't like me, this is true, yes?'

'No, that's not true. I like you. That doesn't mean I trust you. There's a difference.'

Mihai shrugged, and gave a little nod. 'In a place like this, it's a wise way to be. So, I have a suggestion, okay?'

'I'm listening.'

'We shall do an exchange. I will give you one piece of information in exchange for every one that you give to me, yes?'

'That seems fair. Okay—'

Mihai held up his hand. 'There's one thing I must absolutely insist on.'

'Yes?'

'Ladies first.'

Catalina laughed and said, 'I'm no lady'.

'But, we have a deal, yes?'

'Yes.'

'Good.' Mihai nodded. 'So, who invited you?'

'Why does it matter to you so much?'

He shook his head. 'Oh, no. No, no. What was that Catalina?'

'What do you mean?'

Mihai buried further back into his chair. 'Our friendly deal does not allow you to answer a question with a question, see?'

'Yes.' Catalina paused for a moment. 'The deal doesn't say I have to answer any question you pose.'

'You have me there. Okay.'

'Try again, then. Give me another question. This one matters too much to you. We should start smaller.'

Mihai grinned. 'Okay, yes. Let me think.' He rested his chin on his knuckles, looking like an old bronze statue.

Catalina grinned.

'Ah!'

'Yes?'

'I made you smile. It's a minor achievement, I think?'

Catalina laughed, but she shooed his

comment away with her hand. 'My turn then?'

'Oh, no, no, no. Not yet.' He thought for a moment. 'So, who is she? She is not merely, I think, a random tourist. Your Anna. She is not here by chance. Who is this adventurous young woman and what draws her here?'

Catalina watched Mihai for a moment. 'You must promise me one thing.'

Mihai raised an eyebrow.

'You mustn't laugh. This is Anna's tale, not mine.' Catalina looked over at Anna's sleeping form. 'I care for her deeply. Her sense of adventure and willingness to believe is both what brought us here and what I so admire about her.' She looked back at Mihai and said, 'You've got to promise not to mock or belittle her for her reasons. However, silly they sound'.

'This was not part of our deal, but I see that you respect her, yes?' He held his hand to his chest. 'I promise.'

* * *

'Anna's family are storytellers.' Catalina glanced at Mihai before going on. 'My *Bunică* was too, but she dealt more in traditions and morals. In the big truths.'

'This is how my own family are.'

Catalina nodded. 'Not Anna's. Her family spun big, woven webs. We've known each other since we were small children. Not one week would go by without her rushing over to see me, breathless with excitement, her head full of stories. 'She smiled. 'One story they always loved to tell was about one of her very old relatives.'

'Her great-grandparents, yes?'

'No. I don't know.' She sighed. 'I can't be sure. They never made that very clear. It was always "many, many generations ago" or "hundreds of years ago".'

'And what was it that this great man did? Or it was a woman, no?'

Catalina shook her head. 'No, it was a man. A man called Jonathan Harker.'

Mihai's forehead creased slightly. 'Why does this name seem familiar to me?'

'You have heard of Bram Stoker's *Dracula*?'

Mihai laughed. 'Look where we sit, Catalina,' gesturing around him. 'We live in his story, whether we want it or not. Our geography fills each chapter. This stonework is on every page. Even our economy is driven by it ...' He paused mid-sentence. 'Wait. No, no, no. I absolutely could not have this right. Jonathan Harker is a character in his story?'

Catalina grimaced. 'Yes.'

Mihai began to smile but squeezed his hand over his mouth. He did not laugh.

Catalina nodded at Mihai. 'You see?'

'Surely, no. She does not believe him to be an ancestor? He is myth. Fiction. An author's story and nothing more.' He tilted his head in Anna's direction. 'She knows this, yes?'

'Yes. She knows it.' Catalina looked down at her hands. 'As a fact, it is something that she knows. But stories are not facts. Her heart,' said Catalina, 'her heart still longs to believe. Her head is sometimes overruled by the stories her heart wants to exist in. And, you know. There is a James Harker in her family tree. That much is true. Family stories and myths and fantasies.' Catalina shrugged, slightly. 'What can I say?'

'This leads me to many more questions, yes?'

'No.'

'You expect me not to have questions after hearing your tale?'

'Of course you have questions,' said Catalina. 'It isn't your turn. One question, one answer. It's my turn.'

He smiled. 'The sphinx questioner is right. Please, yes? Ask your question.'

Catalina studied him before saying, 'Why have your family sent you here and insisted that you hide from the keeper?'

'No, no. You do not think so little of me, no?' He shook his head. 'That was two questions. I will allow you to try again.'

Catalina screwed up her nose then said, 'Why have they made you promise to hide from him?'

Mihai grimaced. 'This is not a simple question.'

'No. It isn't.'

'I have the right to refuse to answer, yes?'

Catalina sighed. 'Yes.'

Mihai reached across and touched Catalina on her knee. 'You do not trust me Catalina? I trust you. I absolutely cannot tell you why, but I trust you.'

Catalina held his gaze and her breathing quickened, but she said nothing.

'So, I trust you. I'll tell you our story. For free. You will not understand it, but I'll try to explain. Today, today is an anniversary. Today or thereabouts. It was long enough ago that we can't be sure.'

'An anniversary of what?'

Mihai held up his hand. 'No, no. If you interrupt with questions it means I am done. I'll allow you one chance. I will go on, yes?'

'Yes. I'm sorry.'

'Many centuries ago this castle was abandoned. Forever. It had been ruined, destroyed, invaded and abandoned before. This time was different. This was the very last time. Only one man stayed. This man is the keeper.'

Catalina opened her mouth to speak, but snapped it shut.

Mihai nodded and went on. 'I know that this man cannot be that same man, the same keeper. Yet this is our village's tale. That somehow, yes, through some promises made, some deal done, he is still alive. We all, all of us, know this can absolutely not be true. Oh, we know that, yes. But if this man is not him, then who is he? We don't know. We know that *he* believes in the story. And my family know that he has much power and has been alive far too long, yes?'

'It's fear that keeps you hidden?'

'No. Custom. Hundreds of years of living in the shadow of this place. They have lived alongside it and respected it. They honour it, yes?' Mihai took a deep breath and continued. 'It's custom that keeps us, me, all of us in the shadows, yes. It is perhaps fear that makes some of them happy to stay there.'

'So, why come up here at all?'

Mihai crossed his arms and shook his head.

'I'm sorry.' She smiled. 'I can't help myself. Do you want to try another round?'

'You won't answer my questions about invitations?'

'Only if you tell me why it matters,' she said.

Mihai looked at Catalina.

'Well? What will you ask instead?'

Mihai shook his head. 'How did you find the castle?'

Catalina shrugged and said, 'It wasn't easy. We knew roughly where to go, but we had to investigate and question people all along the way. Even people in your village'.

'You were not given clear instructions?'

'You're a good sphinx questioner in training. That's enough.' She looked at him. 'Why did your family send you here?'

'They are good people. The valley is treacherous. This place is full of danger. They let you come, told you the way. They regretted this, yes? So they sent me after you. They did not wish to leave you unguarded. Alone.'

Catalina grimaced. 'Your family. Your village. They seem like good people. But they still let us come.'

'Yes, they are good people. But they are cautious.' Mihai took hold of Catalina's hand and gently turned it over, allowing his fingers to follow the lines of her palm. 'You can see that. You can also sense that you are from here. You can see why you too are a good person, yes? They are your people also.'

Catalina allowed her hand to stay in Mihai's hold. 'Maybe. But Anna is my family too. Perhaps more than my own family, and definitely more than your people. She's family. She's what brought me here and she's the reason I stay.'

* * *

Mihai watched Catalina as she fussed over Anna, who had slipped part-way off the lounge.

'I think you have enough answers now. Yes?'

Without turning around, Catalina said, 'Yes. I'm sure you intend us no harm'.

'You trust me Catalina?'

'I'm not completely certain about that. My words were very measured. I think you *intend* us no harm. Your village, or you, may yet cause us accidental harm. I think there's things you haven't told me that might yet hurt us.'

'No. On my word.'

'I think Anna is her own worst enemy, but I also think other people can help to make things worse. Or better.'

'I hope to make things better.'

Catalina nodded. 'I can see you at least hope that.'

'I'll continue to do my best by you, Catalina. It's absolutely all that I can do.' He clapped his hands together. 'What now?'

'I would like to rest, but I don't think we should all be sleeping at the same time.'

'No. I feel though that my keeping watch over both of you is very much not what you want right now.'

Catalina opened her mouth to speak, but stopped short.

'Please,' Mihai held up his hand. 'Don't say it. So, we'll eat, yes?'

'You know, I think I've developed a cavernous and empty pit in my stomach.' She reached for her backpack.

Mihai walked across the room to pull one of the small tables closer to where they sat. Without turning around, he said, 'What about our young adventurer?'

'I suppose we should let her keep sleeping.' She shrugged. 'I don't know. She'll be angry for missing out on *any* of this.'

'Let her be,' he said. 'She needs her strength.'

Catalina looked at Mihai's back and said nothing.

* * *

'We may never see him again,' said the grey-haired man sitting at the table.

The old woman stood looking out the window, watching the lightning dance across the fields. At length she said, 'It was his own choice. He knows what he has walked into.'

'He knows the castle. He does not know this night.'

'Mihai has been told. There was nothing more we could do for him.'

'Knowledge is not knowing. It is not living.' He ran his fingers through hair. 'I have sent my son to certain death.'

'Nonsense. You did not send him. He chose to go.' She gestured at the sky, her fingers curled and swollen with arthritis. 'The portents are bad, but they are not a certainty. He is no fool. He will take care.'

The man shook his head. 'We could have stopped him. We know what the keeper would do. He has warned us.'

'No, Nikolai. He has hinted. Mihai was right. We are not barbarians. We could not leave them.'

The man buried his head in his hands. 'My eldest son. 'His voice dropped to a whisper. 'What have we done to you?'

As the old woman turned away from the window, white lightning filled the sky behind her.

Silhouetted against the night sky she said, 'No more than any other has ever done to us'.

* * *

Anna woke up and sat bolt upright.

Mihai and Catalina both turned to her.

'Anna! Anna, are you alright?'

Anna turned to look at Catalina. 'Cat?' She looked around the room. 'We're here. In the castle.'

'Yes, Anna. You were sleeping.'

'I was dreaming. There were a lot of dreams. I thought the castle might be a dream too. But you're here.' Anna smiled. 'And you're too real to be part of any dream.'

'You do bounce back quickly, Anna,' said Catalina smiling.

'She seems to jump to many things quickly,' said Mihai.

Anna turned and considered Mihai. She could remember something from her dream. She could remember her mother, but there was something else. Something vague. And it was trying to slip away, but there were people. Two of them. They looked a lot like Mihai. Older versions of the same man.

Under Anna's thoughtful gaze, Mihai eventually said, 'Yes?'

'You. Your family. I think I know them.'

Mihai shook his head; once left, once right. 'I don't think so. Perhaps you need a bit more sleep, yes?'

'Your grandmother has arthritis. Your father, grey hair.'

Mihai raised an eyebrow. 'You're a good guesser, I think, Anna.'

'Was I right? I was, wasn't I.'

'Yes,' said Mihai. 'Where do you think you met them, Anna? Not in the village, no? Then, where?'

'I …'

'Anna? What are you talking about? We haven't met anyone like that.'

'Anna, these are some of my family, yes. Not all. They've never left the village. If they had met you, they would have told me. Who have *you* met since being here?'

Anna shrugged. 'Only one man. A younger man.' She tilted her head. 'Catalina never saw him. He was a very good-looking man.'

'Anna, that's enough,' said Catalina.

Mihai smiled. 'Ah. And so we approach the answer to my question, yes? This young man,' said Mihai as he leaned forward, 'He invited you here?'

'Sort of …' began Anna.

'Anna!' Catalina got up and stood facing Mihai. 'Why does this matter so much to you?'

Mihai sighed and leaned back again. 'I only wanted to know if you were invited.' He spread his hands in front of him. 'It matters because you have avoided this question too often and with much, let me say, enthusiasm, yes? Clearly you were invited.'

Catalina looked ready to interrupt.

Mihai said, 'No. Don't bother. The question has changed, yes? You were invited'. Mihai nodded to himself. As he asked each of the next questions, he counted them out on his fingers. 'Who invited you? Why? When were you to arrive? Did someone meet you? Do you know why you are here?' During the final question, Mihai's voice had raised with every single word.

Catalina sat down and allowed her shoulders to slump.

Anna watched them both in bemusement. She thought something significant had happened while she slept. She felt a small and pitiful pang of jealousy. To Mihai she said, 'It matters that we were invited?'

'It matters. It changes everything.'

Anna looked at Catalina and said, 'It isn't that simple. Cat didn't know everything. I'm not sure I did. Okay. You're right – I was looking for an adventure'.

Mihai kneeled at Anna's feet and grasped her hands. 'You must tell me what you were told. Who told you it? What did you know?'

'I'm starting to get Cat's reluctance,' said Anna as she pulled her hands free. 'You really are desperate to know about this stuff. Why? Exactly what is it that matters so much?'

Mihai looked at both Catalina and Anna. For a long moment no one spoke.

Anna watched Mihai's face darken. She didn't understand why it mattered so much to this intriguing man, but she felt sure if he ever knew the whole story he would leave them. So she said nothing.

Mihai sighed. 'Not here. I'll explain, but not here. Perhaps instead I will show you. I'll share the story. But there is something you should see. Yes.' Mihai got to his feet and walked towards the door.

Anna whispered to Catalina, 'I guess we've got no choice but to follow'.

'No choice.' Catalina stared after Mihai as he left the room. She shook her head. 'Once again we've been given no choice. But still we go ahead.'

CHAPTER NINE

'Where are you going, Mihai?' said Anna, calling after him.

He didn't respond, but paused near the doorway.

Anna looked over her shoulder at Catalina, who shrugged. Anna knew they needed him. She had to try and make amends. She wasn't sure what for exactly, but it didn't matter. 'Mihai, we'll come with you, but help us out, hey? Give us a clue. A hint?'

Mihai didn't turn back, but said, 'We're going somewhere that will help you with your curiosity. This will make you happy, yes?'

Anna couldn't help herself. She grinned and said, 'You betcha'.

Mihai grinned at her over his shoulder.

Anna didn't look back at Catalina. She didn't need to. She knew she would be rolling her eyes.

'I thought you didn't know the castle, Mihai,' said Catalina.

'I've been told many stories. We'll see if this one is true.'

* * *

At the end of a short corridor, Anna stood before a huge wooden door. Dark oak that had bowed and warped with time reached as high as her head, but still, somehow, loomed. The door held all the ferocity of a short and irate man.

A large iron handle, sculpted into the shape of a bird's head, took up the centre of the door. The bird's fierce, pointed beak held a circle of iron. A pair of dark, beady eyes peered at Anna. As she reached out, the muscles in her hand contracted, warning her away. She pushed through it and opened the door. Nothing happened, but she had the distinct feeling that she was lucky that this was so. She gazed through the doorway and took in a vast gallery, high arching walls and an intricately painted ceiling. Even in the gloom, its splendour was impossible to hide.

'Beautiful,' said Catalina.

'Is this what you wanted us to see, Mihai?' asked Anna, as she stared in awe at the delicate patterns on the ceiling.

'I absolutely was not expecting this place,' he said. 'It's intriguing, yes?'

'Oh, yes.'

Anna could see that the first few paintings held a scene from the surrounding countryside. She didn't recognise everything in them, but she knew the landscape. The tumultuous grey slate landslides.

The breathtaking and precarious cliff faces.

'It's amazing, sure, but I wouldn't exactly call it calming.'

Mihai nodded. 'It's here to catch our attention, I think. It's here to impress itself upon us. It is not somewhere you would want to stay.'

Anna stood still in the middle of the room. Since waking up she could sense that she was once again lucid and clear-headed. She never knew when she wasn't thinking clearly, but could see it had been happening once it stopped. This time she wouldn't allow herself to get too close to the walls, even to inspect the paintings. The temptation to feel the stonework under her fingertips was driving her senseless. She fumbled around in her pockets and felt the coin. The coolness and its weight, felt comfortable, ordinary and familiar in her hand.

'I'm astonished by the sheer size of some of the paintings,' said Catalina. 'They seem to go on forever.'

'This is a strange one, no?' said Mihai from the other side of the gallery.

The painting showed a grey, rolling storm front with three ravens in the foreground. The ravens were formed from the wind, their feathers blending and curling into the burgeoning clouds behind.

For a time, no one spoke.

'Have you seen anything like this before, Mihai?' said Catalina.

'No, not seen. But this word underneath?' he

said gesturing at a plaque under the painting. 'Yes, this I've heard of.'

'*Vântoase cetăţilor,*' said Catalina. 'The second word sounds familiar, but not the first.'

'The second means "protector" or something very much like it. But the first word is a rare one. It doesn't surprise me you don't know it. It's a myth.'

'What do you know about it?' asked Anna, trying not to meet Catalina's eye.

'Very little. It's an old, old tale and it speaks of an ability to create storms or winds. I've never known them to be called protectors.' He shook his head. 'I've never seen them in this form, no.'

'That's all?' asked Anna.

Mihai nodded. 'You both seem very curious about this painting, yes? What do you know about it?'

Anna glanced across at Catalina before speaking. 'I think we saw one.'

'You saw …' Mihai paused to gesture at the painting of the cloud-formed birds, 'this?'

Catalina shook her head. 'We heard a raven. I'm unsure of exactly what we saw.'

'Oh, yeah?' Anna looked from Catalina to the painting and back again. 'I'm pretty sure about what I saw. You know what, this picture reminds of some of the more wild stories my dad and his brother used to tell. Ravens and portents and all that. Silly really.'

Mihai raised his eyebrows at Catalina.

'Time to move on, I think,' said Catalina, as she turned to walk off.

'Please, Catalina, do not rush off, no? I think we should talk some more.' Mihai followed Catalina as she marched away.

Anna stood in rapt fascination in front of the painting of the '*Vântoase cetăților*'. Keeping back from the wall, she lingered and studied the painting as Catalina and Mihai moved further down the gallery. Anna knew how rational Catalina was being. She also knew that Catalina sometimes put her rational thinking before anything else. There was rational thinking, there was make-believe, and there was something in-between. What she had seen lay somewhere in the in-between. What she had seen was *this*.

Catalina had come to a stop in front of a large, dark, black painting. The vast image was a triptych, each third holding many smaller scenes. The darkness was peppered with scenes in dull, yellow light.

'What have you found?' asked Mihai, as he approached the same painting.

Catalina didn't speak.

Mihai looked at the painting more closely. He was mute.

They both stood and stared.

After a while, Anna noticed their absence and ambled down the gallery towards them. 'What've you found now?'

Neither Mihai nor Catalina answered.

'Cat?'

Mihai rushed up towards Anna and said, 'It's

nothing. I think that I have absolutely taken the wrong path. We can leave now, yes?' He tried to herd Anna back out of the room.

Anna looked at Catalina over Mihai's shoulder. She hadn't moved an inch. She looked in shock. 'What is it? What's in the painting?'

Mihai tried to hold Anna back, but she kept pushing and eventually he gave up and let her pass.

The enormous painting filled a quarter of one of the gallery walls. Old and covered with dust, it was hard to discern all the details. But there was enough. The three frames held images of dozens and dozens of young women and men. Every one of them was either being tortured or had died from their wounds.

* * *

Anna was the first to speak. 'What's this, Mihai? Some sort of myth?'

Mihai shook his head.

Anna said, 'It's real?'

'No.'

'It's not real and it's not a myth.'

'These things are often overstated, yes?'

Anna looked at the painting and said, 'I sure hope so in this case. Does this mean anything to you, Cat? Aside from the obvious'.

'I think I know as much about this as Mihai,' said Catalina. 'Which is to say, very little.'

Mihai turned to face Catalina and said, 'I see'.

'Well, I don't,' said Anna. 'What's going on?'

'Nothing. We should go, I think. You agree, yes, Catalina?'

Catalina nodded, her face pale.

Anna watched them both. They were hiding something from her. 'You're not getting off that easy. Who's the woman in the middle? In the big, corseted dress?'

'She isn't from Romania,' said Catalina.

'If it is who we suspect, both Catalina and I are troubled by her presence in this room. But her name is Countess Báthory.'

'And …?'

Mihai said nothing, but continued to stare at the painting.

'Come on, Cat. What's going on?'

'Look at what's happening in the picture, Anna. Do you really think I want to talk about it?'

Seeing how unsettled Catalina was, Anna decided to let it go. 'Okay, let's move on.'

Catalina nodded again and kept walking, with Mihai following close behind.

Anna took one last look at the painting. For all that it took centre stage, it wasn't so much revered as ignored. Unlike all the other paintings, it was grimy and dusty. She didn't know why it was here, but she had the distinct feeling that it served as a warning. Not the woman, but the scenes. But for what? And for who? She had no idea. And she hoped never to find out.

* * *

The trio travelled for a while without saying anything. The corridor leant itself to silence. Largely unadorned and unassuming, aside from the occasional flickering torch, it twisted and curled about, leaving Anna feeling like she was walking along a corkscrew. Eventually she said, 'I think if that painting had been the first thing we saw when we got here, we would have left straightaway, hail or no hail'.

'Perhaps. At the very least, I would have had some very pointed and interesting questions for Igor,' said Catalina.

'I absolutely do not understand it,' said Mihai. 'Why is it here? It's a loathsome thing. Why would he not destroy it?'

'You should not ever try to erase history. How else do you learn from it? 'said Catalina.

'I'm not sure what you learn from that picture.'

'That people are capable of great cruelty,' said Catalina, 'both men and women'.

Mihai raised his eyebrows and looked at Catalina. 'I think you have it right, yes. Nothing else makes sense.'

'You're not saying that women can be as cruel as men? Come on.'

'You don't think so?' said Mihai turning to face Anna.

'No.'

'A different kind of cruelty, I think, but just as cruel, no?'

'Nope. I don't buy that.'

'But in vampires and fairytales you will believe.'

Anna held Mihai's glance, curious as to what would make him say it quite like that, but then chose to ignore him. Her eyes drifted to a pair of torches set close together. Unlike the others, these flames burned in sconces made of large, ornate carvings. One, a dragon; the other a sheaf of cut grass and flowers. Anna reached out to towards the wall.

'What are you looking at?' said Catalina.

'They're so beautiful. Like the little gifts Igor gave us earlier.' Anna, knowing full well the castle was once again calling to her and drawing her in, was unable to resist it this time. She rested one hand on the wall and the other on the carving of the many-headed serpent. The curves under her hand was sensuous and all-encompassing. Her fingers started to trace the sinuous tail of the dragon.

'Anna, I don't think that's a good idea. Come away from the wall.' Catalina put her hand on Anna's shoulder.

Anna spun around and said, 'Can't you leave me be? Just once! I'm not doing anything bad'. She shrugged off Catalina's hand and turned back to the wall. She dug her fingers into the carving and tried to get closer to the wall. The sconce shifted and slid under Anna's grip.

Without warning, the floor collapsed beneath them.

* * *

As the floor gave way, Anna's senses rushed back in. She jumped from half-drugged and dozy to overly hyped. But before she could begin to panic, she landed on a lumpy, heat-filled floor. Something pushed into her back. Hard. She lay sprawled across a lump of old, brittle wood. She tried to look around for Cat, but she could only see smoke and dust. The roar and heat from nearby flames flushed half of her face. Something or someone was moving nearby.

'Cat? Is that you? Are you okay?'

'Mostly. My arm is bleeding. I landed on something sharp. Are you hurt?'

'No. Let me get you a bandage or something.'

'It can wait. It's not a bad cut. The dust should clear soon. Stay still, Anna.'

Anna could hear a low groan. 'Mihai! Are you okay?'

There was no reply, but the groaning quietened.

'He's alive. Leave him for now. You never know what you might crawl over.'

They sat in the gloom, waiting for the thick dust to clear. Anna's nose and eyes were streaming from the mixture of smoke and grit. She said, 'You think this is my fault, don't you'.

'I didn't say a thing,' said Catalina. 'Not one

word.'

'You don't have to. I know what you're thinking. Most of the time.'

'I see. And did you hear me thinking "*Please don't touch that, Anna …*"? I know it would have been a tricky one for you, but I imagine the clue was when I said, "Anna, I don't think that's a good idea".'

'Okay, okay. Just because I know what you're thinking doesn't mean I'm going to listen to you.'

'Maybe this was one of those times you could have chosen to listen to me?'

Anna said nothing. She knew the castle had managed to get her full attention. She also knew she'd been stupid. She didn't need to say either of those things to Cat. 'We said no more saying sorry.'

'I think you're getting to use that line a little too much.'

Anna felt around in her backpack until she found a bandage. She aimed for where she'd last heard Catalina's voice and threw.

'Hey!'

Perfect shot, thought Anna. 'Oh, I forgot to say. Here's that bandage you wanted.'

'Thank. You. Very. Much,' said Catalina.

'You're *very* welcome,' said Anna, glad her face was obscured by dust.

Catalina muttered as she bandaged up her arm.

'Pardon?' said Anna. In the greyness she could feel her face twisting into a sort of smile. 'I didn't catch that.'

'Vixen!' said Catalina.

Anna laughed until it turned into a cough. Through the coughing, she said, 'And proud of it'.

As the dust settled, Anna realised they were in some sort of a pit. Here and there, short stumps of broken wood poked up from the floor. A long iron gate covered one of the walls, and behind it was the source of the heat on Anna's face. The flames were small, but intense.

'This must be one of Mihai's central heating ducts,' said Catalina.

Anna patted one of the crumbling piles of wood. 'What's with all this though?'

'I don't think they're connected. We didn't come down here by choice,' said Catalina inspecting the wood. 'What if the little piles of wood were newer and ...'

'Pointier?' said Anna.

'Yes.'

Anna shivered, despite the heat. Everywhere she looked, whatever she looked at – innocent, beautiful, harmless or comforting – eventually everything here was dangerous.

'We were more than a little lucky. It could have been worse'

'You don't think Mihai did this to us on purpose, do you?'

'No. He sounds far worse off than we are.'

'And Igor?'

'No,' said Catalina after a short delay. 'Like it or not, we haven't seen Igor for quite some time.

'That doesn't mean he hasn't seen us.'

* * *

In the darkness, Igor smiled.

He leaned away from the wall and rested his back. He tried to curl up in a corner, but his movements were stiff and awkward. He stood tall and stretched, every joint cracking. After a moment's rest, he twisted his shoulders and leaned forward again, his ear to the wall.

* * *

As the dust thinned out, Anna and Catalina leaned over Mihai's half-conscious body.

'He still hasn't woken up. Can't we do anything?' said Catalina.

Anna looked at her. 'Aren't you the biologist?'

'Biology student. A pre-biologist is a long way from anything as pragmatically useful as a doctor,' said Catalina. 'You're the one with first aid training'

'A half day course!' said Anna. 'And it was ages ago.' She looked at him again. 'I guess we need to get him on his side?'

'Anything's got to be better than how he currently looks.'

Mihai was flat on his stomach, his face partly buried into the packed dirt floor.

'Alrighty. You grab a shoulder and I'll grab a

knee.'

They shoved Mihai onto his side so that his face was clear of the ground. He started to breathe noisily.

'That sounds a little better.'

'Noisy, but good,' Anna agreed. She wiped sweat and dirt out of her eyes. 'I wouldn't mind getting out of this little hellhole.'

'I doubt there's a convenient way out.'

'No, I guess not.' Anna's eyes fell on the iron gate on one wall of the pit. The flames flickered behind it.

Catalina followed Anna's eyes. 'A gate.'

'Why have a gate if you never expect anyone to open it? There's got to be a way out.'

Anna and Catalina went around pressing corners and fiddling with stones and loose bits of wood.

At last Anna said, 'Oh, look. A hatch'.

Catalina looked up at the crooked metal square. 'A hatch above an iron gate? Near the flames?'

'A door's a door,' said Anna, pulling at the hatch above her head. An enormous pile of skulls and smaller bones tumbled over her head. Mingled with it came a river of bugs. Millipedes and spiders, things that wriggled, some that writhed, ones that squirmed, and others that oozed.

Anna held her breath as the bugs and bones fell about her, some cascading down, but far too many finding their way into her hair and under her clothing. As dozens of nightmare feet found purchase on her skin, Anna heard the distinctive squeal of a rat. She didn't see it, but she felt the scrabbling claws.

When the horror finally stopped flowing, Anna tried to open her mouth to scream. But the cascade of wriggling horrors had surrounded her. She was sure if she opened her mouth it would fill with bugs and other nightmares. She squeezed her mouth tighter shut, biting her own lip and keeping it there, in fear of letting go.

As the bones settled around her, the festering smell suffused Anna and invaded her. Her nose, her tongue, and even her teeth, tasted of death and decay. As a young girl, she had found a desiccated mouse corpse. She was thrown back in time, watching her young self turn over the fragile, small body to uncover its remains alive and wriggling. The smell had hit her and she had stumbled backwards, falling over her own feet. She had never forgotten the smell or how fast she'd run to get away. And now she was surrounded by it again. She thought she would suffocate. She knew she would. Overwhelmed and unable to move, Anna allowed herself to disconnect from everything around her.

Seconds later, Catalina started scraping away the bugs and filth, and digging her out from the pile of mildewy and half-gnawed bones. As horrible as it was, Anna kept her eyes squeezed tightly shut. It wasn't that it felt better not to see. If anything, not being able to see made everything worse. She could sense everything and imagine it all the more vividly. She wanted to protect her eyes. Let nothing find a way in. Nothing. Ever again.

After a while, Anna felt the weight of the pile disappear.

'Anna?'

It was Catalina. Anna realised she had moved everything away. She contemplated opening her eyes, but didn't move. She couldn't do it. Not yet.

Anna thought there was something moving in her nostril. Without thinking, she touched her nose and, in response, something squirmed against the inside of her nostril. Bile swarmed to the top of her throat. Keeping her eyes shut, she forcibly and rapidly blew air through her nostrils. She felt whatever it was slither down and drip, at last, onto the ground.

Catalina said, 'Oh. My. God'.

'Never,' whispered Anna, 'Never, ever tell me what that was.'

'I promise.'

'I mean it.'

'I know.'

Anna was about to open her eyes when something made itself known on her scalp. She screamed, bent over, and ran her fingers raggedly through her hair, shaking her head wildly. After a while, when she felt that everything that could be gotten rid of was finally gone, she quieted.

Catalina was silent.

Anna wanted desperately to make a joke of it,

but couldn't. One day, she knew, she'd have to shave her head. It was all she could do to stop herself from tearing out her hair right now.

'Anna? Here. Take my hand. Let me lead you away from it. To another corner at least. Keep your eyes shut for now. Trust me.'

Anna felt Catalina take hold of her hand. She came around behind her, but then stopped.

'Just a minute.'

Anna felt Catalina's fingers flicking against her back. Once here. Two-three-four times there. Once hard. Eventually it stopped.

'Right. I think you're okay now.'

Anna didn't speak. Catalina held her shoulders from behind and guided her along. They inched forward, with Catalina nudging her left, then right, around the different obstacles.

'Stand here for a minute,' said Catalina. Anna heard rustling and then Catalina said, 'Okay, you can sit now,' as she pressed her fingers down on Anna's shoulders.

After she was seated, Anna felt her lower legs being scooped up. 'I've putting your feet on my lap.'

At last, Anna let out a long, deep sigh. She wanted to scream, but didn't have the energy. She also wanted to vomit, but was worried what might come out.

'Do you want to open your eyes now?'

Anna nodded. She opened them one at a time, with great care. In front of her sat Catalina. And a view of a stone wall. And that was all. She looked down and saw that she was perched on their backpacks.

'Okay?'

'No. Fuck, no.' She twisted up at Catalina and said, 'But, thanks for trying anyway. It would have been a hell of a lot worse without you'.

* * *

'What happened?'

Anna turned to see Mihai attempting to sit up.

'I'll see to him. Stay here.'

Anna slumped back down, nodded, and popped her feet on Catalina's backpack.

'Mihai? Are you hurt?'

Mihai lifted his head. He touched his fingertips to a large bruise on his temple. 'I'm not good, no, not absolutely. But where are we? What happened?'

'The floor collapsed beneath us. We're in some sort of a pit.'

'You're hurt.' He rested his fingertips on Catalina's bandaged arm.

'It's not so bad.' She held his gaze. 'I thought you were …'

'I'm okay.' He sat up a little and said, 'See?' As he sat up, he caught sight of Anna, white-faced and curled up on a pair of backpacks. 'Anna? What happened? Were you hurt also?'

Anna shook her head.

Mihai looked to Catalina and said, 'We fell

down. I hit my head, yes. And then?'

Catalina pointed at the pile of mouldering bones, crawling bugs and other festering filth that sprawled across the floor in the far corner of the pit. She whispered, 'That fell on Anna. It smothered her. Almost buried her'.

With Catalina's help, Mihai struggled to his feet. After a moment steadying himself, he walked to Anna. She didn't look up as he approached. He gingerly sat down next to her and said, 'We need to get out of here, yes? Leave the castle?'

Anna nodded.

He drew her closer to him. 'We'll find a way, Anna. I won't be so cruel as to promise success to you, but we will try. This I can promise you.'

Anna leaned into Mihai's shoulder and allowed her tears to escape. The weight of his body shored her up, but she could feel that he leaned as much on her as she did on him.

Catalina said, 'Mihai? What is this place? Is it for heating? Or is it something else?'

Mihai looked at their surrounds. He shrugged. 'It could be many things. A trap. An incinerator. Something for heating. Perhaps all three. It is absolutely not very nice, this is the only thing I know.'

She nodded. 'I don't think we fell far.'

Mihai touched his forehead. 'It feels a long way to me.'

Anna listened to them both as her senses began to return. At first she thought that the smell of the festering bones was still all about her, but as she raised her head she realised that the stench was coming from the disarrayed pile of wriggling decay in the far corner. She said, 'The smell. Please. We have to get out of this hole. I can't stand it'. Bile had filled the back of her throat again.

Mihai squeezed her shoulder. 'We will, Anna.' He squinted above him. 'I think Catalina is right. It's not so very far. Are there any ladders or steps?'

'No. That's what we were looking for before.' Catalina looked at Mihai. 'You and I are the tallest. If I stand on your shoulders we might be able to reach the top.'

Mihai nodded, wincing as he did.

'We'll need a rope.' She looked at Anna. 'Anna, do we have any bandages left?'

Catalina's voice was so strong and comforting that Anna found herself responding without thinking. 'Yeah, but we don't have to waste them on that. I should have some cord in my pack.' After a while, she pulled out a neon yellow roll.

'Hiking cord?' said Mihai.

'Nope, it's not that tough, but it's good stuff. It should hold.'

Mihai stood, bracing himself against the wall. He offered a hand up to Anna. 'Even at your worst, you seem to think very quickly, Anna, yes?'

Catalina smiled. 'And she recovers quickly.'

'If it helps, I don't exactly feel recovered.'

Mihai looked up at Catalina and said, 'Ready?'

'Ready.'

❊ ❊ ❊

Catalina stood on Mihai's shoulders. Her fingertips could just make the top of the pit.

'Can you make it from there?' asked Anna from below.

'I'm not sure. My fingers are strong, but not that strong.'

Mihai said, 'If you get ready, I can boost you from below, yes?'

'How?' Catalina looked down at Mihai, her smile becoming a frown.

'I can stand on my toes, for one thing. Then I can lift your feet up with my hands. Only once you have an absolutely good grip. Okay?'

'I suppose so.' She reached above her and gripped the concrete edge tightly.

'On the count of three, yes?' said Mihai. 'One ... two ... three! 'He stood up and pushed Catalina from below.

Catalina's elbows scratched the edge of the pit. She said, 'I'm on the edge, but I'm not sure I can push myself any further over'.

'Can you hang for a bit?' asked Anna.

'I think so.'

'Mihai, let her go. I'll climb up and try and give Cat a boost.'

'Yes, Madame Adventurer. As you wish.'

Anna enjoyed the moment's release of tension and let out a small chuckle.

Catalina said, 'Could we not joke right now, please?'

'Sorry, Catalina,' said Mihai. 'Are you ready, Anna?'

'As I'll ever be.'

Mihai stepped away from Catalina and the wall, allowing Anna to awkwardly make her way up and onto his shoulders.

As soon as she was up, Anna grabbed hold of her friend's feet, and straightaway Catalina's weight relaxed into her hands. 'Do you need a second to catch your breath?'

'No. I just want to go.'

'Okay.' Anna pushed up as hard as she could.

Catalina scrambled up and clambered over the edge. She rolled onto her back and lay still, breathing heavily.

Anna climbed down and off of Mihai's shoulders. As she climbed down, she could feel his muscles strain. Her face was hot, flushed. She shook her head. They needed to get out. She must smell awful. None of it mattered. She wanted to be held. She caught his eye as she dropped to the floor and could see he knew what she'd been thinking.

Mihai held onto her and did not let her go at first. 'Are you okay?'

'Yes.'

'I'll go find somewhere to tie the cord,' said Catalina from above.

At the sound of Catalina's voice, Mihai pulled away from Anna. She'd sort of expected him to, but still felt disappointed. She wanted to fall into someone's arms, and she didn't mind who.

'Everything okay down there?' said Catalina looking into the pit.

'Yup, we're fine Cat.'

'Glad to hear it. I'll see what I can find.'

Anna stood awkwardly by Mihai. She had only known him a little while, but she suspected he was going to ignore whatever it was that had just happened. It was likely that the thing that happened had been in her head.

'We can tie the backpacks to the cord and send them up first. This is okay, yes?'

Anna rolled her eyes and looked away. 'Yup, that's fine. Great idea.'

'Anna?'

She ignored him.

'Anna. Please? I only wanted to be sure you would not fall. This is a dangerous place.'

'Sure.'

Overhead, Catalina called out something, but Anna couldn't make out the words. 'We can't hear what you're saying, Cat!'

Catalina's footsteps grew louder as she came closer. 'I found a matching pair of sconces. Like the ones that caused this—'. She cut herself off and gestured at the pit below. 'The cord is tied to them.' She threw the thin, yellow line down below. 'Grab hold. I'll help pull you up.'

❈ ❈ ❈

Mihai looked down into the pit.

'I don't think we left anything, Mihai,' said Catalina.

'I didn't know this was here.'

'How could you have known?'

Mihai said nothing.

'I think we all need a rest,' said Catalina.

'I think that I do not agree. I think we all need to get away. Now.'

'Look at you, Mihai. You're as bruised and wretched as the two of us now,' said Catalina, as she gestured at herself and Anna. 'If not worse.'

Anna sat on the floor nearby. Her eyes were shut and her head rested against the stone wall behind her. She had enough of her wits about her that she could still hear Mihai and Catalina, and know that they were right. They should leave. She shut her eyes. *But not yet.* The touch of the castle soothed her. It revived her, even as it took from her and drew her away from the rest of reality.

Mihai, looking at Anna, said, 'I do not think we should stay very much longer'.

'I agree with you, but we need to rest first.' She touched the bruise on his temple. 'You can't save us looking like that.'

He turned to her and said, 'I'm no one's saviour'.

Catalina drew close and said, 'Perhaps not. But you are our friend'.

'Friend?' said Mihai.

'At the very least,' whispered Catalina.

Mihai closed the gap between them. They stayed together for a long and lengthening moment. Their kiss was like a shared breath. He pulled away, but only a little. 'Some of my friends tell me I often don't say quite what I mean, yes?' He took in a deep breath. 'Let me try, this one time, to not do that.' He held her face gently and said, 'I want you. But not here and not now. Before anything else, I want all of us to be safe'.

'I've always liked sensible people,' she said, smiling. 'But did I need to travel halfway around the world to find this in a man?'

He smiled back at her and did not let go.

'I think your advice is very sensible.' And before he could speak or protest, she kissed him again. Deep, silent and intimate, they remained locked together for an endless time. When Catalina finally pulled away she said, 'I don't really believe you're willing to listen to it'.

CHAPTER TEN

'He'll be alright, father.'

He turned to glare at the younger boy. 'You should have told me. Us.'

'It's all so harmless. They'll be fine. He'll be fine. Mihai is sensible. The women too.'

'He's been gone too long. They are not safe.'

'Father, please.'

'You should feel fortunate that we have chosen not to tell the village.'

'They wouldn't care.' He shrugged. 'And why should they care? They know I take him food and other stuff.'

The old woman spoke from a darkened corner of the room. 'This is not the same. Information is different. You have shown him a way out. You have given it to him. You invited these women in. And with them our Mihai!'

'*Bunică*, you don't understand. He's just a lonely old man. He's no monster.'

The grey-haired man sighed and came over to the table. 'He is neither one of those things, Sorin. He's somewhere in the middle.'

The young man wasn't listening. 'No.' He

shook his head. 'Company. That's all he wanted. Someone to talk to. I only gave him a way. Invited some people to stay. It's harmless. He's harmless.' He looked at his father. 'Everything else is nothing but stories.'

His grandmother spoke again. 'A story he has lived and believed in for longer than I have been alive. If people willingly enter his world, he believes he has the right to ask for me. To demand it. It isn't the truth of history. It is the truth of what he believes.'

'You see, Sorin? Whether it's a truth or not is no longer important. He believes it and he will act on it.'

'Okay. Then let me come with you. If there really is danger, you'll need help.'

'The boy is right,' she said in a hushed voice. 'Are there any young men you trust, Sorin? Absolutely trust?'

'A couple, yes. One or two. Most of them are as hot-headed as me.' He smiled at her.

She looked at the grey-haired man. He nodded.

'Gather them, Sorin. Quietly. Bring them here.'

The young man bolted from the room, half-closing the door behind him.

The grey-haired man shook his head and said, 'He thinks this is an adventure'.

'For him it is.'

'I should have taught him differently.'

'And would he have believed you? No. It's not

a lesson that can be taught. They must learn it for themselves,' she said.

He hung his head low. 'Perhaps I'm wrong. Perhaps Sorin is right. Is it possible the keeper will see reason?'

'No.'

He looked at his mother.

'No. He has lived the story too long. His will is bound to the castle.'

'His will, yes. But not my son's. Nor the women. None of us are bound by his story.'

'The story might be stronger than you know.'

'And so? What should I do?'

She had no words.

'So,' he nodded. 'We will go. We will bring him home.'

* * *

The sting of fingers burned into Anna's face. And another. She blinked.

'Anna. Wake up!' Catalina raised her hand.

'I'm awake. I'm awake!'

'You'd drifted off into one of your little trances again.'

She yawned and said, 'It's so cosy here'.

Catalina looked up and down the twisting, stone-walled corridor, dark yet alight with guttering torchlight. 'Cosy?'

Anna gave Catalina a weak smile.

'Okay. Time to get up. On your feet.' When

Anna didn't move, Catalina grabbed her by the arm and yanked her up.

'Yes, Cat. Sorry, Cat. Whatever you want, Cat,' said Anna as she stood.

Catalina ignored her.

Anna knew she was being petulant and didn't care. She wished Catalina would let her be. She was getting used to the feeling of the castle. It reminded her of the first time she had taken sleeping tablets. It made her nervous at first, because she thought she might end up relying on it. It was becoming a sensuous and wonderful feeling, that moment she felt herself going under. Being *pulled* under. As with the tablets, once she realised she didn't need it as desperately, she no longer panicked and just took them whenever she needed a little help. Sometimes she could relax on her own. Sometimes she wanted a little push. She knew she was in control. Then and now. She knew how to control the castle. She needed a hit now and then. To keep her going.

'What do you think, Anna?'

She realised she hadn't heard a word Catalina or Mihai had said. It was Catalina's fault. She always interrupted her when she was with the castle. Always getting in the way.

'Anna?'

'I was still a bit groggy. I missed what you said, sorry.'

Catalina groaned. 'It's like dealing with someone with an intermittent hangover.'

'Okay, okay. What did you say?'

'I want to find somewhere to rest. Somewhere you can lay your head down that isn't against a castle wall.'

'Okay.'

'Mihai would rather we left right now.'

'No!'

'Our adventurer is unhappy again? Why do you not wish to leave now Anna?'

'It's too soon. I mean, we should rest.' She pointed at Mihai's bruised forehead. 'Look at you. You're in no shape to travel down that valley.'

Catalina and Mihai stared at her in silence.

'It just makes sense,' said Anna.

'Too soon?'

'I didn't mean anything by it,' said Anna, a little too quickly. 'I want to rest first. It was your idea,' she said to Catalina.

'Yes,' said Catalina. 'A little more rest and then we can go. I did see a door further down this corridor, but I have no idea whether it would be safe to go in there.'

'We should be safe, I think,' said Mihai.

'I thought you were unfamiliar with the castle.'

Mihai sighed. 'Mostly, yes.'

'Mostly? Precisely what do you mean by that?'

'I have been given some information, yes? But it is not very good or … what would you call it? Thorough? It is incomplete and, clearly, unreliable, yes?'

'What sort of information?' said Catalina.

Mihai hesitated before sliding something out of his pocket. 'This sort of information.' He unfolded a small, blue, faded piece of paper, covered with penned squares. Even though it was a very rough sketch, it was clearly a hand-drawn map. The squares seemed to be floors of a dwelling, and dotted here and there were little red crosses.

'Is that here? The castle's floors?'

Mihai nodded. 'It's meant to show known areas that are of danger. Places to avoid or be more alert, yes?'

'So, you *have* been here before,' said Catalina.

'Me? No. Never. But my family – my ancestors – have lived under the castle's gaze for many years.' He gestured at the map. 'These are the places we have learned are dangerous.'

Catalina looked at the pit behind Mihai. 'I think you need to update the record.'

'This is true, yes. I know now I can't trust what it tells me.'

'Trust, it seems, is hard to come by.'

'I promise I have not lied to you, Catalina.'

Anna, watching both of them, realised there was something going on between them. Something real. She was jealous of him. Of them. She knew it made no sense, but sense didn't come into it. She'd hoped he would fall for her. It would have made such a great story. She couldn't help but be romantic in a place like this. She tried to make her next words sound dismissive, but they came out bitter as she said, 'Oh, but you've lied to me and you're fine with that'.

Mihai shook his head. 'No. I promise. No lies.'

Catalina's face had darkened. 'Time to move on.'

Catalina strode off ahead of them and Anna watched her go. Feeling safe and alone, she allowed herself to wander over to the castle wall again. She was abruptly pulled away.

'Oh, no, adventurer. You've had your fill of ancient daydreams today, I think.'

Mihai prodded Anna now and then to keep her moving along the corridor. As she walked along, Anna's head eventually cleared. She stopped and said, 'It's okay, Mihai. I'm fine now. Let me walk alone'.

Mihai grasped Anna's shoulders and turned her around to face him. He studied her face. Anna wanted to melt under his gaze, even though she knew he was only watching out for her. She allowed herself to enjoy the idea all the same. His eyes were as dark as dark could be. If he had been willing, she would have lost herself there instead of any stone wall.

He nodded. 'You seem okay, I think, yes?'

'Yes.' She gave him her best winning grin.

'You are a resilient adventurer, Anna.' He grinned back.

Anna's smile faded and she looked away. She wasn't about to share it, but she felt different again. She was clear-headed, yes. She was clear in her mind that she wanted to stay at the castle. They could be safe here. She was sure. All of them, not just her.

When they caught up with Catalina they found her staring at a vast double-panelled door.

The door was a wonder. Its broad wooden planks reached from ceiling to floor. Both sides of the door bore massive carvings at the front. The carvings were similar to one of the sconces and the little gift that Igor had given Catalina. They swept majestically from the very foot of the door and curled up and out to every corner. Each wooden stook comprised a bunched gathering of different swathes of wood: some dark and some so yellow they glowed like gold. Long flowing blades of grass had been rendered elegantly in a pale, patinated wood. Here and there, at the very top, sat tiny, pale yellow carvings of delicate flowers. A thick bronze band ran across the middle of each door and over the carvings, like rope binding a bale. The wood was so ancient that the carvings burgeoned out from under the bronze band, swelling with both age and pride.

Catalina looked over her shoulder at Mihai and Anna. No one spoke. They were held sway by the vast, golden carvings. The details in the carvings on the twin door appeared to dance before their eyes.

Catalina shrugged and pushed against a door.

* * *

Igor let the little slot in the wood drop silently back into place.

In the darkness, he smiled and whispered to

himself, 'They are safe. Mistress is safe. They are secure. She is safe, she will rest. I must trust that she will rest'.

Igor grimaced.

'I must prepare.'

❋ ❋ ❋

Anna stood in a dark, small and peaceful room.

Long, high slits interrupted the stonework on the outside wall. As clouds moved across the sky, and the moon came out to shine, a bleak silvery-grey glow flooded the room.

The furniture was unassuming yet somehow comforting. One long bench ran against the inside wall of the room. It faced the gaps in the wall opposite and, under the moonlight, its surface became a shifting kaleidoscope of browns and greys. On another wall stood a number of small, empty tables. A large, heavy table in the middle of the room held a pile of perfunctory books. Old and crumbling, they were not unlike a set of ancient accounting ledgers.

Anna went over to the table to look at one of the ageing books. She almost tripped over a partially rusted, barbed chandelier. She moved to go around it, but felt she couldn't go on. There was something about this room, the books, the furnishings. It unnerved her. Thinking she was being stupid, she looked back to Catalina and Mihai, only to find them still standing in front of the doorway.

Catalina said, 'How can a room be so peaceful and so uninviting?'

'You can feel it?'

'Yes,' said Mihai. 'But we need to rest, and this might be the best we can do.'

'I guess,' she said, half-nodding. She couldn't come up with a good reason for why she didn't want to stay.

'I think you're right, Mihai. We should use the room. It's a little secluded. And it feels unobserved.' Catalina paused before going on. 'And I don't know quite what I mean by that.'

'Yeah, I know. But you're right. Unobserved is spot on, 'said Anna.

Catalina moved further into the room and peered through a gap in the wall. 'The storm's still going. I couldn't hear it for a little while. We must have been in the heart of the castle, not out at the edge. '

Anna came and stood at a nearby gap. The scent of the downpour was metallic when it reached her. She could taste the rain at the tip of her tongue. It was a blessed relief, after the lingering smells of the pit. Her breath slowed and she let the air fill her chest.

'It smells good,' said Mihai moving closer.

Catalina and Anna's agreement was their silence.

Anna peered through the gap again. The sky had broken apart. Some of the horizon was a maelstrom of rolling clouds and hazy walls of rain.

Occasional gaps in the clouds allowed runnels of sky to appear, sometimes the stars, sometimes the moon. The landscape below was awash with water. 'The storm might be quieter, but that ground looks like a wild, stony river.'

'It looks more than a little terrifying out there. It's here or nothing.'

'Yes,' said Mihai, his voice hoarse.

Anna stood transfixed. The view tugged at her heart and drew her closer. The scene was, as ever, dark, grey and imposing. But it had its own peculiar grace. There was no need to leave the planet to find alien landscapes. It was right here, tumbling away below her. The land was old and untouched. It had been hewn from towering slabs of slate and stone. To Anna, it showed how the earth was born. Crashed together from its stony, imploding beginnings. Anna leaned closer towards the cold, flint wall, seeking comfort and familiarity as she watched the ancient mountain below.

'Anna!' said Catalina.

Anna jerked away from the wall. 'What? I wasn't doing anything!'

'I wasn't saying you were.' Catalina shook her head. 'We want to know if you think we should rest here.'

Anna, still annoyed, turned to look again at the room. She shrugged. 'I guess it's the best thing we'll find for a while.'

'So, we agree? Yes?'

Catalina stepped over to the long bench and

sat down, grimacing as her legs folded beneath her. 'One last thing, Mihai.'

'Yes?'

'What does your little map say?'

He shook his head. 'No. I have explained. We can no longer trust it.'

'It's all we've got, Mihai.'

He reluctantly pulled out the folded blue paper. He was silent for an uncomfortable length of time.

'Mihai, what's wrong?'

'Do you know what this is?'

Anna looked at Catalina who shrugged.

'It's a map?'

'Yes, yes. Absolutely it is.' He sighed. 'But that is not my question. You saw the red crosses, yes?'

'Yep.'

'It shows the traps and secret pitfalls, I imagine, Mihai.'

'No. Possibly, yes.' He sat on the long bench and took in a deep breath.

Realising that this was probably not going to be a short conversation, Anna sat down as well. The feeling as she lifted the pressure from her feet was a pleasant shock, and one she allowed herself to savour. Blood rushed in, the veins in her soles throbbed intensely, as it returned sensation to places she normally ignored. She swung her feet back and forth, skimming them along the floor, and enjoyed the feeling of movement and air.

Mihai spoke. 'Long ago, long before any of my

living family were born, many people died here. It had always happened. It is not so, unusual, yes? In truth, many castles hide a bloody history. Some deaths were ritual or expected. Some deaths were not. There was intrigue, there was war. There were many ways to die.' He stopped talking.

After a moment, Catalina squeezed his hand and said, 'Go on, Mihai'.

Without warning, he continued. 'When our people died within the walls of the castle, they were left where they died.'

'They left them here? Like some sort of—' said Anna.

Mihai looked at Anna, his eyes dark and heavy.

Anna fell silent.

'When they died, they called for us. For the people of the village.'

✳ ✳ ✳

The old woman walked along the winding stony corridor. A young voice behind her said, 'How many times have you been here before, Oana?'

Oana stopped moving, and the young woman stopped too so she wouldn't walk straight into her. 'I do not know. I know the names of those I have collected, but I do not count them. To make them numbers,' she said, 'is to erase their presence as humans.'

'I understand, Oana.'

The old woman raised her eyebrows, but said nothing. She continued walking. 'It is a heavy duty that we bear, but it is better this than if we were to leave them to the castle.'

'Why do they not return them to us?' she said.

'They do not consider us important. We must be grateful that they allow us this,' said Oana.

'Grateful.'

'Alin is not one of your family. If he were, you would understand my meaning.'

She nodded politely.

'You should at least be grateful he is not young.'

'Alin? Alin was young. He was only in his third decade.'

'He is not a child.'

She put her hand to her mouth. 'Oh, Oana, I am grateful. I am terribly grateful.'

The old woman stopped walking again and held the young woman's shoulder. Looking at her, she said, 'This duty may come to you yet. You must try to be ready'.

'How can I know I will be ready?'

'The only way you will know for sure is when the call comes. You will know this more clearly than anything you else you have known. You will feel it in the darkest pit of your soul. You will know.'

Tears welled in the young woman's eyes. 'I will do my best to honour you, Oana.'

The old woman nodded. 'I think we are close now. We should go on,' she said. 'Silence will follow us the rest of the way. And silence will follow him home.'

After walking for a while, they came upon his body. The young woman gasped and covered her mouth to quiet herself.

His body was piled in a corner, against the wall. It appeared that he had simply been pushed out of the way. For no other purpose than to keep the path through the corridor clear. He lay unconsidered and alone.

One item at a time, and with neat precision, the old woman began to unpack bundles of linen. After a long moment staring at the corpse, the young woman bent down to help. Together they laid out the shroud next to his broken and disarrayed body.

On his front, the young man bore several small wounds. As they straightened his body, they rolled him over to find three gaping wounds in his back.

The young woman looked at the ceiling above where his body had fallen. A terrible wrought iron chandelier swung above them. Its decorations were simple. Its pointed iron barbs sharp and fierce.

The women rolled him onto the shroud and dressed him, ready for his return. Together, they lifted him, the old woman bearing most of his weight.

And the three began the long journey home. In silence.

❋ ❋ ❋

Mihai sat in silence.

Catalina reached out and, with great care, slid her fingers up and around his forearm.

He did not stop her. Neither did he acknowledge her.

The three sat in quiet contemplation,

watching the shifting sky through the gaps in the castle wall.

Mihai unfolded the papery, blue map. Pointing at a particular small red cross, he said, 'This was him.'

The women were silent.

Anna realised that each of the crosses must be someone from the village. It was a terrible thought. But it was sensible, all the same. If a life was lost, of course you would want others to know and, if possible, maybe even save them from a similar fate.

Catalina said, 'And you know who each of the crosses represents?'

Mihai shook his head. 'No. Many, yes. But not all. It goes too far back.'

'Each cross a human being,' whispered Anna.

'No.'

Catalina said, 'Mihai?'

'The smaller crosses, yes. The bigger crosses ...' he paused, unable or unwilling to say more.

'It's okay Mihai. We understand.'

'I was not wise, yes? I thought that with this we would be safe. That I could look after myself and, yes – incredible fool that I am – somehow protect you also.' He held up the paper. 'This is absolutely not true. It's part of why we must leave. As soon as we feel able, we must go.'

No one spoke. Anna felt too exhausted for words. She was sure that anything she said would be the wrong thing.

Mihai looked at Anna and said, 'You must

listen to me, Anna. Hear me, yes?'

She looked at him.

'This place is no adventure. It's not safe. It has a long history of blood and lost lives. We know this.' He gestured out towards the window and said, 'Down there, we live in the modern day. But we never forget. This place is older and remembers more than we ever can. We no longer live under its rule, but we continue to live in its shadow. It's not safe'. He looked at her. 'We must go.'

Anna could hear the sense of what he was saying but still didn't want to go. And she knew neither of them wanted to hear her say it. Desperate to delay things until she could figure out some sort of plan, she remembered Mihai's earlier words and said, 'But you wanted to show us something'. She looked around the room. 'Surely it wasn't this place? Where were you heading?'

Mihai ignored her final question and nodded. 'You're right. After we rest, I'll show you one more place. Then, when the storm is at least quietened, if not gone, we'll go. You won't argue with me, yes?'

'I can't promise that.'

Catalina said, 'Argue all you like, Anna. You have one more stop on your little adventure and then we're going home'.

'Okay, okay. It makes sense. I'm just saying I can't promise I won't argue with you. Where's the fun in not at least putting up a fight?' Anna grinned at Catalina.

Catalina grinned. 'I suppose we can't ask the

impossible. Surely you agree, Mihai?'

A smile flitted across Mihai's features. 'It's hard to resist either of you when you grin like that. Very well, Anna. Prepare your argument.'

Catalina nodded. 'But for now, we can get a little rest. Anna in the middle?' she said looking at the cold, polished floor before them.

'Anna in the middle,' he said.

Anna smiled, but did not feel its warmth. So, they had decided they were her nannies now, both of them. As much as she cared for them, she wouldn't allow it to continue like this. Anna knew it wouldn't matter what the next stop held. She was not going to let it end there. It was safe here. She knew it. It already felt like her home. History was just that: history. Old, forgotten and long in the past. But if she couldn't make them understand, she would stay here without them.

But she would never feel on her own.

❉ ❉ ❉

Anna was dreaming. She knew it. And she allowed it in.

The castle was young. Her external walls did not crumble. They soared. Her highest peaks were masterful and elegant. She was carved from the ground to the sky. Her architecture was exacting and for it she was worshipped. Her presence was both enchanting and terrifying.

Anna stood at the base of the great castle.

The doors stood gaping and open. Through them she could see dozens of people. Row after row of elegantly coiffured denizens, waiting for her.

But she hesitated.

The doors were open. The castle pulled at her. It longed for her. But only her.

Anna looked behind her. There was no one there. She was alone. She was the last.

The castle, the people, they called to her. She stepped forward. She could her its song.

She took another step. She could hear their pain.

She hesitated again.

And the doors swung shut.

She screamed.

* * *

'Anna, wake up!'

Anna woke to find Catalina looking over her.

'You were screaming. In your sleep. Are you okay? What was it?'

'I thought I had lost both of you. And ...,' Anna said, pausing, unsure of her next words, 'I don't know. Someone. I lost someone else. I lost everyone'.

'My poor Anna.' Catalina gathered her close.

Anna curled into her arms. She didn't entirely understand what it was that she might have lost, but she knew that she never ever wanted to lose her friend. The thought startled her a little. She was sure that a few short hours ago – before she had rested – she had been willing to leave Catalina and to stay here. In the castle. The sleep had done her more good than she could ever have expected. Yes, the castle was wonderful. It seemed to welcome her. To embrace her. But she would never want to leave Catalina. No. Her mind was, again, just for this moment, as clear as it could be. The last few hours began to seem like yet another haze. She could remember the horrors and the delights, but she no longer felt entangled by them.

'Do you feel better after a rest?' asked Catalina. 'You look better. I say better, but you don't exactly look great.'

Anna moved back from Catalina's arms and felt every bruise and aching muscle as she did so. She grimaced at the thought of ever having to move again. Despite the pain, she smiled at Catalina and looked her up and down. Her friend was bruised, had dark circles under her eyes and wherever there was flesh, there were scrapes and scratches. She said, 'Well, gee, thanks. You don't look so hot yourself'.

'Oh, yes. You're definitely better.' She smiled. 'I'm not sure now whether I like that or not.'

Anna slapped Catalina on the arm. She aimed for somewhere Catalina was not already beaten up. It wasn't easy. 'You're starting to look like a patchwork bruise.'

'You should be grateful, Anna, that there are no mirrors in this castle. You are little more than an explosion of purple and blue.'

A voice from behind them said, 'I can say that,

bruises or not, you both look good to me, yes?'

'Well, hello, Mihai,' said Anna. Mihai was digging through their backpacks. 'Please, help yourself.'

'Mihai is looking for whatever food we have left.'

Anna considered both of them with an obviously exaggerated attention to detail. 'Did you two get *any* rest?'

'Anna …' said Catalina shaking her head.

'Yes, yes. Absolutely. I have never felt so good.' His grin was as wide as it was foolish.

Anna rolled her eyes. 'So, no sleep at all then.'

And Catalina smacked Anna. Catalina, though, aimed for – and hit – a fresh, good sized bruise.

'Hey! That really hurt.'

'Serves you right,' said Catalina.

Mihai laughed and said, 'Well, we have no coffee, but let's see what we can turn into food.'

'Are you also a master chef Mihai?'

'With food, perhaps, yes.' He waved about a plastic-wrapped packet of freeze-dried nothingness. 'With whatever this is? Well, I think my answer is absolutely no.'

'Men,' smiled Anna. 'Always blaming their tools.'

A square plastic packet of nothing hit Anna on the side of her head.

* * *

Igor sat before a bench covered in bottles and untidy stacks of books.

Sweat dripped from his brow, traversing its way along his pockmarks and scars. He ignored the sweat and blinked often to clear his vision.

The raven sat on the windowsill, his pointed beak following Igor's manoeuvres across the workspace.

From time to time, the raven would caw or ruffle its feathers and Igor's hand seemed to automatically change course.

At one point, as Igor reached for a particular book, the black, feathered beast cawed loudly. Loudly enough to break Igor's concentration.

Igor went to a bench on the other side of the room. It was laden with offal and thick, gristly pieces of meat. He selected a fresh, bloody piece and threw it into the air behind him.

The raven leaped across the room and caught the food mid-flight. The meat was devoured before the raven landed beside Igor.

Igor looked at the bird thoughtfully.

The raven tilted its head and looked up at Igor.

'Food,' said Igor. 'It is an offering. A sacrifice. Yes, raven?'

The giant bird tried to peck at the towering pile of meat on the tray.

Igor knocked the bird away.

The feathered beast flew into the air and rushed down at Igor who unthinkingly tossed another sliver of red meat above him. The raven twisted mid-air and caught up the torn flesh.

'Mistress, yes. This is fitting. There is a way. Mistress, I promise I will ease your way.'

The raven flew back to the windowsill. It sat silent, looking out to the storm, its feathers moving with the wind.

Igor looked at the silent bird. He scowled at it. Its silence seemed to offend him. 'There is a way. I can find it. For the Mistress.'

The raven turned back towards Igor and the room.

Igor stood up and stared at the feathered nightmare.

The raven was silent.

'I will find a way.'

The raven cawed once and quietly. And then it said no more.

* * *

Thunder rolled.

Anna looked out through a gap in the stonework, being careful not to touch the castle's walls. The sky was alive. Lightning struck and arced across the sky. Sometimes the bolt would earth itself on the mountain and streams of light would bind the sky to the ground. Hail and rain lashed at the surrounding countryside and the heavens echoed with the rolling noise of the storm.

Catalina looked up from where she sat, packing and reorganising their backpacks. 'It's good we planned for one more stop.'

'Yeah, I know. It's like the country is giving us licence to stay.'

'You say the strangest things, Adventurer Anna,' said Mihai. 'It's a pity, no? That we can't leave. If the storm was not like this, I would say we should go now. And not make our final stop.'

'You sound more worried than when we first met, Mihai.'

'The longer we stay, the more worried I will sound.'

'We could risk it,' said Catalina quietly.

Mihai watched Catalina for a moment. He came closer and kneeled beside her. Just as quietly he said, 'We could, yes. We may yet have to. But I want our friend to be sure, yes? To make sure that she will not ever come back'.

Catalina reached out and held Mihai's hand. 'We'll get out. Somehow.'

Anna pretended not to listen. She tried not to intrude on what had become an intimate moment. She could still remember her thoughts. It scared her to know how willing she was to leave them and stay here. And how easy it was for her to lose herself. She only hoped Catalina was right. She didn't understand what was happening to her, only that she knew she was powerless to control it. And that the lure of it – the lustful, comforting, all-pervading intimacy of it – was already calling to her. The castle was her drug. She had been a willing addict. And like most addicts she feared its lure but wanted it all the same. She was terrified and out of control. She had to help Mihai and Catalina get out. And somehow she had to hope they would take her with them.

CHAPTER ELEVEN

The way ahead was narrow, dark and low.

At first it had been yet another long, winding, stone-encased corridor. As Anna moved along, the walls closed in around her and the ceiling seemed to crush down. Mihai stopped, then Anna, and Catalina, stopped behind him. 'Mihai?'

After a moment, he let out a long breath. 'I'm not sure. I'm no longer certain this is the right path.'

'It's the only way forward now,' said Catalina. 'None of us want to go back near that pit.'

'No, it is not the right word. You misunderstand me, yes?' He sighed. 'I'm unsure if this now is the right way. The right thing.'

'After all we've been through, you honestly think that now, *now*, you can stop someone like Anna?'

Anna mugged a grin at Mihai.

Mihai's face and body were stock still. 'What right do I have to do this to you? The storm is bad, but when isn't it?'

Catalina said, 'Are we close?'

'I think so, yes.' He tapped on the creased blue paper. 'This is not from maps. It's from our oldest tales. It is not a direction from the inside, but something we've seen from outside,' he said. 'I think I am lost, yes?' He shook his head. 'No. We must be close.'

'Well, that makes everything clear as mud,' said Anna.

'You were sure before, Mihai. Is it because we're getting close? And you're having doubts.'

Mihai looked at Catalina. 'Yes.'

'Mihai, come on,' said Anna, 'Whatever it is, if you think we need to know, then we need to know. '

'She's right, Mihai. Whatever's going on – it doesn't matter how bad it is, it's not up to you to choose. We need to know.'

'Okay. So it is. We shall go on, yes?' Mihai sighed and ducked down low, ready to move ahead.

Catalina put her hand on his shoulder and said, 'No'.

Mihai stopped and turned back.

'This time we'll go first. This isn't your choice alone. Whatever we find, we won't blame you.'

Mihai bowed and let her pass.

✳ ✳ ✳

A different double-panelled door stood before them. Catalina, Anna and Mihai all stopped in front of it.

The doors were dark and, at first glance,

seemed unadorned. On coming closer, Anna could see that the wood bore a shallow, bevelled carving. The carving was of a many-headed dragon. A sinuous serpentine tail wound its way around the door, reaching into every crevice and corner of the panels. A portion of the tail wound its way back to the middle where it split and became the door's handles. The dragon's many heads had dark, metallic tongues. Its heads were tilted away from Anna, with some eyes obscured from her view, and the others open and staring. Open and staring at her.

Anna realised that as she stepped closer to the door to inspect it, Catalina and Mihai hadn't moved. She glanced back at them before reaching out to open the door.

Catalina said, 'Anna—'

Anna shook her head without looking back. 'I recognise it. This is meant for me. It doesn't matter. It's okay. Because it's my decision. You can stay here or not. Whatever. I'm going in.'

She reached out and grasped the dragon by a tail. As she stepped in, Mihai and Catalina followed.

✿ ✿ ✿

It was a simple place, a sombre place.

No more than a chamber, small and round, the space huddled in close. It had an effortless grace and presence that belied its simplicity. Inside, Anna could see a window and two small, crescent-shaped marble benches.

The room did not exist for its view, not for what it contained. The scenery was like a living painting, beautifully framed in the curving stone windows of the castle's walls. The sky still raged in the throes of the eternal storm, but it was changing with the pre-dawn hues. The mountain lived and breathed, lit by an eerie, shifting light. The landscape cleaved in half before the roots of the castle. Both sides of the mountain enclosed the stone walls and disappeared from view at the edges. In the middle of the split, the tumbledown rocks and moss-covered slate made way for a small clearing.

Far below, a mossy ground snaked and dug its way into the mountainside. The tiny valley was a small oasis of green, nestled in the unrelenting dark grey walls of the mountain. Anna could not see its end. What she could see were graves. An unnatural number of them. Every few feet there stood a simple gravestone and an undecorated grave. Most were ancient and crumbling, some were newer, but still quite obviously old. The graves were a long way down, but they were unmistakable.

The graveyard was the centre of the landscape, the centre stage.

For the longest time, none of them spoke. All that could be heard was the steady drizzle of rain and the occasional caw of birds in the distance.

To Anna, it was quite possibly the most beautiful place she had ever seen. It was also, without question, the most terrifying.

* * *

'We can't keep going.'

Nikolai Troester said, 'I will not go back'.

'I don't want to go back. We need to stop. The storm is out of control.' Sorin spoke louder and louder with each sentence. The sound of the rain was deafening and all-encompassing.

'Please, father, we've got to take shelter. We need to rest. We can't help him if we get ourselves killed.'

Around them the storm raged. It was impossible to predict and prepare for whatever faced them. None of them could see more than a few feet in front of them. The rain came in lashes, beating at them relentlessly. The wind and hail merciless.

All of the men were experienced climbers, and experienced with this treacherous mountainside. Yet every single one of them had already slipped and fallen at least once.

The grey-haired man looked up. Above him, there was a narrow ribbon of sky. The path they followed stood in a deep valley, with high walls of slate towering up on both sides. The walls of stone appeared to cascade on them from above.

Right now, the view of the sky the grey-haired man was used to seeing was completely obscured. He sighed. 'I can't argue with you. I cannot see forward or above.'

'Good. Come with me,' Sorin said, pulling him

backwards. 'We saw a safe spot, a small cave, just a little way back.'

Nikolai resisted.

'You haven't got a choice.' Sorin gave up. He turned to speak to the three young men that followed him. 'Go. Go back to the shelter. We'll follow later.'

The other young men didn't hesitate. They didn't run, but took each step with careful precision, until they made it back to the sheltered cave.

Sorin turned to his father. 'Father, I'm willing to beg. We can't just stand here and we can't go on. Not yet. It isn't safe.'

'If only I knew *he* was safe, Sorin.'

'We've got to presume he is, father. Or else, why are we doing it? What's the point?'

His father glared at him.

Sorin paused for a moment before he spoke again, 'Father? Would you know if he was not ...' Sorin stopped speaking, seemingly unable to finish the sentence.

'If he were dead? Yes. I would know.' He looked at his son. 'I would know it of both of you.'

'Then please, rest. You can't know he's safe. But you know he's there. If he needs you, he'll need you at your best. 'The young man grasped his father by the shoulder. 'I need you at your best.'

Nikolai's head dropped. 'I'm sorry. I have driven you and pushed you when I did not even want you to come. We will take shelter. And rest.'

Sorin guided his father slowly back down the

path. His eyes tracked every step that the older man took. His father, a man normally sure-footed and considered in his movements, paid no attention to the treacherous ground beneath him. His eyes were for the castle back behind his shoulder.

In the pouring rain, Nikolai's tears slid away, unseen.

❋ ❋ ❋

Anna spoke first.

'But who are they? Cat, didn't we see a cemetery in the village—'

'I'm sure we did. It was beautiful and well-tended. Ancient, but loved.' Catalina looked to Mihai. 'What is this place? It feels … well, more than a little unusual.'

The storm roiled past the window and the disquieting shades of pre-dawn light battered the gravestones below.

Mihai sighed. 'What I tell you next is an ancient tale, yes? There is no certainty of truth, beyond the evidence you can see here. And this truth is not absolute. It's a tale. A story. But it has truth at its heart, yes?'

Catalina nodded. 'We understand, Mihai.'

'And, remember also that this is not a whole thing. I tell you what I know, knowing it isn't all there is to know.'

Catalina nodded again.

Mihai nodded and said, as simply as possible,

'These men were sacrifices'.

Anna looked at the graves. She couldn't believe it. There were so many of them. She felt her chest tighten. She wished they hadn't come to this room. Why did Mihai think she needed to hear this? She wasn't going to die here. None of them were. It wasn't an easy place, it wasn't safe, but they were hardly going to die. She didn't know what he had to say, but she didn't want to hear it.

She looked at Mihai and realised that he hadn't continued with the story. He was watching her.

'Do you wish me to go on, Anna?'

'Look. Do you want me to answer honestly?'

'Yes.'

Anna found that she couldn't speak when she had the graves in clear sight. She turned her back on them and said, 'No'.

Mihai raised one eyebrow.

'I don't understand any of this. Why do I need to hear one of your village's tales. I mean, come on. You've even said it's untrue and incomplete. Even looking at these graves is disturbing enough. I've spent so much time feeling unnerved that I'm pretty sure I don't want to hear any more. I know I came here, but I don't belong in your tale. In fact, I wouldn't be surprised to find out that whatever you want to tell me is just a fantasy. Something long dead that belongs to the past.'

'I see.'

Catalina stared at Anna. 'This isn't like you.

Normally so curious. Needing to know everything.'

'But I know a lot already,' said Anna.

'How?' said Mihai. 'What do you know?'

Mihai's tone annoyed Anna and without thinking she spat out the words, 'I lied about not knowing the name of the person who invited me. It was your own family. Sorin, was his name. He invited me, for Igor. And he said to come this week. Yeah, he was relaying messages for Igor, that much is true. But he had added a few words of his own. Your own brother told me it would all be okay.'

Both Mihai and Catalina were speechless.

Looking at Mihai's face, Anna immediately regretted her words. His face had paled. He didn't look angry, like she'd expected. It looked more like he'd turned white with fear.

Catalina said, 'What's going on? It isn't good that she lied'. She paused to glare at Anna. 'But you look like a ghost. What is it?'

Mihai's hands had curled into tight fists. With deliberate precision, he straightened his hands before speaking. 'Are you certain, Anna? Are you sure he said to come this week?'

Anna, though unnerved, said without reservation, 'Yes. He said it was the best time of year to be here. He said Igor had promised to put on some sort of special welcome if we came this week'.

Mihai turned away from the balcony. He shook his head and under his breath uttered the words, 'The fool. My brother, the absolute fool'. He turned back to Anna and said, 'Sorin Troester, yes?

You are sure, absolutely sure, that it was him?'

Anna nodded. Now she'd released them, the words tumbled out without pause. She said, 'Yep. That's his name. I also met him in the village. He's a great guy and he looks a bit like you'. As much as Anna found it uncomfortable to look at Mihai, she held his gaze. The alternative was far worse. She could feel Catalina's stare at her back. Mihai might have his own reasons to be angry, but none of them could match whatever thoughts would be going through her friend's mind right now.

Catalina came around in front of Anna. Anna looked away, to avoid seeing the look on her face. 'What has your brother done to us, Mihai?'

'Done? He has done nothing, yes?' Mihai paused. 'This is what *he* would tell you. He trusts the keeper. He supplies him with what he needs. He has befriended him. He believes he is nothing more than a lonely, old man. Absolutely nothing more. He is a fool. He doesn't understand. He doesn't know about this night. No. Even I only know some of it. My father, my grandmother, they would think him too young, too rash, to even tell him. He hasn't done anything to you, yes? You see? Just as our young adventurer, Anna, has done nothing by coming here, yes?'

'Then—' began Catalina.

'They have done nothing. No, that's the truth. There has been no intent. No plan. However, whatever the keeper has planned for you, he has it planned for this night, this day. This time is the time of sacrifice.'

The women stared at him.

'And what that means I cannot say.'

✻ ✻ ✻

The raven was gone.

Igor was alone.

He stirred a small cauldron full of dark and ominous liquids. Now and then, he would add a drop of something from a bottle.

At specific points, he would scoop up some of the mixture and, with great care, bring it to his nose. Another small drop from another bottle would be added. Not once did he sip from the spoon.

He hummed quietly to himself as he worked. The humming had the rhythm of words.

He smiled and reached for another bottle.

✻ ✻ ✻

Nikolai Troester stood by the entrance to the cave. The rain was a wall. A solid sheet of water cascading past the entrance.

'Father, you should sit. You should rest.'

After a few more minutes spent staring at the rain, he came to sit with the small group of young men.

'*Domnule* Troester?'

The grey-haired man looked at the young,

209

fair-haired boy called Petre. 'Yes?'

'Why are you so concerned?' Petre paused. 'I'm sorry. I don't mean that like it sounds, obviously. But the keeper. He's been quiet, my family tell me. For a really long time. So, why are you so worried now? Why tonight?'

'Petre. You have put the question to me right. It is not the women. It is not only that it is my son. It is this night. It is a night that my family remember as being a night of sacrifice. We do not remember it. The keeper has been with us too long. Sorin's grandmother recalls the tale. But her memory is good. It is this night. She is certain. Or certain enough. This night or soon.'

In another corner of the cave, Sorin had gone very quiet.

'Isn't that just an old story?' said Petre.

'Yes. But, as we say, it is a story that he lives. Who can say what he will do with them so close, so usefully close, on a night such as—' Nikolai stopped mid-sentence, having caught sight of his son's face. The colour had drained completely. Sorin's hand was to his mouth. The other young men followed the grey-haired man's gaze.

'Sorin,' said Petre. 'You have to tell him.'

He said to his son. 'No.' He put up his hand. 'Do you think I cannot guess, Sorin?'

Sorin opened his mouth to speak, but his father's gestured hand silenced him.

'Yes. A coincidence. The women. The date. My youngest son, the errand-runner. My youngest son, the kind-hearted, unwitting fool; the message bearer.' He shook his head. 'Yes. I know it would not have been deliberate, Sorin. I also know how much more you think you know than any of us.' He paused before going on. 'None of that. Not the blame, not the how, not anything. None of that matters. It is done. We will do our best to stop it. We will do everything we can to get your brother back.'

'Father—' began Sorin.

'No. Do not tell me you are sorry. It is far too late.'

Sorin stared at his father, seemingly lost for words.

Nikolai moved towards the mouth of the cave. Before heading out, he turned back to the group and said, 'Do not follow me. Do not dare'.

The young men watched him leave. All but Sorin. He stared at his feet.

Nikolai Troester walked outside. He didn't even seem to notice the rain as it crashed down around him. He didn't go far. But he did not look back. He stood. Quiet and still. And the sheets of water washed down over him.

* * *

Mihai sat on the marble bench, his head buried in his hands. Catalina sat next to him, her arm around his shoulders.

At last, Anna managed to say, 'I'm so sorry. Both of you. I'm so sorry'. She knew her words weren't enough. They were worlds away from being enough.

Catalina shook her head. 'Why would you keep this from me? We're meant to be in this together.'

'Honestly, Cat, it wasn't my idea. Sorin asked me to keep it quiet. He's young. I guess he didn't want to get in trouble.'

Mihai snorted.

Catalina squeezed his arm.

'I know I've been an idiot. But, Mihai, is Igor really that dangerous? Would he ...' Anna stopped and made a futile gesture towards the gravestones.

'I don't know what he's capable of, Anna. My young and headstrong brother may be partly right, yes? Perhaps the keeper is absolutely nothing more than an old man. But if so, he is a very old man who has been alone with his torturous tales for longer than anyone in my village can remember. So, you see, yes? He's lived the tale. He believes the story. He is the story. And for it, to serve it, he's brought you here. For whatever he plans next, I think he sees you as part of it. Yes? Yes?'

'Yes.'

Mihai studied her face. As fatigue washed across his face, he looked away.

Watching him, Anna at last realised what had driven Mihai so hard. He was afraid for her. For all of them. The word *sacrifice* hovered in her thoughts and she tried to push it away. But she couldn't hide from it. Because no matter where she looked, the evidence was everywhere.

* * *

Igor walked alone.

The passage was narrow and unlit. Igor's body was at ease in the dark. He didn't stumble. His feet didn't falter.

Unsmiling, he carried an enormous tray of bottles and containers.

'All will be well, Mistress. I promise you.' His voice faltered as he whispered to himself. 'W-well.'

He frowned.

'Yes. All will be well.'

* * *

Anna stared out at the graves far below. They were so depressing. She'd heard Mihai's words, but she couldn't bear to think that all these graves were sacrifices. Staring at them, she noticed one was different. All of the others appeared to be the same size. This was one was far larger.

'Mihai?'

Mihai, his voice thin and cracked, said, 'Yes?'

'Why is one of the gravestones so much bigger than the rest?'

Mihai and Catalina came to her side and looked out at the grey, mossy graveyard. Anna pointed in the direction of the largest stone. It was hard to tell from so far away, but she thought there might also be wilting flowers around the base.

'I'm not sure I should share this with you.'

Catalina said, 'Please, Mihai. Don't hide it from us. Don't try to shield us'.

'No. You misunderstand me. It's not that you shouldn't know. It's that I'm not sure I believe this tale. It's a child's tale. A bedtime horror story, yes?'

'Come on, Mihai. Given everything else we've seen and heard today, I don't think it matters. So, it's a kid's story. We'll listen to it like it's nothing more than that. Like scared little kids. Okay?'

A slight smile crept into the corners of Mihai's mouth as he looked at Anna. 'Yes. Okay.'

Anna could hear the warmth returning to his voice. She was relieved. She couldn't undo what she'd done by bringing them here, but if she could somehow make amends, bit by slow bit, she would try.

Mihai coughed and cleared his voice. 'That is the grave of the last man to die.'

As he spoke, the unrelenting rain eased and the sky burst apart with lightning. An immediate and deafening boom of thunder followed. Anna watched Mihai's face as the sounds died away. She knew he wanted to speak, but was struggling with what to say next.

'They say it is the keeper's grave.'

'But …' said Anna.

'Pardon?' said Catalina.

'You see? It is – ah, yes – a ghost story. Nothing

more.'

'But the grave's there,' said Anna.

The thunder boomed again and Mihai nodded.

'So, you're saying that Igor is—?'

'No, no. I absolutely do not say this. I think it's an unlikely and ancient tale. Told and passed down long before words were written. No. I think it's a story. A myth.'

The trio looked out at the raging storm. Lightning cracked out of the sky, sometimes surging across the mountains, sometimes the valley of graves.

'Does Igor believe the story?'

'Sorin thinks so, very much, yes.' Mihai pursed his lips.

'Mihai?' managed Catalina, before another bout of thunderous rolls drowned her out.

'Sorin says that the keeper believes he is trapped here until he can be released.'

Anna looked at Mihai. There was no doubt there was a lot he was leaving out. If she were him, she probably would too. It was too much. But the intensity of his words left her in no doubt. They had to leave.

'We have to leave,' said Catalina.

'My thoughts exactly,' said Anna.

Mihai's face lit up. 'You mean this? You are willing to leave, Anna?'

'Yes.'

As she spoke, the sky cracked apart with the loudest peal of thunder, the clouds rolled in, and the hail drummed and roared.

Anna knew they couldn't hear her, but she needed to say the words all the same. 'I might fail, but I've at least got to try.' Looking into the hellfire storm she said, 'I won't give in. I won't'.

Catalina had been watching Anna's face as she spoke. She seemed to understand. She reached over and embraced her. Anna pulled her close and, without speaking, together they ran back to the heart of the room and away from the noise of the storm.

* * *

The three stood unmoving in the long, dark and winding corridor.

'Okay. Now what?'

'Good question. It feels like it's taken us all night to get to where we are,' said Catalina. 'I'm not sure I could find my way back out.'

'I have an idea, yes?'

'All ideas welcome, Mihai.'

He gave Catalina a lingering look before continuing. 'The graves. We know where they are on the outside. I think I can figure out where we are from what I've seen below, yes?'

'Um. Not sure I follow you, but okay.'

'There's something else. I've never seen it used, but I know what it is. And where it is.' Anna gave him a confused look, so he hurried on. 'A staircase.'

Both Anna and Catalina groaned.

'No way. I mean, come on, Mihai. There are stairwells and ladders in every damn part of this maze-ridden castle. Finding a stairwell isn't a problem. It won't end there. We'll probably end up trapped inside another strange and eldritch room.'

'No. You misunderstand me. This stairwell, it's on the outside of the castle wall.'

* * *

Nikolai Troester walked on ahead. He stopped when he found another outcropping of rock to use as shelter from the rain, where he crouched inside and waited for the younger men to catch up. Each time they caught up, he waited to allow them a moment's rest from the rain, and then set out again.

Sorin stayed at the back. His face was grey and his mouth pinched tight. He walked on, each step heavy with the weight of determination.

Each of the men walked without speaking, taking one small step after another. Each foot careful, considered, yet treacherous with the rain. But with each step, they carved away the vastness of the heights before them.

Step. And step again.

* * *

'Is it far away, Mihai?' asked Catalina.

'I don't think so. I'm not so sure. I'm trying to imagine it.'

'Okay. Draw it for us.' Anna dug around in her backpack until she pulled out a pencil and notebook.

'Old school, adventurer?' He smiled as he took them from her.

'She's so quaint, isn't she,' said Catalina.

Anna rolled her eyes. 'Oh, come on. You've got to have something you can rely on.'

'Your mum would be so proud. Such a sensible little daughter.'

Anna poked her in the arm. 'Shut up.'

Ignoring their banter, Mihai drew a rough outline of the castle as it appeared on the outside. He sketched in the towering mountains.

Anna was astonished. There was very little else around the castle but mountains. Never-ending mountains. Forests were mere outlines or ways to connect the mountains. She'd walked those same mountains, but she presumed her imagination had gone wild. But the castle truly was carved into and out of the landscape.

Mihai tapped the pencil on his sketch. 'Here is where we are, by the graves.' He traced his pencil around a corner. 'I think this is where the stairs start.' He continued tracing around another corner. 'It ends at the back. There's another way out of the mountains from there. It's further, but I think it's better than back the way we came, yes?'

The women looked at the tiny sketch.

'It looks like quite a long way.'

'It is, yes.'

Anna said, 'But that's okay, since taking the front way might be as long. It might mean we're easily spotted or that we never even make it out'.

'I think, yes, that if I'm right, it's not too far from here to the entrance of the stairwell.'

Catalina looked at Anna. 'At least this time, we're making the decision.'

Anna smiled. 'Yep.'

Mihai nodded and said, 'To the stairs, yes?'

Anna groaned and got to her feet. She put out her hand to help Catalina up. They both groaned as she stood.

'Lead on, Mihai,' said Anna. 'Lead on.'

* * *

After a brief walk, the corridor took a sharp turn.

'This isn't good. There should be a door here.'

'Oh, come on. In this place? A door out in the open where anyone could see it and use it?'

Catalina smiled. 'It's good to see that Nancy has decided to make a return appearance.'

Mihai tipped his head, bird-like. 'Nancy?'

Catalina smirked.

Anna blushed. 'Just ignore her, Mihai.'

'Oh, no. I think it's time for something not dreary and grim. Yes?' he grinned.

'Okay, okay.' Anna couldn't help herself. It thrilled her to see him smile. 'There's these old mystery books I grew up loving. They're silly, really.

There was a girl detective and—'

'No.' Mihai held up his hand. 'No? The Nancy Drew Mysteries?'

'You know them?!'

Mihai's face flushed red.

'Oh, Mihai, no,' said Catalina. 'Don't tell me you've read them.'

Mihai turned to Catalina. 'I can tell you I haven't read them, but this would not be the truth, yes?'

Catalina winced and buried her face in her hands.

'But only one or two!'

'Sure, Mihai. Only one or two. That's what they all say. 'Anna laughed. 'Anyway, there you go. That's why Cat calls me Nancy.'

'I approve. The ever-curious mystery solver. Well, dear "Nancy". What now?'

'Sleuth extraordinaire, that's me.' She shrugged. 'Poke things with a stick until we find something?'

'Actually, I quite like that idea.' Catalina and Anna set about prodding and poking the walls.

After watching them for a moment, Mihai leaned his ear to the wall and, every few centimetres, tapped and moved along. He was forced to stop now and then to wait for the thunderous noise of the storm to die down.

Anna stood and stretched. 'What if it isn't here?'

Catalina stood up and said, 'We'll find another

way. There'll be more than one way out. There's bound to be'.

Anna half-smiled and half-grimaced at her friend. She tried to be optimistic, but could only think about the danger that she'd put them all in. She closed her eyes and began tipping her head back towards the castle wall. And as she was about to make contact, she jerked her head forward, like an addict throwing away a syringe. She slipped to the ground and hugged her knees to her chest.

'Anna?'

'We have to get out.' Anna's voice was barely audible.

'We'll find a way. We will.'

Mihai had continued moving along the wall, ear pressed to the surface, tapping again and again. The thunder that struck reverberated along the walls and across the ceiling. Mihai reeled away from the wall and clutched his ear in pain.

Catalina ran over, kneeled down and held Mihai's face in her hands. 'Are you okay, Mihai? Can you hear me?'

He held his ear and shook his head. He grinned at her.

Catalina pulled back from him and said, 'Why are you grinning? Have you gone mad?'

He looked around and shouted, 'Perhaps so, yes? I think I may have found the stairs'. He grinned at her again.

She grinned back and whispered, 'You're the perfect man, Mihai. Perfect'.

He nodded and said, 'Yes. And I can read your lips'.

Catalina smacked him hard enough that he stumbled sideways. But even as he went, his grin grew even wider.

* * *

They stared at the blank wall.

Looking close, Anna realised that the stones were subtly different to the ones nearby. Similar in colour, it wasn't until she ran her fingers over the surface that the bubbles and pockmarks became obvious. She thought of limestone, but she wasn't a geologist. They were different. That was that. She pushed around the edges, but found no magical depressions, no mystical buttons.

Mihai said, 'I think we'll need to force our way in. Out. Through, yes?'

'Yes 'said Catalina. 'But, what if this little oddity isn't the way to the stairs?'

Mihai had to lean forward to hear her words, but seemed to understand what she said. 'It's something, no? It can be one last mystery for Nancy if it is not our actual stairs.'

Anna sighed. 'You know, I think I've had my fill of mysteries today.'

Catalina raised her eyebrows in mock surprise. 'No, surely not. Is this the end of Nancy Drew?'

'Look, I just said for today. I didn't say forever.'

Catalina smiled. 'So, what do we have that's heavy?'

Anna looked at her feet. 'My boots?'

'It's somewhere to start,' she said. 'Yours are quite a lot sturdier than mine. Off. Yours too, Mihai.'

Mihai looked shocked. 'My boots? You would have something better in your backpacks, no?'

'Sure, we're carrying something heavier and bigger than hiking boots in our backpacks.'

'Yes?' Mihai looked sad and hopeful, all at the same time.

'You're ridiculous, you know that?' She shook her head. 'Come on, boots.'

Mihai bent and unlaced his boots.

Anna reached out to stop him. 'Let's try mine first. It might be enough.' She painfully removed her boots and looked at her swollen, bandaged leg. She sighed and said, 'I mightn't ever be able to get that boot on again'. One at a time, she handed her boots to Mihai and stood back.

Mihai tied the boots together and swung them like a man getting ready to release a slingshot. He wound up, let go and cracked the boots into the middle of the patch of stones. On the first thud, the stone crumbled under his attack. In a very short time, the thin, porous layer of stone had all but disappeared.

The fresh scent of rain rushed through the gap in the wall. It was the outside.

Anna had never smelled anything more beautiful in all her life.

CHAPTER TWELVE

The air tasted alive.

One after another, Mihai, Catalina and Anna squeezed through the gap in the wall.

Lightning stormed and arced in the distance. The rain had eased from a raging torrent to a steady downpour.

Water cascaded down Anna's body, washing away the grime, blood and incestuous smells of the endless, terrible hours just gone. Long, thin rivulets traced their way along her body and over her face. The feeling of fresh water cleansing away all the filth from her matted hair allowed her to, for a moment, forget where she was. She shut her eyes and let the sensation of the chilled liquid to envelope her.

'Don't let go of the banister,' said Catalina, jolting Anna back to reality. 'And you'd best get your boots back on.'

With great care, Anna complied. She slowly stood back up, her legs shaking the whole time.

Anna grabbed the banister and looked out at the view in front of her. She swayed back. The height was sickening. A 'long way up' just didn't cover it. She didn't think she'd ever been this high before. And never standing unsheltered on the outside of a windblown wall. Her knuckles turned white as she gripped hold of the stone siding. The ancient staircase appeared to run around the outside of one wall of the castle. Anna couldn't see around the corner of the wall and didn't know whether the stairs turned the corner or ended in a terrible architectural nightmare. She was so high up she felt she could touch the mountains. But even at this height, they soared into the sky and towered over her. She tried to look to the top, but it made her dizzy.

Anna followed the glacial twists of the mountains down to the ground. A small trail, if it was a trail at all, meandered like a drunken caterpillar until it reached the earth at the foot of the castle, where it disappeared from view. The vastness of the mountains dominated the scenery and made everything seem small or far away. The scale was unfathomable.

Catalina had taken a first few steps before glancing back and seeing that Anna hadn't moved. 'Coming?'

Anna nodded and said, 'Mm-hmm.'

'You can't stay there, Anna.'

'Yeah, I know,' said Anna looking down. 'Aren't you scared? Shouldn't you be scared?'

'Perhaps, yes, but look at the view,' said Catalina. 'It's breathtaking.'

'Yep. You're right. I think I've forgotten how to breathe.'

'One step at a time, Anna. Take it slow. I'll be with you the whole way.'

Anna smiled tightly and attempted her first step, her leg shaking still. She groaned. She hated this place. But she stepped again. And again.

* * *

Mihai looked back at the slow-moving women.

Catalina, during a break in the thunder, said, 'How can you go so fast?'

Mihai grinned. 'Look around you. This is my home. These are my mountains. A long way up is a good thing. A familiar thing, no?'

'Do you want to go on ahead?'

'No. I want to be near you.'

She smiled.

'That, yes. But also, you might need help.' He looked around her at Anna. 'Or our adventurer friend, perhaps.'

'Thank you, I'm not deaf,' said Anna.

Mihai smiled. And waited.

* * *

The three made their way down the stairs, one slow

step at a time.

Mihai paused every now and then to allow the women to catch up.

Anna found if she concentrated on the act of stepping, she was better able to tune out the surrounding view. The stone steps were peppered with tiny patches of moss, making them bumpy and slippery in unexpected spots. The falling rain meant she had to push her foot in place to stop herself slithering away. Each step that contained no sliding was a small victory. She thought about the details of how she stepped, how each muscle worked. The momentum of swinging her leg in front of her and the pull as the weight of her foot dropped her hip low. One foot. Then another. Again and again. She became so focused on the step in front of her that she nearly didn't notice when Catalina stopped. 'What's wrong?'

'I don't know. Mihai?'

Mihai had turned back to look at the women. 'There's a gap.'

'A gap?' said Anna.

'Yes.'

'A gap, you say.'

'Yes, Anna.'

'How big a gap are we talking?'

'No more than one step. A half step, crumbled away. And with it a part of the banister, yes?'

Anna's breath caught in her throat.

Without warning and with effortless grace, Mihai leaped over the small gap. Before Anna could even think to look away, Catalina had taken a similar, if not as deft, leap.

Her legs shaking, Anna approached the gap and looked down. She knew she shouldn't, but she couldn't stop herself. It was far worse than she'd imagined. Her body felt as if it was being drawn down into the gap. The blood rushed from her head. Bitterness roiled through her mouth. She coughed and spat. The bilious drip plunged into the depth below. She couldn't think for the sound of her own blood thrumming in her ears. Nauseous and giddy, she still couldn't look away.

'You have to look up, Anna.'

At the sound of Catalina's voice, Anna looked up. Her heartbeat slowed and returned to normal. She drew in a deep breath and, keeping her eyes level, took a long and deliberate step over the gap. She didn't slip and didn't stumble. She placed both her feet carefully on the lower, solid steps that followed.

'You're here, Anna. You're safe.'

Anna started to smile, but stopped, letting her smile falter.

'Anna?'

'I just realised that's probably not the last time I'm going to have to do that,' she said.

'You've done it once, yes? You can do it again.'

Anna grimaced and nodded.

They continued their relentless march down.

* * *

When Mihai slowed his pace, Anna looked up to see they had reached a corner of the castle. She had a desperate hope that the stairs would reach all the way to the ground. It was too easy to picture a vast gap with a pile of despair and rubble far below. It wasn't the thought of climbing up the stairs that bothered her. She was more worried about what they'd face if they went back inside. And that wasn't the ghastly traps, it wasn't Igor, or the deathly omens. It was herself and her own untrustworthy thoughts. They were a traitor to her own will. Her own intent. Even out here, standing in the cleansing rain, chilled and level-headed, she could still feel the pull of the castle. She should be running from this place, desperate to get away. She understood that. Instead she was constantly shoving down a feeling of loss and something else that she didn't want to name. It was something approaching lust. She had to get away.

'Good news, fellow adventurers. The stairs seem to go all the way down across the wall,' said Mihai.

'No gaps?' said Catalina.

'It's dark, but I think not, no. Not big gaps,' said Mihai smiling, his face shining in the rain. Distant lightning briefly lit up part of the sky and the castle.

Anna peered around the corner. The staircase made its way along the wall at about the same height as the windows they had stood at to see the graveyard. The stairs veered down and under the balcony they'd been standing on, then appeared to continue around to the next corner of the castle.

'I'd sort of hoped the stairs would reach all way to the ground at the bottom of this wall. I can't believe there might be a whole extra wall of stair climbing to do.' She looked down at the grey-slated mountains below her. She spotted a small meandering path and recalled seeing it earlier, from the balcony. The path doggedly continued on until it reached the graveyard and crumbled away. It wasn't the same path they'd taken to get here, Anna was certain, but it might be the one they could take to get out.

'That's quite a lot of stairs,' said Catalina, as another long and all-too-close bolt of lightning fully lit up the castle wall and stairwell below.

Blinded, Anna heard Mihai say, 'At least I saw the stairwell before the lightning fell away. It looks good. I think we'll be okay for a while, yes?'

'Yes,' said Catalina. 'Once we can see again.'

'We all can't see. We should rest, yes?'

Anna heard the sounds of someone sitting down. Her vision was clearing, but was hardly great. Her legs pleaded with her to rest and she obliged. She allowed them to collapse under her. She thought could see the form of someone, probably Catalina, nearby.

'It might be a good idea to rest anyway,' said Catalina. 'Igor doesn't seem to be giving chase and we have a long way yet to go'.

'Come on. Would he chase us? Do you really

think so? 'said Anna. In the momentary silence, she shook her head. 'That's it though, isn't it. We can't know. Not for sure.'

Mihai said, 'I suppose we have absolutely run out of food?'

Catalina said, 'There's nothing substantial, but I might have a little something'. She started to dig around in her backpack.

'I can't believe how hungry I am. We keep eating and I keep being hungry.'

'Ah, adventurer, this is what adrenaline and action will do to you, I think.'

Anna smiled warmly at Mihai.

'Ah-hah,' said Catalina. 'I think I've found some nuts. 'She waved a small packet in the air.

'Victory!'

Mihai said, 'Please, both of you. Eat. I can go without'.

'No way. We all eat or no one does,' said Anna.

'Yes,' said Catalina. She tore open the bag and counted out the nuts.

Anna ate slowly and enjoyed the tang of salt as the nuts rolled around on her tongue. She dragged in a deep breath, the fresh air hitting the back of her nostrils, a heady mix of stone, tin, and rain. For one heady moment she felt as if she was in the world's greatest cinema and the landscape was there just for her. She embraced the moment and relaxed. For whatever reason, this was her mountain. And it felt like home.

* * *

Mihai started to hum. A moment later Catalina joined him. As she joined him, they both gently broke into song. Sounds became words, words became song. The sound of their voices echoed across and down the mountain.

Anna followed them in silence. It lent a rhythm to her steps. After a while she said, 'What are you singing? I don't know it, but it seems sort of familiar'.

Mihai continued to sing, deep and low.

Catalina answered Anna softly. 'It's a *doina*. It's hard to explain. It's different each time. You might have heard my grandmother do it.'

'It sounds sort of mournful. What's it about?'

Catalina shrugged. 'It's not about the words. It's about the sound and the feeling. It's often sung alone.'

'I thought I could recognise individual words,' said Anna.

'You probably can. But the sound's the focus. It's been a long time since I sung this way, but I don't need to know the words.'

Mihai continued to sing, his sonorous words filling the valley and catching the wind.

* * *

Nikolai Troester rested against a stony ledge. The young men sprawled across the stones behind him.

Sorin made his way past his exhausted friends. 'You need to rest, father.'

Nikolai looked at the young men. Their shoulders drooped, but most of them were awake. Every time he had moved on, they had followed. 'You could perhaps convince me of this, but not your friends.'

Sorin turned back to look at them. 'You're right. They're even more stubborn than you.'

Nikolai smiled wearily.

The wind roared and with it came the hint of a sound. Sorin looked at his father, eyebrows raised.

His father pressed a single finger tight against his lips.

Both men stood still and silent, leaning into the wind. The wind rushed down the valley again. A fleeting moment of sound raced by. Sorin turned to look at his friends. They were smiling, all of them. Each one sat still, leaning forward. Ears to the wind. Once more came the wind, whistling through the valley. And with it a taste of a sound. A song.

'Mihai,' whispered Nikolai.

All of a sudden, the group of young men were on their feet.

Sorin opened his mouth to speak. He shut it and looked away.

His father watched him.

Sorin started to hum. At first his voice was cracked, hoarse. He pushed on and raised his voice in song. Short seconds later, one after the other, all the young men joined in. As one, they continued their climb.

Nikolai, his eyes moist with the sting of the wind, followed behind them. He did not sing. But he carried on.

* * *

Mihai stopped. His song had been strong and melodic, but it drained away.

'Another gap, Mihai?' asked Anna. They had found several more crumbling, dissolving steps, so Anna had been keeping a careful eye on him. She was getting quite good at stepping over the most terrifying of depths.

'No.'

Catalina and Anna walked down the stairs to stand behind him.

When Anna glanced over his shoulder, she realised he was staring at the graveyard.

'What's up? It's the same one we saw earlier, isn't it? 'said Anna.

Mihai didn't respond.

Anna followed his line of sight. In the near corner of the graveyard stood a small gravestone. Far smaller than any of the others. Too small.

Catalina said gently, 'Mihai?'

'Can you imagine what the keeper's seen? You see why he chose to stay here, yes? It doesn't matter what is real and what is not. This,' he gestured down, 'this is what he thought he could stop'.

* * *

Igor stood on top of a rocky outcrop of the castle. He stared at the trio on the stairs below.

Snippets of their conversation carried to him on the wind, but Igor did not strain to hear them.

He did not need to hear.

He could see what they could see.

He could remember.

* * *

The villagers had gathered at the graveyard. The sky was relentless, the sun shone fiercely.

The visitor, curious, wandered closer to listen to their conversation. He settled down behind a vast headstone. The once foreign language washed over him. He watched the villagers, paying as much attention to their gestures as to their words.

'What were you thinking, Radu?' said one woman.

'I thought it was a game,' said the young boy. 'It is only a game, mama? Yes?'

His mother looked away, seemingly unable to speak.

A man near him said to the crowd, 'He doesn't know what he's doing. We must stop this'.

Several people tried to speak at once.

'You know what will happen. This young man was an accident, but you saw his face. The hunger. He won't stop with your son.'

'Your son will die and many others will follow him.'

'None of us want this. We have no choice.'

The father said, 'I will offer myself'.

'We know it won't be enough. It won't work,' said another man pointing at a small grave. 'We know that. Accident or not.'

'I will offer myself,' said the father again.

Those around him shook their heads in silence.

The visitor stood up.

The small gathering of people looked at him and began to back away.

'Perhaps I can offer another way.'

* * *

The three of them stared down at the tiny gravestone.

Mihai continued. 'We don't know if he personally witnessed the death of this young man. But we know one thing: he knew he was no more than a child. Not a sacrifice, they say. But intentional or not, this young one died in the name of the castle. And somehow, we don't know how, the visitor – the keeper – managed to stop it from ever happening again.'

'He was an outsider?'

'Yes.'

'But,' said Catalina, 'what could he possibly offer that the villagers couldn't?'

'We do not absolutely know. It was too long ago and too much has been forgotten. It's clear to me now though, yes, that we have neglected him. It may be an ancient tale, but it's one he believes. One that he lives. And if this is his view,' said Mihai as he faced the small grave below, 'if this is what he remembers, perhaps my brother was right. Perhaps he is nothing more than a very lonely old man'.

'And maybe he isn't,' said Anna.

'Yes,' said Mihai. 'You see now? It's not one single story. No clear truth. The lies and uncertainties are twisted and hidden with the truth.' He shook his head. 'No. The only certainty is that you are here on a night you shouldn't be. And that you're in danger. Whatever that danger is, it's real and terrible.'

'I wish we knew,' said Catalina.

'Hell, I don't.'

'It doesn't matter. What matters now is that we leave. And, with any luck, we won't ever know.' He turned away and, without looking back, continued his climb down the stairs.

✻ ✻ ✻

Igor looked up at the sound of Mihai's final words.

'It is not for you to know,' he said. 'Only one need ever know. I was wrong, Mistress. This is my burden. Then, now, and forever more.'

Igor watched them linger, watched them consider.

As they turned to leave, he simply watched them go.

* * *

The trio had fallen into a shared silence since seeing the small grave.

Mihai's pace had slowed. It was clear Igor was not in pursuit. Anna couldn't see any point in hurrying.

And with the monotonous regularity of each step, the travellers slowed, their fatigue apparent and growing.

Mihai stopped.

Not far behind him, Catalina and Anna stopped as well.

Anna almost hadn't seen it. And it was clear that Mihai almost hadn't seen it either. A gap. Not a near-crumbled stair as before. A sizeable, harrowing breach. The half dozen missing steps formed a yawning crevice.

Mihai edged his way back up the staircase. 'I'm sorry. I was so tired ...'

Catalina took hold of his shoulder as he came closer. 'You did see it, Mihai. It's okay, we're safe.'

'Safe, now, maybe. But look at that. We're stuck. There's no way past that,' said Anna.

Mihai looked from Anna to the gap and back again. 'No, Anna.'

Anna gazed down into the plummeting depth. Unlike the previous gaps, she could clearly see the details of the ground below her. Real, and almost touchable, the depth was still bone-crushing. She looked back at Mihai. 'You've lost it. We can't jump that.'

'It's a short distance, no? Imagine jumping over a small creek. It is not so very much wider than that.'

'Cat? Come on. You can't think this is a good idea?'

Catalina shrugged. 'I think going back is a far worse idea.'

Anna threw her arms in the air and said, 'Okay, Ms Brave. After you.'

Mihai raised an eyebrow at her. 'Perhaps this is not such a good idea.'

'What do you mean?,' said Anna.

'Catalina is tall and strong, yes. If she goes first she can help you. You though. You're stubborn and flighty.'

Anna opened her mouth to interrupt, but Mihai waved her to silence.

'You can promise that you would not give in, if we left you this side of the gap? Promise not to return to the heart of the castle?'

At the mention of the castle, Anna's blood rushed to her face. 'I can promise,' she lied.

'You're a terrible liar, Anna. At least to me,' Cat said smiling. 'I'll go first. Mihai can stay this side to encourage you across.'

'I'm not a misbehaving child.'

'No?' said Mihai.

Anna's lips tightened. There were some arguments she wouldn't even bother trying to win.

Catalina said, 'So, I go first.'

* * *

Mihai and Anna held Catalina by the feet.

Catalina lay flat out, head pointing down towards the gap. Her long, blonde hair tumbled past her face and over the edge of the gap.

'I think it's okay. The bottom step should hold.'

'Are you sure?' asked Mihai.

'As sure as I can be, yes,' said Catalina, her voice thin. 'I'm getting a little dizzy. Help me back up.'

Anna held Catalina's feet as Mihai moved down to help her. As he moved, he slid his hands along her body, never letting go. 'The other side looks quite sturdy as well,' she said as Mihai helped her up. When she was upright, she swayed a little and leaned into him for support.

After a long and lengthening moment, Mihai pulled back from their embrace and said, 'You are okay now, yes?'

Catalina looked herself up and down, smiled and said, 'Yes'.

Anna coughed. 'Sorry to break you two up. But what do you think, Cat? Can you make it?'

'I was quite confident before we looked. Now I'm sure. 'She climbed up a few steps and stood still, steadying herself and catching her breath.

'Be careful, okay?'

Anna watched Catalina. Smiling, Catalina glanced back, ran down the steps and jumped. She sailed across the gap and landed on the other side, her feet slipping and skidding, but she was over. And standing, eventually, firm and safe across the way.

Mihai grinned.

Catalina turned back, her face split open in a wide smile.

Anna, despite herself, laughed. 'And you call me the adventurous one'.

'With each step we get closer to home, and I get more brave. Perhaps I'm a homeward-bound adventurer.'

'Tell yourself whatever you like, Cat. When you stop grinning we can chat some more.'

'Alright, Anna,' said Mihai. 'Your turn, now, yes?'

Anna's face, pricked with the cold, had drained of all colour. 'Yes.'

Like Catalina before her, she didn't give herself time to think. She ran, and she jumped. Her feet faltered on the rain-soaked stonework.

And she didn't quite make it.

* * *

Anna's fingers clutched at the crumbling stone. The

rain made the stones slick and her grip failed again and again.

A strong hand encircled her arm. She looked up as Catalina grabbed hold of her jacket. 'Reach up, Anna. I have you.'

Anna pulled herself up, grabbing at her friend's arms. The skin on her wrists scraped against the broken stonework. Halfway along, she lay her upper body flat against the steps. Her breath rushed out, hot and rough. She felt Catalina's presence – her warm, strong arms – and clambered the rest of the way. She sat up and caught her breath, and curled tightly into Catalina's hold. Her feet dangled down into the gap below. She watched her boots sway back and forth and tried to let free the image of herself as a crushed body far below.

'Okay, dear Anna?'

'Yep,' she looked over to Mihai. 'I'm okay.' As she said it, she was surprised to find that it was true. She smiled and she said, 'Your turn.'

Anna walked down a half dozen steps to make way for Mihai. Catalina stayed close, but to the side.

Mihai turned, jogged up a few steps and faced the gap again. He stood for a moment and shut his eyes, the rain in his face. His eyes flicked open, he grinned, and then ran and leaped across the gap. He soared across the abyss and the steps that followed it. And crashed into Catalina, and then Anna as he landed. All three tumbled down the stairs together. When they came to a stop, they had travelled quite a way from the break in the stairs. The second corner of the castle was a few steps away.

'I guess that saved us a lot of slow climbing,' said Anna, as she rubbed her neck.

Mihai winced and said, 'I think I was a little over eager in my judgement, yes?'

'It was a beautiful thing to watch,' said Catalina, 'until you landed.'

Mihai grimaced and clambered to his feet. He put out his hands as an offer to help the women up. 'Are you both okay to stand?'

'Yep, I'm good,' said Anna, as she stood. She looked down at her scraped, bruised and battered body. 'Okay. Um, I'm going to go with "good enough".'

Catalina took Mihai's hand and leaned into his shoulder as she stood.

'You okay, Cat?'

'My knee has seen better days, but there's nothing broken. I'll be fine.'

The three huddled together and looked down at the corner of the castle wall.

'I think we're nearly there, yes?'

'Don't say it out loud. Don't jinx it,' said Anna.

'Anna?' said Catalina. 'Are *you* okay?'

'Yes. I just want to go home.'

Catalina and Mihai smiled briefly at each other.

'Let's go,' said Catalina.

Anna led the way.

❋ ❋ ❋

As they turned the corner of the castle, the bottom of the stairwell appeared. The ground coalesced into a palpable and touchable presence. Still an incredible distance, it had become perceivable and no longer a distant horror.

'The ground. I can see the ground!' said Anna.

Anna, Mihai and Catalina broke into a run. Their exhaustion forgotten, the stairwell dissolved under their feet.

Anna smiled as she ran, half-stumbling. The air and rain swept across her face, and tears were swept away with it. She was free. She could feel it. She was going home.

CHAPTER THIRTEEN

Anna stepped onto the ground.

Her legs trembled and she reached out for something to lean on. Instead of a wall, she felt Catalina's arm. Anna leaned into it and felt Catalina lean back. As they stood together, the cool rain ran down Anna's sweaty back and the breeze pricked at her skin. Anna's head spun as though she were standing on the deck of a boat. She'd been up in the clouds so long that the ground felt foreign. She wondered if anyone had ever had reason to use the phrase 'stair legs'.

Mihai looked up at the steps and said, 'I will be happy if I never again see this place or this castle wall'.

Anna stayed silent. They were out, but nothing like safe.

'So what now?' said Catalina. 'Do you know the best way from here?'

'Not from here, no. I have never been this way before. But we will find our way.' Mihai looked at the landscape ahead of them.

Unlike the heady climb to the front of the castle, the immediate ground was mostly level. The mountains still surrounded the castle, but a a small, dense forest covered the distance to the castle wall. Several meandering paths ran in different directions, each one disappearing into the forest after a few feet. One path stood apart from the others, well-used and well-trodden.

Anna pointed at it and said, 'Oh, hey! There's a couple of broken branches'.

'Does that mean we want to use it or avoid it?' said Catalina.

'I think we shouldn't overthink it, is what I think,' said Anna walking away.

'Mihai?' said Catalina.

Mihai followed Anna down the more used path. 'This time, I'm with the adventurer, yes? I'm taking the path of less thinking.'

Catalina shrugged and followed.

* * *

Anna screwed up her nose. Something new had caught her attention. Not only the fresh air after the mustiness that had been haunting her waking hours. Something else, something refreshing. Sweet and somehow familiar. 'What *is* that?' She sniffed at the air. 'Can you smell it?'

'The trees?' said Catalina, a little way behind her.

'No.' Anna breathed in again. 'There's something else. 'She waited for Catalina to catch up to her. 'I swear I can smell tomatoes.'

'Now I'm hungry again,' said Catalina.

'What have you found, adventurer?' said Mihai, walking up behind them.

'Nothing yet,' said Anna, distracted. 'A smell. A scent.'

Mihai breathed in deeply and sniffed heavily at the air. 'Have you heard of deadly nightshade?'

'No,' said Anna.

'I know the name,' said Catalina. 'It's also called belladonna, I think.'

'The deadly part is in the name for a reason, no? A few berries could make you very ill, even kill you. If you spot them, don't even think of eating them.'

Anna stared at Mihai. 'Are you serious?'

'I thought you would know about something like this.'

'We know better than to eat random food, but not the specifics,' said Catalina. 'We're not from here, remember? Perhaps you should lead, Mihai.'

'Oh, come on, Cat. Mihai shouldn't have to do everything,' said Anna. 'Neither of us would've eaten something without knowing what it was.'

'No, but still …,' said Catalina.

'No. We're only going to get through this if we rely on each other, not merely on one man.' Anna looked at Mihai. 'Even if he is a damn fine man.'

Mihai grinned.

'Oh, shut up,' said Anna and walked away.

Mihai and Catalina walked on also, side by side. Their hands touched. Mihai sought and held Catalina's fingers in his own.

Anna forged ahead, grateful to be on solid ground again. The rain still fell, but in dribs and drabs. By comparison with the overnight storm, it was welcoming and calm. The path began to close in on her and the low scrubs thickened. The surrounding thickets ran and rambled until they met the approaching forest. Anna pursed her lips as if to whistle, but for some reason thought better of it. She scrunched up her nose. She longed to sneeze, but couldn't. She paused and, unpleasant though it was, took in a long, deep breath. She called back to the others, 'Can you smell that? Something musty?'

Behind her, Mihai stood very still. He filled his chest with air. He exhaled and said, 'Do not move'.

Anna carried on ahead, distracted and fascinated by the smell.

Mihai's voice stayed at a whisper. 'Anna. Please. No.'

Catalina stood still, but her head flicked between Anna and Mihai. 'What is it? What's wrong?'

The tendons in Mihai's neck stood out, his jaw clenched. 'How did she smell it so soon? Who is she?' His hands curled into tightly bunched fists.

'Mihai?' said Catalina. 'What is it?'

'That,' he said. 'That is a wolf.'

* * *

A movement in the shrubs ahead caused Anna to stop.

A wolf walked across the path and stopped as it caught sight of her. It lowered its head and peeled up one corner of its lip to reveal a pointed canine.

Anna had never seen anything so domineering and yet so beautiful. The wolf's coat was grey with flecks of white and brown. Its dark eyes followed her every movement. The eyes were beautiful; mesmerising. She walked closer.

Behind her, Catalina whispered, 'Anna, come back'.

'She can't hear you,' said Mihai. 'Or refuses to hear you, yes?'

'Are we safe, Mihai?' she said

'If we'd stayed back and let it be, yes, probably,' he said. 'Be ready to run.'

Anna stared straight at the wolf. As she came closer it hunkered down and began to back away. She put out her hand. The wolf stared at her hand, unmoving.

'You can trust me,' said Anna softly, stopping a few feet away.

The wolf stopped and Anna approached it again. She moved forward, one cautious step at a time.

The wolf growled a low, rumbling sound.

Anna felt it in her gut and in the base of her

spine. She paused, but then started forward again.

The wolf stood its ground and let out a long, slow and uncertain growl. A sound that was more like a whine.

Behind her, Anna heard Catalina's quiet, sharp intake of breath. It didn't stop her. Instead, she made soothing sounds at the wolf as she moved forward. Her whispers blended with the gentle sound of the rain.

The wolf fell silent and tilted its head. Just a little.

And then, in the softest of voices, Anna started to sing.

The wolf's ears pricked forward as Anna's voice rose. The beast lowered itself to the ground and, putting its chin across its front paws, appeared to settle and listen keenly to Anna's voice.

Still singing, Anna turned back and smiled at Catalina and Mihai.

Mihai and Catalina stood stock still. Catalina's mouth hung open. Mihai's face was as dark as the gloomy night just gone.

On seeing Mihai's face, Anna's voice faltered. At the same moment, the wolf leaped to its feet and ran.

When Anna turned back, the wolf was absent. Without thinking, she cried out. 'No, come back. We won't hurt you. Please come back'.

As Anna moved to follow the wolf, both Catalina and Mihai ran forward to stop her. They caught up with her and each grabbed a shoulder.

'What are you doing? What in all hell is wrong with you?!'

Mihai said, 'If we knew the answer to that, we'd have the answer to everything'.

* * *

Igor stood at his bench, fingering the pages of an old, crumbling behemoth of a book. He whispered to himself as his fingers traced the words, as a wave traces the movement of the earth.

'Mistress, I long to let you go, but I know you will return. You belong here. I *wanted* to let you go, but you cannot. It is not my choice. Nothing is of my choosing.' His body swayed along with his meandering fingers, his movements increased in intensity, shuddering and juddering.

'You will come back to me. You will have no choice, Mistress. The castle. She needs you.' He laid his hands flat on the pages of the tome. 'We need you.'

As he closed the great book, parts of the pages came away in his hands, crumbling like an ancient ruin. He glared at his hands and brushed the useless remnants to the floor.

'Without you we are nothing,' he whispered. 'Without you, Mistress, we are the past and we are lost. What else can I do?'

'Mistress.' He looked out at the soulless grey sky, as tears filled his eyes, 'What do I do?'

❋ ❋ ❋

Anna stood in silence, avoiding Catalina's glare.

'Anna,' said Catalina. 'What were you thinking? I mean ... Exactly what were you thinking?!'

Anna ignored her and tried to break free of their grip.

'She was thinking only of herself, as ever,' said Mihai. 'No?'

Anna wrenched herself free. 'No. That's not true.'

Mihai shook his head sharply. 'Anna, you approached a wolf as if it was some sort of pet dog. Only minutes before you were telling us we needed to be able to rely on each other. That you could be sensible, yes? That you would not be so unwise as to eat unknown things. What do you know of wolves? How could someone like you know about such a thing?'

'Anna, you're scaring me. What's happening to you?'

Anna ignored Catalina and turned a glare at Mihai. 'What do you mean "someone like me"?

'Anna, he's only saying that we're strangers here. How could you know you would be safe? When have you ever even seen a wolf?' said Catalina.

'That's not what he was saying. He doesn't trust me.'

Mihai said, 'I continue to try though, no? And

you continue to make it an impossible task'.

'Seriously, Anna. You could have got us all killed.'

Anna knew they were right, but she didn't want to admit it. She hadn't thought. She'd just felt. And she'd felt safe. More than that, she'd felt a deep connection with the beast and its home. She knew it as surely as she knew the touch of her own feet on the ground. She also knew they would be safe. That the wolf wouldn't harm them. She thought desperately and tried to build a logical defence for her own behaviour. It wasn't easy because there was no such thing and she knew it. She said, 'I once read somewhere that wolves respond to music. I knew we couldn't outrun it, but I thought if I could calm it and soothe it, we might be able to walk by, unharmed'.

Mihai raised an eyebrow and said nothing.

Catalina said, 'Is that true?'

'Cross my heart and—' began Anna.

'Don't say it. Not here,' said Catalina.

A smile flicked across Anna's face. 'Okay, fair enough. Honestly, I remember thinking it was amazing. I guess it's about the way they howl with each other. Their ears are attuned to music.'

'All the same, Anna.'

'What difference does it make? We're all okay.'

'Another adventure for your list, yes?' said Mihai.

'It wasn't like that.'

'She's right, though, Mihai,' said Catalina.

'None of us were hurt.'

Mihai nodded, but grimaced as he did so.

'Come on, Mihai,' said Anna, as she poked softly at his arm. 'Let's keep moving. Okay?'

'Yes,' said Mihai. 'We should walk on. And everything is absolutely okay.'

Anna winced at his final, bitter words. She turned and walked away.

Catalina watched as expressions shifted across Mihai's face. She pulled him close and said, 'Do you still trust us?'

'You. I trust you. Your friend,' he said. 'Your friend, I cannot say. And neither can you.'

* * *

Anna meandered along the path, looking for signs of the wolf.

As she walked she found herself hoping it would return. She knew they'd been safe. As much she was tired of her own thought, she was tiring of Catalina's logic. Her demand that everything make sense. Everything be measured and weighed. She had grown up listening to Mrs Dalca's stories too, yet Catalina had rejected all of it. Anna wanted to believe. Especially here and now. She wanted it to be to true.

Anna stepped over a gnarled root in the middle of the path and started muttering to herself. 'I'll never understand what happened to Cat. Why can't she feel things the way I do? Why doesn't she believe the stories? What's wrong with her?'

Anna glanced at a shrub that had a carved hole in its branches, like an above ground burrow. Curved and lined with traces of white fur, she couldn't quite look away, so she kneeled down to inspect it. As her eyes adjusted to the dark, curving space, she saw a flash of white. Moments later she glimpsed a pair of eyes blinking back at her. She smiled. 'Hi there, little one. Mind if I call you Alice?' She sat up and looked behind her. Catalina and Mihai were making their way along the path. They walked close to each other, chatting, and Mihai didn't look anywhere near as angry as before.

'Does your leg still hurt, Anna?' Cat asked, gesturing at Anna's bandaged leg.

Anna blinked and said, 'Oh, hey. No, not really. I'm surprised. I guess adrenaline can push you a lot further than you realise.'

'It looks a little that way. So, um, why are you sitting on the ground?'

'Oh,' said Anna smiling, 'I found a rabbit hole. I mean, I guess it's a rabbit hole.'

Mihai walked up and peered over Anna's shoulder. 'You're right, no? It's a bit strange that it's so out in the open, I think.' Mihai looked up and down the path. He stared at the ground.

'Would someone like to give me a hand up?'

Mihai grunted and held out an arm to Anna.

'Thanks,' said Anna, as she felt his strength pull her effortlessly to her feet. Sometimes she resented her short, slight body. Frequently.

Occasionally it was a small delight.

Mihai was still staring at the ground.

'Hello? Earth to Mihai. Are you giving me the silent treatment?'

Mihai glanced at her. 'No, but perhaps I should, yes?'

Catalina said, 'Mihai. Please. We have to work together. I know you're still angry about the wolf, but we've got quite a long way to go'.

'It's so tiring. We build this trust – all of us. Then one of us puts us and it at risk. Then we build it up again,' he said. 'I'm not sure I want to be part of this game anymore.'

'It isn't a game, Mihai. Nothing I've done was meant to harm you,' said Anna.

'So you say' he said.

'I promise you,' said Catalina. 'I've known her all of my life. Anna would never intentionally hurt anyone. She can sometimes be a little silly, as you say —'

'Hey!' said Anna.

'— but it's always with good intent. Please, Mihai. How can I help you see that?'

He smiled warmly at Catalina. 'You can stand there and say the words you have said. I trust you.'

'But not me,' said Anna.

He turned halfway towards at her, 'No, adventurer. But I will do my best once again, if you can promise me the same. Again.'

Anna thrust out her hand and said, 'It's a deal'. Even in the face of Mihai's surly features, they shook hands. 'What were you looking at before, Mihai?' said Anna, changing the subject before the conversation could have a chance to go wrong again.

'The path,' he said pointing. 'It's newly turned.'

He walked back a few metres staring at the ground. 'Yes, and here. You see here?'

The women walked over and stared at what seemed like an ordinary corner of damp earth.

After a moment, Anna realised what she was looking at. Loose earth. Up until now the path was tightly-packed, covered in moss, flattened tree roots and levelled stones. It was not smooth and engineered, but it was old. Very old.

This path was mostly clear and, in a way, well presented. The difference wasn't stark, but once she realised it was there, it became more and more obvious. 'I don't know what's going on, but I don't like it.'

'You're not alone, adventurer.'

'We should backtrack and see if there's another way, 'said Catalina.

'I may as well say it out loud,' said Anna. 'We all think this is a trap, right?'

Mihai said, 'I am still thinking. But, yes, absolutely this could be a trap. Or it might be something else'.

'Oh, come on. You think Igor comes down and lays convenient getaway paths for people like us?' said Anna.

'No. But he is not the only visitor to his castle,

as we know, yes?'

'Do you mean your brother, Mihai?' said Catalina.

Mihai sighed and said, 'Yes'.

* * *

Sorin stood looking up at the twisting path ahead of them.

'There is another way, father.'

Nikolai Troester turned to his son and raised an eyebrow. 'This is the only way I have ever known.'

Sorin grimaced. 'You know what I've been doing. I couldn't have done it as often as I did if I'd had to make this twisting climb every time.'

'I am listening, Sorin.'

'Can we rest?' Sorin said, gesturing at himself and the weary group behind him.

Nikolai closed his eyes and, after a pause, answered. 'Yes.' He ran his fingers through his grey hair and watched as all the young man sat down, some collapsing to the ground. They were wet, shivering and exhausted. But not one of them had complained and none of them did so now. For the first time since starting their journey, Nikolai sat with them.

Sorin sat down and said, 'You know I visited him. You know I ran errands. What you didn't know is that I ended up his friend'. He turned away from his father's look as he said this.

'I couldn't have done this and taken this climb

every time. I complained to the keeper early on. To my surprise he said he'd fix things. And he did. The next time I came, he greeted me at the bottom of the valley. He showed me another way.'

'There has always been more than one way, Sorin,' said Petre. 'All of them are dangerous.'

'This is a new way.'

'He built you a new path?' said Nikolai.

Sorin breathed out, and looked up into his father's face. 'Yes.'

'So, you truly were his friend. You trusted him.'

'Yes, father.'

'And now?' he said staring at his son.

'And now I don't know. I thought I knew him,' said Sorin his voice cracking. 'I don't know.'

There was silence in the group.

'*Domnule* Troester? Which path should we take?' said Petre.

'This is not a question for me,' said Nikolai.

'No. It's for me,' said Sorin, as his father nodded.

Sorin spoke directly to the small group of young men. 'You all know Mihai. If he travelled a path, would he notice it was new? If he noticed it was new, would he take it?'

Petre spoke again. 'Yes, we know him Sorin. I suspect we all know the answer and that it's the same as yours.'

Sorin stood. 'I'll show you the way.'

* * *

Anna pushed the toe of her boot back and forth along the damp new earth. She watched the rivulets of rainwater drizzle down the tracks that her boot left. 'It's new alright. The other path was packed so tight I was barely even making a dent with my boots.'

'I didn't think there was anything new here. Everything feels so ancient,' said Catalina, crouching on the ground. 'I don't understand why the trees and shrubs aren't broken or cut.'

'I think whoever made the path used a place that was wanting to be one anyway, yes?' said Mihai.

'Well, I guess that means it's the safest bet,' said Anna.

'We can't be sure, Anna 'said Catalina.

Mihai shook his head. 'If Sorin was involved it will be safe. I'm sure of that.'

'That isn't what I meant, Mihai,' said Catalina. 'It might not have anything to do with your brother. It might still be a trap. It might also have changed since he was last here.'

Anna said, 'No, I don't think so. Why would Igor have let us leave the castle so easily only to trap us out here?'

'It's interesting to see what you consider easy, adventurer.'

'Oh, come on. You know what I mean,' said Anna. 'He could have stopped us if he wanted to.'

'Maybe. But as you put it,' said Catalina standing up, 'he *let* us leave the castle. He might even have led us here. If you were going to let us die, wouldn't it be better to have it happen out here, where it might be thought of as an accident'.

'Do you really think that's what he's done? Seriously?'

'I don't know for certain, Anna. That's my point. I do feel he isn't a man to be trusted. Beyond that ...'. Catalina shrugged.

'It doesn't matter what we think. Not truly,' said Mihai.

'Mihai?' said Catalina.

'We have to choose. Either way, it might be bad. Either way, it's not a path I know. We have to decide our own fate. Yes?'

Anna and Catalina nodded.

'Okay. Let's take the rabbit hole as a sort of good luck thing. Yeah, a good omen.'

'Are rabbits good luck, Mihai?'

'Let us say that they are, yes?' He reached down and pushed his hand into the sharp, tangled bristles. His fingers scraped and scratched as they came back up, but he managed to hold on to a tuft of rabbit fur. 'For luck.'

In turns, Anna and Catalina did the same.

'For luck,' said Catalina.

'Hey! You don't believe in luck.'

'Perhaps today I do,' she said. 'Or I need to.'

'Yeah, that's fair. For luck.' Anna tucked the tuft into her back pocket. As she did so, her fingers felt the coin she had found earlier. She pulled it out and looked at it.

'The coin,' said Catalina. 'I'd forgotten about it.'

'It's such an ordinary thing. It's easy to do. I don't even know why I kept it.'

'Did you find it in the castle?' asked Mihai.

Anna nodded.

'Leave it here,' said Mihai.

'Why?'

'We've taken something,' he said rubbing his fingers around the tuft of fur. 'Is it so bad to leave something in return?'

'I like that.' She placed the coin by the entrance to the burrow. As she stood up she said, 'Okay. Who's going to lead this time?'

'No one,' said Catalina. 'We'll go together.'

* * *

The old woman sat at a table, trying to eat stew.

'Liliana, please. You must tell us what is happening,' said Toma, brushing away his long grey fringe.

She glanced up at the visitor. 'You tell me I must?'

Toma grimaced. 'Please, Liliana. The rest of us, we're only concerned.'

She sipped at the stew and winced. She put down her spoon. 'It is good stew, but it is hot. Too hot. I do not like food so hot.'

'I am sorry. It will cool fast, I'm sure,' he said.

'Do you feed your mother food this hot?'

'No, of course not. I said I'm sorry, Liliana. Leave it and it will cool soon enough.'

'It is thick. It will not. You cannot make me eat it while it is like this,' she said. She glared at him. 'You also cannot make me talk of them.'

'Liliana, they are our sons also.'

She stared into the heat of the stew, steam curling up into the cold air. 'You were not meant to find out. Not yet. How did you find out?'

'Does it matter how?' he said

Liliana didn't speak, but picked up the spoon instead. She began stirring the stew, releasing great curling ribbons of steam.

'Liliana, please.'

A hot cloud of steam rushed from the bowl as she scooped the stew and turned over a large heap. 'It's still too hot.' She glared at Toma. 'This is not a gift, this is a nuisance.'

'I think it's you who's being a nuisance. Are you trying to hide something?'

'I am only an old woman. The small things trouble me. 'She scooped up another large heap and food spilled onto the table. 'Now there's a mess.' She began to stand up.

'No, no. Let me.' Toma walked to the sink to get a cloth. As he turned, Liliana smiled to herself. When he turned back she was levelling a sullen stare at the mess on the table.

'I am a useless old woman.' Her eyes brimmed

with tears.

'Oh, Liliana, no. These things happen to all of us as we get older. Do not feel bad. My mother's the same.' He cleaned up the mess and turned away again. As he walked he continued to natter in an uninterrupted stream of words.' We should do more than merely respect our elders. We too often expect too much of them.' He rinsed the cloth and continued chatting as if she were no longer in the room.

Back at the table, Liliana watched him and allowed herself a small sneer.

'"Find out what she knows", they said. It's not right. She's nothing more than a harmless old woman. What do they know of trust? Of respect? Nothing. Less than nothing.' He turned back to face her.

Liliana smiled at him, her eyes dark with sadness.

'It's alright, Liliana,' he said as he came and sat back down again. He reached out and patted her on the wrist. 'Whatever has happened can wait. I will be here for you. I promise.'

She smiled and gripped his hand. 'You are a good man and I am old. Too old. You should not trust me.'

He smiled and shook his head. 'It will be alright. Everything will be alright.'

The look in her eyes hardened. She whispered to herself, 'A fool's fool. Nothing will ever be alright again'.

Toma spoke again, 'Everything will be alright'.

Liliana let her face soften again and said, 'Thank goodness for you, Toma. What would I do without you?'

Toma smiled and nodded. He said, mostly to himself, 'The rest of them can wait'.

* * *

Anna stood at the top of an enormous slab of grey slate. The path ahead twisted and snaked before disappearing into a rocky and mountainous terrain. She couldn't even see a way down. She waited for Mihai to move past her.

'Here, you see?' he said pointing.

Anna peered past him. A thin line of flat ground thread its way between two towering and cavernous rocks. She was grateful for her slender build. The gap was laughably narrow. 'You've got to be kidding. You'll never fit through there.'

'I will, absolutely, fit through there.' He smiled. 'I might need to hold my breath for a while, of course.'

They both looked at Catalina who, in turn, looked down at her own chest. 'No one say anything.'

Mihai grinned. He opened his mouth to speak, but was cut short as Catalina held up a single finger. 'No one.'

'Sure you're that brave, Mihai?' said Anna.

Mihai shook his head, and smiling, turned

away.

The women shook off their backpacks. They spent some time rearranging the contents so that the packs were slender, tall bricks, instead of their usual dishevelled lumpy form. Mihai buttoned his shirt at the cuffs and collar, making sure he covered as much skin as possible. The women did the same, or as close as they could manage with their jackets.

Anna said, 'I'll go first. If I can't fit, none of us can.'

Mihai nodded, but said, 'I'm absolutely sure we'll fit. It's clearly a path. One that Sorin would make. There's no rubble, no stones or other sharp or slippery things. We'll be okay'.

Anna squeezed her way into the gap, one arm first and then dragged her backpack along the ground behind her. It was awkward and a little tight, but she found she was able to move at a pretty fair pace.

'Are you okay, Anna?' said Catalina.

'I'm fine,' she said wincing. Wherever Anna wasn't covered with clothing, the stones grazed and scraped at her skin.

'Are you certain of that, adventurer?'

Anna didn't speak and instead concentrated on pushing through. The stones were damp and in some places it allowed her to slide along, but in other spots it made her stick like glue. She glanced up at the steady, grey sky and was grateful that the storm hadn't returned in force. She had begun to tune out the light drizzle. Its constancy had long since stopped being annoying and had sort of become a comforting and familiar friend. Anna slid between the rocks, but paused all of a sudden. Her stomach rolled and she felt an odd vibrating queasiness at the very base of her spine. She waited for it to pass.

'Anna?' called Catalina.

Anna jumped at the sound of Catalina's voice. 'I'm okay. I'm just concentrating,' she said. The last thing she needed was to worry them again. She needed them to trust her. She didn't trust herself, but she needed them to.

Mihai called down the gap, 'I'll follow you now'. He sidled in, one careful limb at a time.

Away from Anna and Mihai's view, Catalina began to pick out the some of her precious bandages from the first aid kit in her backpack. She picked out a wide, long bandage and began winding it tightly around her chest. She held her breath for as long as she could and when she finally exhaled it was from an elegant and much flattened breast. She packed away the rest of the bandages and walked towards the gap.

'You are following us, yes?' called Mihai.

Catalina looked at the forest behind her, a gentle and fleeting sadness falling across her face. She turned away and called out, 'Now or never'. She took a deep breath and slid in.

❈ ❈ ❈

Igor tied the last strap on a leathery package.

He picked up the bundle and slung it across his back. He looked back and forth around the empty room before settling on the curtain-covered corner.

'The castle has forced this upon me, Mistress. I wanted to let you go.'

He stood tall and unravelled his knotted posture. He reached up and took a flaming torch from the wall and pulled back the heavy, dank curtain to reveal a dark, shadowy entrance beyond.

Igor glanced back over at the bleak sky, framed in the stone-grey window and said, 'I am coming, Mistress. I am coming'.

Igor approached the entrance and the flames of his torch flared to reveal a sturdy wooden stairwell.

As Igor left the castle, the curtain fell shut behind him.

❋ ❋ ❋

A cool breeze swirled past Anna's face and she realised she must be near the end. She rushed ahead, scraping her cheeks and fingers, joyous at the thought of escape. She could see a sort of grey light, not sunshine, but light all the same. She pushed forward towards it. Her fingers curled around a corner and she felt the wind and drizzling rain rush by. 'I'm near the end! I can feel it.'

Mihai said, 'Keep going, Anna. Push through'.

Anna dragged herself out of the gap and

crashed to the ground, dragging her backpack behind her. She let out a squeal of delight.

'You're okay, yes?' said Mihai.

'Yep, yep. Very okay. Super glad to be out,' she said. 'Are you okay? It was rough for me, but it must be awful for you.'

'It's not my favourite day,' he said, as he continued pulling himself along, 'I've done this sort of thing many times before, but I would never say I enjoyed it, yes?' Mihai fell silent as he concentrated on the narrowing final few feet.

Anna scrambled to her feet and moved away from the exit to make sure he could easily get out. She could see his fingers as they curled around the corner of the grey slate boulder. He stopped moving and she could hear a change in his breathing. 'Nearly there, Mihai.'

'Hold me,' he said.

Anna walked closer and put her hand to his fingers. His fingers clawed, sought and, at last, interlocked with hers. 'It's okay, Mihai. You're nearly there. Come on. One last push.' She ran her fingers down his arm and down the gap so she could lock hold of his arm. 'Let me help. I'll pull when you're ready, okay?'

Mihai's voice cracked as he said, 'Yes'.

'Ready?' she said.

'Yes.'

Anna pulled on Mihai's arm and felt him push and scrape himself out. They stumbled together out onto the path ahead. 'Are you okay? Mihai? Really?'

'Yes. It was only that last moment. I allowed myself to think about it, yes?' He grinned at her. 'Not so good an idea, it seems.'

'Well, Cat can't be far behind. We can help pull her through too.' As she stood, she offered Mihai her hand. He took it with grace and gratitude, and stood next to her. 'Sure you're okay?'

'Yes, absolutely,' said Mihai. He wrapped one arm around her shoulders. 'Thank you.'

She smiled. 'It's the least I can do.'

'Hello?' came Catalina's voice.

'Cat?' Anna ran to the stony exit. 'Are you okay?'

'I wouldn't say okay. Not exactly.'

Mihai was by Anna's side. 'Catalina? What happened?'

The sound of a deep and extended sigh rolled out before Catalina spoke. 'I can't believe I'm going to say this.'

'Cat. Come on. Tell us what's going on,' said Anna.

Catalina didn't speak, but made more sounds of pushing and scraping, mixed with muttering and cursing.

'Catalina?' said Anna.

'Remember how I said I think we need to work together,' said Catalina. 'But what I really meant was you two need to work together?'

'Yes, we're trying, I promise you,' said Mihai.

'I'm very glad to hear that,' she said. 'Because I believe I might be stuck.'

CHAPTER FOURTEEN

'You are kidding, aren't you?' said Anna, staring into the rocky gap.

Silence was the only reply Anna received. She stood and lingered in the rain for a moment. After the hot, sweaty push through the rocky gap, Anna allowed the rain to fall wherever it wanted. She had no idea how she could help Catalina, but held a quiet desperation that Mihai would.

After a thoughtful delay, Mihai said, 'How exactly are you stuck?'

'I can't ...' Catalina began and stopped. 'How am I meant to answer that?! I'm stuck.'

'I am sorry, dear Catalina. I mean to say, is it all of you or just one part of you, you see?'

'I'm too tired to say,' she said. 'Everything is stuck. It's not that my foot is trapped under a rock.' She spoke the next words with slow and meticulous care. 'I. Am. Stuck.'

Mihai looked at Anna, but fell silent when he saw her face. He whispered, 'Are you alright, adventurer?'

'I just feel a little queasy.' Anna's stomach had started to tremble and roll again. Her back ached and itched. She shook her head and tried to put it out of her mind. She whispered back to Mihai, 'How on earth can we help her?'

He said to Catalina, 'We're moving away to a flat surface to look in Anna's backpack, okay, yes?'

'There isn't a lot of choice in that question,' said Catalina.

'Promise we won't be long, Cat,' said Anna.

Mihai and Anna moved a short distance away from the entrance. Anna said, 'That looks pretty flat'.

Instead of agreeing, Mihai said, 'You realise I have no idea what to do, yes?'

'Oh.'

'Couldn't we just throw a rope in?'

'It could damage her almost as much as help her, no?' he said. 'We'll try it if we have to, but my heart is not filled with great hope.'

'Damn.'

Mihai stared up the sky. 'I grew up here, yes. But these gaps, no. It's never a thing I sought out. Sorin was always doing it. If there was a gap or a hole, we couldn't stop him from burrowing inside. I've more than once pulled him out of some very small spaces.'

'Well, what did you do then?' she said.

'He was always near an entrance or an exit, with half a limb sticking out. I could grasp him, like you did for me and I could protect him. Catalina is a long way in.'

'Surely it's the same thing?' said Anna.

'No. He would often get stuck towards the end. But then, with me grasping and helping, if he relaxed his body …'.

Anna said, 'Well, that's it. Not the grasping, but the relaxing. We need to get her to focus. To talk her down, get her calm and relaxed'.

'Relaxed?' said Mihai. 'In there? You surprise me, adventurer.'

'Come on. You haven't noticed yet? She's very bloody-minded. More stubborn than anyone else I know.' She paused as Mihai grinned at her. 'Okay, okay,' she said. 'Maybe I know a lot of bloody-minded people. But that's the point. I know how to recognise it because I've got such a good supply myself.'

They clambered their way back up the path. Anna was grateful they were taking this path now on the way down. The climb up had been treacherous and awe-inspiring, but this path gave her terrors in new and unexpected ways.

As they approached the gap in the grey boulders, Catalina said, 'I could hear everything, you realise'.

Mihai and Anna exchanged glances. This time, Anna shrugged. 'Sorry, Cat'.

'Never mind. You were right. There isn't a lot you can do. I see that I'm pretty much on my own.'

✳ ✳ ✳

'Are you ready?' asked Anna, her hands wrapped around a hiking rope.

Ahead of her, Mihai stood braced against one of the towering rocks. He nodded at her as they waited for Catalina's reply.

For a long moment, Anna could hear nothing but the steady susurrus of rain falling gently on the ground. When Anna focus her hearing, she could just pick out Catalina's slow and level breathing. She'd spent the last ten minutes focusing on her breath. In the meantime, Anna and Mihai had dug out the rope and got themselves as well braced as they could, given the slippery, muddy and loose stone-covered ground.

'Yes,' said Catalina with a clear, calm voice. 'Throw the rope in.'

Anna tossed the rope along the gap and heard it fall to the ground. 'No good?'

'No. It's close though,' said Catalina.

Anna tried again and felt the rope whip by her own face on its way past. This time the sound was different. She hoped that it meant Catalina had caught it or that it had fallen within reaching distance.

Catalina didn't speak, but reached above her head and pulled the rope down towards her. She tried, without success, to wrap the rope around her waist, but eventually gave up. She took in a deep breath and let it out again. She wound the rope around her forearm, her wrist curling sinuously as it turned in the tight, stony space. She pulled on it.

Gentle at first, then with a sharp yank.

Anna felt the rope tighten. 'Got it, Cat?'

'Yes,' she said, in a measured tone.

'Okay, then, I guess it's on the count of three.' She nodded at Mihai, who took up the slight slack of the rope between them and pulled it firm. He braced again and nodded.

'One ... two ... Three,' said Anna. And they pulled. She slid a little but fell straight back into Mihai's body, who didn't budge. Anna grasped at the rope again and pulled. She tried to put the picture of Catalina's scraped and tortured body out of her mind. She focused on the rope, pulling and pulling at it again. Slowly, Mihai and Anna were moving back from the entrance.

Catalina's fingers appeared at the wall.

Without dropping the rope, Mihai and Anna ran back to the entrance and grabbed hold of Catalina's fingers and arm. They worked with caution and precision to pull Catalina free. They stopped for a moment to remove the rope from her wrist. Her skin was bruised and bleeding, but she was alive. She would live.

When Anna saw Catalina's face through the gap, it was all she could do not to cry out in joy. Mihai held her steady.

Catalina's eyes were closed and her breathing was shallow and controlled. Far from panicked, she looked tranquil and calm.

At last, she broke free of the gap, rushing and tumbling out in the final seconds.

All three stood together and held each other close.

Tears rolled down Anna's face and she couldn't tell whose they were. And she didn't care.

* * *

The trio sat on the ground.

They had no food left. But little containers surrounded them, each one collecting the rain.

Anna tended to all of Catalina's wounds. None of them were bad. She knew Catalina was allowing her to help to make her feel good. She didn't care. Because she did feel good.

One of the little containers was full. Mihai picked it up and offered it to Catalina. 'Drink.'

She drank and then smiled at him. 'I'm okay, you know. 'She looked at both of them and said, 'I believe I'm doing better than both of you'.

Mihai and Anna smiled.

'She's right,' said Anna. 'I'm so glad that's over.'

'You realise there might yet be more paths like that,' said Catalina.

'I was trying not to think about it,' said Anna. 'But, yeah, you're right. There might be. If there are, we'll get through it. 'Her stomach lurched and her face blanched. It was as if the ground beneath her was trembling.

'What was that?' asked Catalina.

'You felt it too?' said Anna. 'How could you feel

my stomach ache?'

Mihai's face had darkened. 'The ground, Anna. We felt the ground.'

'What's going on?' said Anna.

'Mihai please don't say what I think you're about to say.'

'It might be a single tremor. A foreshock. It might mean absolutely nothing,' he said.

'A tremor? You mean an earthquake?' said Anna, getting to her feet.

'Sit down, Anna. We have tremors here all the time, yes?'

'Still ...' she said, still standing up.

'We'll leave, Anna, but rushing now, exhausted as we are, won't help. We need to be at our best, if it's going to happen. If it's not, then there's absolutely no rush.'

Anna sat down. She wasn't happy. She wanted to go. She wanted to be at home. If she was in the castle, she would be safe. She wanted to be in a hotel. She wanted to be dry. She wanted everything, all at once. She was angry and realised she was going to cry. That only made her all the more angry. She refused to cry. She buried her head in her hands and curled up her knees.

Catalina patted her on the back. 'It'll be okay ...' Catalina shook her head. 'Actually, I don't know that. But whatever it will be, we'll go through it together.'

Anna looked up at her, and through red-rimmed eyes, smiled at Catalina. 'You're no good at trauma. If you're going to be a victim, you need to be a lot more useless than that.'

Catalina laughed and punched Anna on the arm.

As ever, it hurt. But in a good way.

* * *

Sorin stopped and said, 'Did you feel that?'

Nikolai nodded. 'Yes.'

'Do you think it's—' began Sorin.

Nikolai ran his fingers through his grey hair. 'I do not know, Sorin. It could be nothing.'

Sorin nodded in silent agreement and turned to speak to the group of younger men behind him.

Before he could speak, Petre said, 'We felt it too. None of us are willing to turn back now'.

Sorin looked at them all. 'You realise what it could mean?' he said, shaking his head. 'I'm sorry.'

Petre walked over to stand by his side. He grasped Sorin by the shoulder. 'It's okay, Sorin. I know you only meant to help the keeper. You only wanted to make him less lonely. Your heart's always been in the right place. We're your friends. We're here for you. The whole of the way.'

Nikolai said, 'You have good friends, Sorin. Only a good man is surrounded by such good friends'.

Sorin stepped in front of his father and looked back at all of them. 'Okay. So, let's go.'

One by one, they all followed. They moved

at speed and without pause. They ran full pelt wherever the ground was flat and yet still at a strong pace even when climbing up the side of the mountain, clambering up and through gaps and towering stones.

The ground beneath their feet was steady, but they ran as if it could change at any time.

❉ ❉ ❉

Igor stopped.

He dropped to his knees and pressed his hands and ear to the ground. Lying with his face on the damp, rocky ground, Igor smiled.

After a while, he sat up.

'You see, Mistress. She knows. The castle. The country. She knows and will not let you go.'

He stood up in one terrifyingly fluid movement.

'You belong with us.' He looked at the earth below. He smiled again.

'She is calling you, Mistress. And she will bring you home.'

❉ ❉ ❉

'Should we stop somewhere and try to take shelter?' said Catalina.

Mihai shook his head. 'Look around you.'

The mountain had made itself fully known.

They were in another forest; a forest that appeared to be in mid-landslide. The path no longer meandered, but jutted and turned sharply as it dodged monstrous slabs of grey-toned rocky boulders and monolithic trees. The trees loomed so high that their canopy became a patchy, secondary sky. Occasional glimpses of wan, dull light sneaked through whenever the boulders overcame the trees, but overall it was dark, dank and green.

Anna was no longer certain whether they were travelling by day or by dusk. She recalled the night before, and it seemed so very long ago. She knew how dark the night had been, but wondered whether daylight still existed or if it was only this perpetual string of dark nights and dull in-betweens.

Anna leaned against a tree and looked up. The slab of grey-brown bark towered above her.

Mihai said, 'There are no safe places. There are no verdant fields up here in our valley, our mountain. If what we felt is going to be more than that little tremor, we would not stand a chance. Even the castle has been ruined by landslides before.'

'The castle has been rebuilt?' asked Catalina.

'Time and again, yes. Always there is something left behind. Sometimes much remains, sometimes very little. But it has always been rebuilt of itself and back into itself.'

'You use the same bricks to rebuild the castle? Wouldn't they be destroyed too?' said Anna.

'Not completely. My ancestors have done this

many times and with the same bricks. They are no ordinary stones. They are carved from the side of the mountain. Sometimes new bricks have been hewn, but much of the castle goes back into the castle. All of the small rubble stays as it is and eventually returns to the mountainside from where it came.'

Anna had closed her eyes as Mihai spoke. From her sleepy spot against the tree she said, 'It feels like we're never going to make it. Have we gone any distance at all? How can we even be sure we're heading in the right direction?' Her words came out in one hurried, muddled string.

Catalina yawned. 'We're still heading down. Down is the right direction.'

'If we don't leave soon, we may end up moving down faster than we would like,' said Mihai.

'I wish there was a way to know for sure,' said Catalina.

'We felt a small tremor. That's all we can know for sure. It could be a sign of more. It might be that and that alone. 'Mihai sighed.

Anna suddenly said, 'Do you have a mobile phone, Mihai?'

He shook his head and said, 'Up here? What would be the point? There's no signal. In the village, yes'. He looked at Anna with a mock-serious expression and pushed a pretend pair of glasses up his nose. 'We're not savages you know.'

She smiled and bowed an apology. 'I guess I was half-hoping.'

'That I had a working phone with me and was

not using it? To call for help?'

'Sorry. I don't even know why I asked.'

'It's absolutely fine, adventurer. It's only hope that you were expressing.' He stopped to look up at the slivers of grey sky visible through the treetops. 'A bleak hope, but hope all the same.'

'No food, no rest, no hope,' said Catalina. 'All I want to do is rest and we have to keep pushing. I thought that once we got out of the castle we'd be okay. That as long as we stopped and took little breaks we might be safe, and could meander our way down.' She shook her head at herself. 'I even thought it might be quite nice.' As Catalina spoke she stopped to look at a dense little crop of delicate pink flowers. She wearily walked over to them. 'These are so pretty.' She looked at Mihai and half-jokingly said, 'I don't suppose these are edible.'

'I can't be sure. They're all over the forest and they're very lovely, but I've never heard of anyone eating them. Although, I've also never heard of anyone dying from eating them, no?'

Catalina picked one anyway. She handed it to Anna, and they shared a weary smile.

Anna poked the flower through a hole in her jacket. Everything had been so bleak and dark and grey, it felt good to hold something with colour. She picked one herself and returned the favour to Catalina, who smiled and wound and plaited the delicate stem into a thick lock of hair.

'It's quite lovely, but I still wish we had something to eat.'

Watching both of them from the corner of his eye, Mihai yawned before turning away. He crouched down and curled up tight, stretching his back. As he stood again he paused to look at the ground. In the rich, dense earth around the base of a tree, a patch of brown, spongy forms gathered. He picked up a handful of them and grinned. 'Your wish, my lady, has been granted.' He walked to Catalina and, smiling, handed her a small cluster of mushrooms.

'Food!' said Anna, jogging over.

Catalina held back. 'Are they food?' She looked at Mihai and said, 'Are you sure?'

His ridiculous smile became even wider than usual. 'Not merely edible. They are a delicious sort of edible, oh, yes.' Before anyone could protest, Mihai picked one up and popped it his mouth. His face lit up as he savoured the taste. His eyes closed, he said, 'It's okay. If you don't wish to try, I will happily take your share'. He grinned again as he felt the whack on the side of his arm that Catalina delivered.

'I thought it was ladies first around here,' said Anna.

Mihai laughed. 'You find me a lady and I shall absolutely let her go first.' He was quicker this time and ducked both Anna and Catalina's blows.

❊ ❊ ❊

Lilliana sat in a chair by the fireplace and snored.

Toma stood at the front door and stage whispered to a new visitor. The man's wiry body rested against the doorframe, almost melting into it. 'Nothing yet, as I have already told you.'

'But Toma, you were sent here ages ago. What have you been doing?' he said, as he ran his hand through thick salt-and-pepper hair.

'We've been chatting,' said Toma. 'What would you have me do, Marian? She is a harmless old woman.'

Marian raised his eyebrows. 'Harmless old woman?' He stuck his head around the corner to see who was in the room behind the door. 'That is Liliana Troester you have in there?' he said, with a joking smile.

'Yes,' said Toma, not budging from the doorway.

Marian raised his husky, dry voice. 'That's quite a snore you have, dear Lili.' As he spoke, the earth shuddered and both Marian and Toma stumbled. Toma caught the older man by the elbow and held on. They both stood under the doorframe until the ground settled and they had steadied themselves.

The snoring came to an abrupt halt. The old woman said, 'Come in, *Domnule* Popescu.'

Toma turned to look at Liliana. 'Are you sure you want me to let him in?'

The old woman sighed. 'I am sure that I no longer have a choice.'

'How long did you think you could hold us off?' said Marian.

Her expression did not change. 'Not long,

Domnule Popescu. But long enough. You will not hunt down my grandson.'

'You can't be sure of that, *Doamna* Troester. This might be when I see fit to lead the pack.'

'You felt the same thing that I did. Your intent is no longer my worry.'

Toma looked back and forth between them. 'What's going on?'

'Toma, you felt the tremor too,' said Marian sighing. 'Would you go up into the mountains now?'

'No, of course not,' said Toma. 'How little do you think of me? No one would go up there now. Not with forewarning of a possible—' He stopped mid-sentence and turned to *Doamna* Troester. 'Is that where they are?! In the mountains? Right now?' He looked between Liliana and Marian. 'My son?'

The old woman looked into Toma's eyes and said, 'It was their choice. He is their friend and they chose to go'.

Toma raised his voice. 'Chose to go and rescue your family and these strange women. My son! It was bad, Liliana, but now? Don't you see what these women have done?!'

Marian put out a hand and said, 'Stop, Toma. It's too late. They're already there or on their way back. We can only wait. *Doamna* Troester was only trying to protect her family. Her grandson.'

'Try all you like, Lili. It will be the worse for him, if he returns. You know what will happen if he returns,' said Toma.

The old woman was on her feet and inches

away from Toma's face. 'No! Again you speak to me of things that "will" be. Just because they once were, doesn't mean they will always be so.' She stepped back and drew in a deep, ragged breath. 'You are wrong. Nothing is decided. Only fate!'

The earth lurched again. A brief jerk that unsettled no one, but caused the old woman to pause and slow down.

'This is no longer in our hands. The portents were bad. It was as I spoke,' she said. 'They exist now only in the hands of fate.' The old woman fell silent and moved to stand in the frame of the door.

'Wait, Lili,' said Marian.

She looked back.

'We'll stand with you,' said Toma. 'You aren't alone. This burden belongs to all of us.' Toma and Marian came to stand with her at the door. Aside from the steady background hush of rain, everything was silent and the earth was still.

* * *

The trio trudged through the woods, walking at a steady, yet exhausted, pace.

Anna caught sight of a wolf running through the trees. Unlike the wolf she had seen closer to the castle, this one didn't approach her. She'd caught glimpses of other wolves as she walked through the forest, but only fleeting. Catalina and Mihai hadn't noticed any of them yet and she was grateful for it. She didn't want to hide it from them, but she also didn't want to have the topic come up again. She didn't want to return to the awkwardness of that moment. Anna no longer felt the same pull towards the castle. The feeling had been diminishing all morning and was now becoming more of a distant thought. She could remember *how* it felt, but as more of an abstract idea, not something burning in her heart.

Catalina and Mihai walked together nearby, in a relaxed and comfortable silence. It was calming for her even to be in their presence. Anna didn't know what she had done to deserve them as friends, but she would try to do whatever she could to keep it that way. They had returned some sort of sanity to her and safely seen her through an adventure that was beyond even her own all-too-vivid imagination. She knew she wouldn't be able to share what happened with anyone else. Not the whole truth of it. But she didn't care. Whatever happened to them now, she had to protect them. Eldritch feelings could go to hell. She smiled to herself. Strange and beautiful though it was, she realised it had been a self-centred and selfish feeling. Anna watched Mihai and Catalina for a moment longer and allowed herself to enjoy the feeling of being with them. Their steps looked as heavy as hers felt. But they kept going. And they kept her going. She sighed to herself.

'Are you okay, adventurer?' said Mihai. 'You seem thoughtful.'

Anna smiled. 'I was thinking how good you

two are.'

Mihai tipped his head sideways.

'Good to me, I mean,' she said. 'Come on. Just imagine what might've happened to me if I hadn't had both of you.'

Catalina said, 'Imagine what might've happened to all of us, if we didn't have each other, Anna'.

Mihai nodded. 'Yes. But I am glad to see you clear-headed, all the same, adventurer.'

'I just want to go home,' she said.

Mihai said, 'And home is not the castle?'

'Home is *home*. Home is where we've come from.' Anna pointed. 'Home is not up there.' And she was relieved to know that, for once, she meant it. She didn't know what would happen if she returned, and she didn't ever want to find out. She wanted to take Catalina and Mihai and leave. Take them all home. She looked up at the all-encompassing, rambling castle. It had been obscured while they were in the forest, but it was becoming visible once again. The castle dominated the sky, but not in the same way as it had on the climb up. It was heady and filled her vision. It threatened. It was not the entire world, but it was still a terrifying corner of it. She shook her head. Memories of the feeling still remained, but she knew what she had to do. And she began to hope she could make it.

'Come on you two,' she said. 'We have to keep moving if we're ever going to get home.'

Mihai looked behind her to Catalina, whose

face was a studied vision of relief.

* * *

The wolves ran at speed through the furthest reaches of the forest.

They stopped at a point and gathered together, with the pups cowering in the middle of the pack. They stood still, heads low and ears flattened. Their sound started as a nervous mixture of growls and barks, building in intensity, and changing to a strange and uncomfortable bark-howl. The voices of all of the different wolves joined in, one after the other. The barking and howling raised in volume and drifted across the land. Beyond the initial pack, the howling was picked up and continued by other distant wolves.

As slowly as it had started, the howling rapidly ended. A large wolf broke away first, running like a blur through the trees.

The rest of the pack broke away too, leaving only the land behind.

* * *

Igor stopped.

The sounds of distant barks and howls crawled towards him and finally reached him. Embraced him. He stood still and listened, allowing the noise to flood his senses and wash his last doubts away.

Eventually the sounds of the howl passed him by. Igor moved on again, his pace slower, his gait steadier.

As he continued on, he smiled.

As he walked on, he nodded, swayed and hummed.

* * *

The eerie, distant barks and howls reached into the depths of the forest.

The trio had been walking at a steady pace through the thinning forest, but as the sound of the howls hit them they stopped.

'Oh, my,' said Catalina.

'Will they attack?' asked Anna.

'I don't think so, no. I think it means they're afraid. That perhaps the tremors are going to get bigger, yes? If the animals are unhappy, we should be that way also.'

Catalina nodded.

'I'll go ahead and try and pick the best path,' said Mihai. 'I'll find Sorin's way quicker.'

Neither Catalina nor Anna protested. As he moved off, they followed without speaking.

Mihai half-ran, half-walked ahead, dashing around trees and clambering over boulders. The forest had become less dense; the mossy floor thinned out giving way to greater and greater stretches of slate. The descent had also become steeper again.

'Is it safer under the trees or out on the rocks?' called out Catalina.

Not stopping, Mihai said, 'Out in the open, as much as we can. We have to keep moving, yes? I promise you if we get somewhere safe, I will stop'. He rushed on.

Anna looked up as she ran, jagged and stumbling. The trees seemed to be vibrating, but she thought it must be her imagination. 'I think I prefer the rocks to the trees.'

Catalina looked up at the sound of Anna's words.

The sky blurred.

Far from the earth shaking them to the ground, it buzzed and caused a steady vibration all around. The rocks rumbled and the trees whirred overhead. The landscape distorted, like an ill-tuned station. All the details were lost and the grey sky merged with the even greyer landscape.

Catalina stumbled and fell, crying out.

Mihai looked back over his shoulder and ran towards her. In almost the same moment, Anna raced forward.

As he rushed over, the vibrating stopped. 'Are you hurt? Catalina? Please tell me you aren't hurt.'

Catalina looked up at him with a wry smile. 'I'm not hurt …?'

Mihai looked at her ankle. 'I did not ask you to lie to me, yes?'

Anna picked up Catalina's backpack and felt

around for a bandage. She said, 'Are we out?'

'I think I've got one,' said Catalina, as she pulled a bandage out from inside her shirt.

'And that was there because ...'

'I needed it for squeezing through the gap,' said Catalina.

Anna held up the bandage and inspected it. 'I see ...'

'I'm injured and exhausted,' said Catalina. 'Neither of you will say a single word or even laugh.'

Mihai and Anna exchanged glances and managed not to speak. Anna raised her eyes mischievously at Mihai. In turn, they both grinned at Catalina.

Catalina rolled her eyes and ignored them. She tried to stand, but only managed to wince.

'I think you need that bandage, yes?' said Mihai.

Catalina glared at him.

'For your ankle, no? Your ankle,' said Mihai.

'It's not too bad, really,' said Catalina.

'Okay, if you say so. But it won't do any harm to have it strapped up.' Anna inspected the ankle as she wound the cloth around it. 'You're right though, it doesn't look too nasty. Do you want to try again?'

Anna and Mihai each held out a hand and together helped Catalina to her feet. Catalina stood and with great care tested the strength in her ankle. 'It feels pretty good,' she said inspecting her foot. 'Thank you, both. I'm quite okay.'

'At least the tremors stopped,' said Anna.

'Yes,' said Mihai. 'But that doesn't mean we're safe.'

Anna looked at him. 'Mihai?'

'Is it about to get worse?' said Catalina.

'I don't know,' he said, 'The wolves, the small tremors. 'He shook his head. 'What can I say. If we're to be safe – if there is more to come – we have to get to open land, yes?'

Anna and Catalina exchanged a brief glance. Anna knew what they had to do, but she was exhausted. They all were. It didn't matter. They had to go on. And fast.

Mihai said to Catalina, 'Can you run?'

'Probably faster than you.'

Without another word, they ran. Mihai sprinted away, then Anna and Catalina. Shortly after they'd gone, the forest was empty of all animal life.

* * *

Anna stumbled out from between two trees.

The landscape had changed again.

She stood at the top of a long, winding stony crevice. A short way down, the mountain split the rocky pathway in two.

Further down the slope, Mihai yelled up to her. 'I can see a better way, I'll run ahead and come back.'

Anna tried to yell back, but her voice was hoarse and she wasn't sure he could hear her. Without hesitating, Mihai chose a steep, wide-open crevice. It was mesmerising to watch him find a safe way through all the chaos. She decided to take the slender, less steep route just to see whatever she could. She stepped up onto a small plateau and her legs strained to make the small step. She clambered onto the grey surface and stopped to catch her breath.

Looking back over her shoulder, Anna caught sight of Catalina as she came out from between the trees. She waved at her and watched her stumble forward, clearly exhausted. Catalina's shoulders were slumped, but kept half-running, half-stumbling, as bloody-minded as ever. One foot was far steadier than the other, but she persisted.

Looking down, Anna could see Mihai making his way deep into a long contour of the mountainside. She wasn't sure when he was going to turn back, but she kept on and tried to find the next safe place for her feet. The grey sliding landscape became more treacherous, more perilous with each step. She absently put her hand against a nearby outcropping of rock and felt it slice into her palm. Anna stared at the blood seeping out. She suddenly wanted to stop. She resisted, and stepped again anyway.

The land shook under Anna's feet. Like before, it started as a small vibration; small enough that she thought it was her own body trembling. This time though, the sensation built until she knew it wasn't coming from her own fatigued legs, but from the earth itself. The intensity built rapidly until her whole body shook and her vision blurred. The ground heaved.

Catalina called out from behind her. 'Anna, get down!'

Exhausted to the point of confusion, Anna responded to Catalina's words and fell to her feet, grateful to be forced to stop walking. She looked back at her friend, adrift on a giant sea of slate just like her. Without having taken a step, Mihai had almost disappeared from view. Anna cried out to him, but there was nothing she could do.

The earth moved like liquid and Mihai was being washed away.

The mountain had become an ocean.

The world dissolved around them.

❋ ❋ ❋

Anna watched as Mihai was thrown around by the giant boulders and slipping land. Tears streamed down her face.

It took a matter of seconds for Mihai to lose his footing.

The earthquake tore apart the mountain, fracturing it like a shattered vase. The crevice that had held Mihai tumbled down like molten lava. Plumes of dust thundered into the gloomy sky as the chaos below her dissolved a great slice of mountain. Between the shuddering rubble and chaos, she soon lost sight of Mihai, though she continued to search desperately for him.

Behind her, Catalina cried out.

Anna turned to see Catalina falling, as an edge of slate crashed away from beneath her. Anna stood and ran to her, but it was all happening too quickly. Catalina's head bounced as it hit the ground. Catalina's body started to slip over the edge into the rolling nightmare below and Anna launched herself across the remaining distance to make a desperate grab for her. Anna caught hold of Catalina's clothes and, lying flat against the grey slate, dragged at handfuls of clothing and then body parts. Slowly and painfully, Anna dragged and scraped Catalina's deadweight form back up over the edge. She clung to her, her fingers bloodied and white, not letting go until the shaking of the earth subsided.

Noise rushed back in. She hadn't noticed it was gone. Still part-deaf, Anna could no longer tell one ache from another. Her entire body was awash with pain. She ignored it all and dragged her friend's body upright. Touching her lips to her face, she screamed at her. 'Wake up, Cat! Please, please, please wake up. Wake up!'

Catalina lay limp in her arms. Anna tried to pick her up, to carry her, but she was too heavy. Anna gently lay Catalina's body back down on the quiet, still ground.

* * *

Cracks opened up in the ground and the land rushed down.

The men stood in the middle of a large oasis of steady ground. A great carving of the mountain rushed by in a raging torrent. Their safety was far from certain, but moving guaranteed nothing but danger.

Petre pointed and yelled, 'Mihai!'

Everyone turned and looked up. Above them, Mihai struggled to stay upright in the river of tumbling rubble. Nikolai Troester watched as his eldest son stumbled and rolled, falling down the mountain amidst a terrifying snarl of boulders and rubble. The shuddering and grinding of the earth stopped. It had lasted only minutes, but the devastation was immense. An entire section of the mountain had washed away. The land wasn't anywhere near steady, but the earthquake was done.

Nikolai scrambled up the remnants of the mountainside, Sorin straight behind him.

None of the younger men tried to stop them or go with them. They stood, stony-faced, and waited for their return.

※ ※ ※

Anna stood and looked wildly around her, desperate for help.

In the hazy distance, Anna thought she saw a couple of men. She waved to them and cried out, 'Please! Up here! We need help!'

A tall, older man stood and peered upwards. Anna waved her arms again, but he seemed to turn his back on her. Anna watched in confusion as he and the younger man picked up something from between the tortured rocks. It was, she realised, a body. A man's body.

'Mihai,' she cried softly, holding her hands to her mouth. Anna fell to her knees. She looked below her. The way down was now a near vertical drop. Even if the men had seen her and wanted to help, there was no way up.

There was also no way down.

Anna let the tears fall as she watched the pair carry Mihai down and around a curve in the mountainside. Within moments, they had all but disappeared from view. She knew she was on her own. They might come back, but she couldn't rely on them. And having seen Mihai's body, even from here, she honestly couldn't see any reason for them to return. She wanted to lie down and sob. Her chest ached with the pain of Mihai's suffering. But ignoring it, she turned back to Catalina instead.

Catalina's strong, tall body still lay nearby. She was bruised, battered and filthy. Anna moved back to her and lay down beside her. She gently lowered her head onto Catalina's shoulder and folded her arms tight around her shoulders. 'I'll get you out of here, Cat,' she said. 'I don't know how, but I promise. Somehow, I'll get you help.'

Anna watched the last of the dust dissipate into the sky and her eyes filled with tears once more.

CHAPTER FIFTEEN

Anna sat up. Shocked, she realised she had been about to drift off to sleep. Anna shook her head, trying to clear it. She realised she might have been asleep. Something had woken her up. When she thought about it she realised it wasn't a noise, but the absence of something. She looked around her.

Catalina's breathing had stopped.

Anna jumped to her feet and rolled her friend's body gently onto the side. She slid Catalina's hand underneath her head and pulled one of her knees up. 'I think that's right,' she muttered to herself. Anna sat back and ran her fingers through her short, messy hair again and again. She watched Catalina's abdomen. She couldn't hear anything, but thought she could see her stomach gently moving up and down.

'Ten seconds, that's all you get. Otherwise, I'm coming in.' She tried to joke with herself, but it didn't work. She'd give all of herself to see her friend live.

After the longest moment, Anna could hear Catalina start to breathe again. Shallow, steady, but there.

Anna looked over her friend's bruise-covered body. Catalina bled from countless shallow cuts. Anna inspected her own body and unravelled the cleanest bandage she could find. She tore it into smaller strips and set about patching up what she could. Anna sat back to survey her handiwork. It was still a mess, but some of the bleeding had stopped.

'Hell. Now what?' she said. 'I mean come on! Look at you. How the heck am I going to move you?' she said. 'I don't even know if it's safe to move you.'

Anna stood and surveyed the surrounding landscape. There was definitely no way down – not from here – but there was a way back up. She stood, her legs burning and shaking, and went to look for the best path out. A thin line of rubble and slate led back into the forest. Anna tentatively put a foot on the first boulder and tested it. It didn't move and was firm. She looked at it for moment, her brow creasing.

'Great,' she said, looking back at Catalina's unmoving form. Even curled up and unconscious, Catalina's body was an intimidating sight. 'Why couldn't you have been the tiny one?'

❊ ❊ ❊

'Mistress?'

Anna jumped and turned around, looking behind her. Igor stood at the edge of the forest.

'Igor!' said Anna, standing up.

'You left us, Mistress.'

Anna was speechless. Igor spoke as if she were a naughty, misbehaving child. She stared at him. He seemed taller than before, strong and domineering. He also looked like someone more than able to move Catalina. Maybe not to safety, but at least to somewhere less unsafe than where she currently lay. Maybe not on his own, but between them they could do it. She needed him.

With no small amount of foreboding and reluctance, Anna said, 'I'm sorry, Igor. We should have at least let you know'.

Igor stared at her.

Anna felt compelled to talk into the gap that Igor's silence provided. 'Look, I know you must be angry with us, but I need your help Igor. Catalina's hurt. I've got to get her down to the village. I need to find her a doctor.'

'There is no way back, Mistress. Not now.'

Anna looked at the ravaged mountain behind her. 'I know there's no way down from here, but surely there's another way.'

Igor was silent again.

'Igor, please. I know you know this place. Surely there's a way?'

'Yes, Mistress. I know this land. There is no way back now. If you wish me to help, you must choose to return.'

Anna looked up at the forest and beyond. 'To the castle?'

'Yes, Mistress. This is your choice.'

Anna looked at her friend's body. 'It's not much of a choice, Igor.'

Igor sighed. He turned, as if to leave.

'Okay, okay. Wait, Igor. Please.' She sighed. 'We'll come back. We'll do it your way. Whatever it takes. Please, just help Catalina.'

Igor nodded. 'Yes, Mistress.' He walked over to Catalina and, gently, carefully, picked her up body. He awkwardly arranged her body over his good shoulder.

Anna was amazed. 'Igor, surely you can't carry her all the way back like that? And she's not breathing well. Hang on, don't you have a horse?'

Igor shook his head. 'Not this way, Mistress. Not at this time. No. We are on our own. Do not fear, I will not carry her this way. You will help. There is more than one way to make our way back home. This is just to get her to the forest.'

Anna winced. She knew Igor meant the castle when he said home. She didn't say anything. She would listen to him. She'd help him. Nod politely if that's what it took. She would do whatever he demanded. Catalina needed her and that was all she had to know.

Without speaking, Igor turned and, with care, carried Catalina back into the forest.

* * *

The rain fell, light and gentle, above the trees. More a

mist than a downpour. Now and then, large droplets broke through.

Igor dragged a makeshift sled behind him.

Catalina lay stretched on a blanket tied between two long, sturdy branches. Behind her, Anna stumbled along, carrying their backpacks and the other supplies that Igor had brought with him. She had no idea how long they'd been travelling. Her head was a fog and she preferred it that way. Anna's foot caught on a sharp, mossy stone. She stumbled and paused to catch her breath.

'I can't believe how many jumped-up rocks there are in this forest,' she said, mostly to herself. Her voice surprised her. Thin and reedy, she didn't quite recognise it as her own.

Igor stopped walking and turned to look where she had tripped. 'Not rocks, Mistress. Castle.'

Anna looked at the shard jutting up from the wet, green ground. 'This used to be part of the castle?'

'Yes, Mistress. The castle has fallen many times. The castle and the mountain are entwined, for eternity. They are bound.'

Anna put out her hand to touch the stone and pulled back, stopping herself just in time. 'Is it much further?'

'No, Mistress.' Beginning his relentless trek again, he said, 'You must trust me. I know the best way. I can help the tall one. We must not stop again'.

Anna nodded. She was numb. She couldn't let any thoughts in. Nothing mattered more than getting Catalina help. She couldn't bear to think about what might have happened to Mihai, so she didn't. She refused to. He was with his own people now. He was either beyond help, or he had it already. The only job she had was walking. One foot. Then the next.

Step. And step again.

* * *

Liliana stood up straight as she saw the group of men approach.

They carried a long makeshift litter between them. Liliana held her breath as they drew closer.

Her son and youngest grandson led the group. They held their heads low. Nikolai looked up and met his mother's eyes. He didn't speak. Liliana turned to the old men standing by her and said, 'The doctor. Fetch him. Now'.

'Lili, it does not look good—' began Marian.

'You heard me. Now.' She stood and watched as the weary group closed the distance between.

The old men shrugged and left, glancing hopelessly at Mihai's battered form as they rushed by.

* * *

'Anna? Mihai? Mihai!'

Catalina's panicked voice broke through

Anna's dreary, muddy thoughts. 'Cat? Are you awake?' She hurried over.

Igor paused to allow Catalina to speak.

'Cat? Talk to me, please.' Anna reached out and rested a hand on her friend's ashen face. Catalina's eyes flicked open as Anna's fingertips caressed her face. 'Where am I?' Catalina pushed her shoulders back against the sled. 'Who are you?!'

Anna leaned forward and tried to reassure her. Her words tumbled out in a tangled, breathless string. 'You remember me, Cat, you know me, we grew up together, remember the first time we met, remember?'

'I don't know you,' Catalina said, turning her head away. 'Leave me alone,' she said, her voice fading, 'please leave me alone'.

Anna watched helplessly as Catalina slipped away and lost consciousness again. 'She doesn't even know me,' she whispered. 'How can she not know me?'

Igor reached out and, with a surprisingly firm hand, held Anna's shoulder. 'It is only for now, Mistress. She knows you. She will remember.'

Anna stood up, tears threatening. He voice cracked as she said, 'I have to get her help. I can't bear to see her like this'.

'Then we must continue on, Mistress. I can help our tall one. We must return to the castle.'

Anna nodded in resignation.

Relentless, she carried on.

* * *

A small number of men and women, both young and old, gathered outside the Troester household.

'They brought this on themselves,' said Toma shaking his head, his voice heavy with sadness.

'You're saying he deserves this?' said Petre sharply.

'No, not precisely, Petre—' said Toma.

Petre stood and spoke quickly, 'No, not precisely – not at all! I'm tired of this. All of this,' Petre gestured at the house and the looming valley. 'It's no excuse. Living under the castle doesn't mean we deserve to be treated this way.'

'What do you want, Petre? It is history. This is the way it's always been,' said Marian.

'Then things have to change,' said Petre. A number of the younger men and women also stood, nodding and muttering in agreement.

'Life here is how it is. We live under the myth. A centuries old oppression is our neighbour. It will never change,' said Toma. 'It is too dangerous for us to try. Mihai is evidence of that.'

'No,' said Petre.

'No?' said Marian.

'What do you mean "No"?' said Toma.

'What happened to Mihai is evidence of nothing more than an earthquake. Whether he lives or dies isn't fate. It's luck, good or bad. It's not a curse. It's nothing more than chance.'

'Surely you don't believe that,' said Toma, running his fingers unsteadily through his hair.

'I don't *need* to believe anything. It isn't a punishment,' said Petre shaking his head. 'It's just what happened.' He turned to the group of women and men behind him. 'None of us need to believe it.'

'Sorin believes,' said Marian.

'No. I don't.' Sorin stood, pale-faced and shaking in the doorway of his parent's house.

'How is he?' asked Petre.

Sorin shook his head. 'It's too early to say.' He looked at Petre directly. 'I heard some of what you said. Are you planning to go?'

'Yes,' said Petre looking down at his feet. He looked up, quickly adding, 'But not yet'.

'No. You're right,' Sorin said, looking at Petre's group, 'All of you. If you're going, go now.'

Toma, Marian and a couple of other elders looked on speechless.

'But Mihai …' said a young, fair-haired woman in the small crowd.

'I'll stay,' said Sorin. 'He's my brother. The earthquake is no punishment, but he was there because of me. I can't leave him. I won't.' He turned to the older men and women and said, 'But, you. You'll all hear me now. If he is able,' Sorin's voice croaked and he coughed before continuing, '*when* he is able, we will leave'.

'All of you?' said Marian, his voice little more than a whisper.

'Yes,' said Petre and Sorin together. Sorin

looked sombrely at Petre. They embraced, and Sorin stood rigid and unyielding. Petre stood back and studied Sorin's face. His deep-blue eyes were as dark as they had ever been. His face was pale and motionless.

In silence, Sorin turned away and went back inside, closing the door behind him.

* * *

A large gathering of the villagers stood in the heart of the town.

'You can't convince us to stay, 'said Petre. 'Surely we've made that clear.'

'How can you leave your friend like this?' said Marian, as he struggled to be heard above the voices of several other old men and women.

'It's not him we're leaving. It's this place. You can choose to live like this, under that old tale,' Petre said gesturing up to the top of the valley. 'We choose not to. Today.' Behind him, a dozen or more young men and women stood together. They were silent. But they were clearly with him. 'Mihai will live. Or maybe he won't. Our staying won't change that.'

'Our leaving at least means we change our own lives, 'said another young man.

'This town *is* your life,' said Toma, in a pleading voice.

'No. The so-called-curse, the story. None of that's ours. Not anymore. The village is your life. You chose this. And, in the end, you've chosen their fate.

Those women. Mihai.' Petre shook his head. 'We've had enough.'

'We can't abandon the keeper. You can't abandon us.'

'We can. We are. And ...' Petre turned to his friends, seeming to seek confirmation, 'we'll be letting the keeper know that we've gone. For all that he's tried to do, it's the one thing we can do for him.' At Petre's words, the entire group fell silent. They turned and walked to the outer edge of the village.

As they passed an ancient, crumbling church they stopped. A young, fair-haired woman went inside.

Moments later, the sounds of a bell tolling rolled out and up the valley.

* * *

Igor stopped. The wind roared. With it came the subdued and sonorous sound of a tolling bell.

'Igor?'

Igor stood a little taller and turned to look at Anna. He looked thoughtful.

Anna felt the hairs on the back of her neck rise. Her heart felt as though it was beating in time to the sounds of the bell.

Igor hadn't moved. He stood as still as a statue and, without blinking, studied Anna's face.

She said, 'Igor? Has something happened?'

Igor seemed to come to a decision. 'No, Mistress,' he said. 'Nothing has happened. Nothing of note.' He walked on.

The wind dropped away and the sounds of the bell vanished.

They moved on, ever closer to the castle.

* * *

'Mistress. We are here.'

In a fog of exhaustion, Anna looked up. Somehow, they were once again back at the castle. She didn't quite understand how she'd gotten here. It was a different route from all the others and she knew that she'd never be able to find the same path again.

Igor set Catalina's makeshift sled on the ground. 'Please, Mistress. You are tired. The castle waits for your return.'

Anna looked at Catalina's slumbering form. 'Cat. I can't leave her.'

In one swift movement, Igor picked up Catalina's unresisting body. 'We will follow you, Mistress.'

Anna stared at the grey, stony wall. After a moment staring, she realised there was a door made of the same grey slate as the castle and the mountainside. Without noticing she was speaking out loud, she said, 'I ... I can't'.

Igor stood in silence. Waiting. Eventually, he said, 'Mistress. This is your choice'.

Anna looked up at the towering monolith above her. She shook her head and half-turned away.

As she turned she saw Catalina; beaten, bloody and near lifeless in Igor's arms. She turned back and muttered, 'My choice'.

Anna pushed the door open. Her pulse throbbed in her ears and her blood rushed.

She stepped back inside the gloom.

* * *

As they walked along the corridor, Anna tried to keep herself away from the walls and the stones: the beating heart of the castle. Instead she focused on staying close to Igor.

Igor carried Catalina as he walked. She was starting to stir, but never actually woke.

'Can I help, Igor?' said Anna from behind.

Without turning, Igor said, 'You are too tired, Mistress. She is no burden. It is not far'.

Anna grimaced. He was right to say she was too tired, but she was annoyed all the same. Catalina was her responsibility. She winced as she thought it. She'd let them all down. She shouldn't be responsible for herself, let alone another person. She winced again, but this time from the ache in her legs. Her feet, her shoulders, her back, they all throbbed. She shook her head. She couldn't keep pushing on. She needed to rest. 'Okay, Igor,' she said quietly.

Anna moved a little closer to Igor. She would follow in his footsteps until it was done. Until both of them were okay. Then she'd get them both the hell out of here.

* * *

Igor stopped in front of a familiar wooden door. 'Mistress?'

Anna walked up behind him and said, 'What's the matter, Igor?'

Igor nodded towards the door.

'Here?' She shrugged. 'Okay.' She opened the door and walked through to a near forgotten sight of silken blues and tall, beautiful stained glass windows. Anna stopped in the doorway. 'No.'

Igor tilted his head. 'Mistress?'

'Uh-huh. No, not in this room, Igor. It wouldn't feel right.'

Igor pushed past Anna and said, 'She will rest here. We can keep her safe here'. Igor gestured up at the room with his chin as he spoke. 'It is a sanctuary, Mistress.'

Anna had not moved from the doorway. She hadn't ever understood what had made her so uncomfortable in this room. There was nothing ominous here; it was a feeling. And because it was only a feeling, it was something she couldn't explain, even to herself. She watched as Igor lay Catalina's body gently on the fur-strewn lounge in the middle of the room.

Igor begin arranging the different silks and fineries around Catalina. He placed her head on a small, overstuffed pillow. He stood and said, 'I must prepare'.

'You're going?' said Anna.

'Mistress. Your friend needs help. Rest is not enough. I will bring medicine. Herbs.'

Anna's brow furrowed. 'Herbs ...'

'Mistress?'

'Okay. But, herbs could mean anything. What sort of herbs, Igor?'

'They will heal. They will ease her pain. She is fitful now,' he said. 'The herbs will allow her to rest.'

Anna looked at Catalina. Her breathing was shallow and irregular. Her face twitched now and then, jumping and jolting.

'Right. Whatever you give her, you have to give me.'

Igor nodded and said, 'Yes, Mistress. You should both sleep'.

Realising exactly what it was that she had asked for, Anna added, 'Only a drop. For me. You can give Catalina what she needs, but I want to try it first'.

'As you wish, Mistress.' Without another word, Igor turned and left the room.

❋ ❋ ❋

When Igor returned, he held a small, greyish-green bottle with a carved wooden stopper. The stopper was carved into the shape of a tiny, papery flower.

'What's in the bottle, Igor? I thought you said herbs,' said Anna, rising to her feet.

'Mistress, yes. Herbs must be prepared. As with many foods.' He held the little bottle aloft and said, 'These are liquified, Mistress. But they are herbs.'

'Yeah. If you say so, Igor,' said Anna, after a brief pause. 'I guess I don't have much of a choice.'

'You do not need to do this, Mistress—' began Igor.

'No,' said Anna, 'I'm first. I'm definitely not giving Cat something that might be poisonous without trying it out myself first'.

Igor's face had fallen as Anna spoke. 'Mistress.' He nodded and sighed.

Anna screwed up her face and said, 'Igor, I'm sorry. Look. I just need to feel okay about it. It might be something new to us and it might cause a reaction even you weren't expecting'.

Igor looked away. 'Yes, Mistress.'

Surprising herself a little, Anna reached towards him and touched his shoulder. Igor flinched, but she said, 'I'm sorry, Igor. Really'.

Igor turned and looked ponderously into Anna's eyes. He held the small bottle out to her.

Anna held the small grey-green bottle up to the dull light falling from the coloured windows. The stopper had a small glass nub that extended into the top of the dark liquid contents. Before she could think too hard about what she was doing, she grabbed the stopper and allowed a small, ichorous drop to roll down and drip onto her tongue. Warm, bitter and nutty. She looked up and said, 'It's warm,

Igor'.

'It is a tea, Mistress. A brew.'

Anna smiled at herself, 'I'm drinking herbal tea?'

Igor nodded. 'It is very strong, Mistress.'

'Right, okay.' She handed the bottle back to Igor. She didn't feel anything. She had felt nothing but fatigue for so long that she wasn't sure she was capable of feeling anything else. She also wasn't sure how long she had to wait. Anna yawned and sat at the edge of the lounge, next to Catalina.

'Mistress?' said Igor, after a moment's pause.

Anna stretched and yawned again, saying, 'Go on, Igor. I guess it can't hurt'.

Igor nodded and sat across from Anna on the other side of the lounge. He raised Catalina's head and let the entire mixture drip slowly onto her tongue and away.

Anna tried to keep watch, but her eyelids were heavy and she found it hard to concentrate. She wasn't sure what she was even looking for. If he wanted to hurt them, it would be all too easy. It always had been. She just felt better for staying close.

Igor sat back and, with Anna, watched Catalina's face as the tension drained away. Her breathing became even and more steady. And, at last, a little stronger.

Catalina's face relaxed in her sleep, an image of contentment.

Anna watched her for a little while more

before looking around the elegant room again. As at peace as Catalina looked, nothing had changed for Anna. Everything about the room still made her feel trapped.

Igor sat down next to Anna. She hadn't even noticed him move. As he spoke his warm breath fell against Anna's cheek. 'Mistress, yes. I know this room is not for you. I know your needs. I will see to them.'

He stepped away and said, 'She must rest'. He held out his arm for Anna.

Anna ignored his offered gesture of support and stood, wobbling as she went. She started to move, but turned again and took one final glance at her friend's tall form, lying still, but at peace, among the beautiful architecture and scenes of Catalina's old country. With reluctance, she moved away.

Her head low and shoulders drooped, Anna left the room. Igor followed close behind.

* * *

Walking along a dark and gloomy hallway, Anna dragged her feet, stopping and resting now and then. Her head was heavy, her eyelids heavier still. The proximity of the stone soothed her. She wanted to reach out. To be absorbed by it, but she didn't. She stood and rested. She could happily have stayed right there, and allowed her cheek to rest against the stone, her face bathed in the flicker of torchlight. But Igor would not allow it.

'Please, Mistress. You must rest.'

'I can rest here. It's okay.'

'You must move, Mistress. You are more tired than you know.'

Anna moved on again, dragging her feet each step of the way. 'It is only a little further, Mistress.'

* * *

Anna walked and allowed herself to embrace the castle's presence, but only a little. It smelled like no other place. In part it smelled of earth, in part musty and old. She breathed it in. The ancient dirt was at the back of her throat, nearly making her choke. Her tongue, her teeth and her lips tasted of an old, old earth. She breathed in deeper and as she released her breathe, she imagined she was tasting the absolute heart of the castle.

Behind her, Igor had stopped again. He turned her around to face him. He tilted his head and spoke to her, but his words came through as if filtered through cotton wool.

'Mistress? Mistress?' he said. 'Can you hear me, Mistress?' Igor reached past Anna's exhausted form and opened a door. He turned her back again and tried to guide her through the doorway. She slipped out of his grip and stumbled forward.

As Anna lurched through the doorway, she tripped over a deep step inside the door. Igor reached out to try and stop her fall, but was too slow. Like an unhinged statue, Anna fell forward.

The sound of skull on stone reverberated from ceiling to floor.

* * *

Anna woke up.

'Mistress, you are home.'

Anna shook her head, and looked around her, eyes blinking. 'This isn't home. This is some sort of hell.'

'Mistress, no. You are home.'

'Are you saying "yes, this is hell" or "yes, this is your new home"?'

Igor was silent, his head lowered.

Anna tried to catch Igor's eye. 'Where's Cat? I want to go and see her.'

'She is where we left her. She is safe. She is secure.'

Confused, Anna sat straight up and said, 'What do you mean?! Where is she?' As she sat up, tiny, coloured lights swam in front of her eyes. She sat still, waiting for her sight to clear.

With her eyes closed, Anna took a few slow, deep breaths to try and calm herself. When her vision settled, she took stock of herself and looked around the room.

Igor, it seemed, had lain her out on one of the biggest lounges she had ever seen. Plush and velvet brocade-covered, the cushioned behemoth stood as tall as it did wide. It more closely resembled a long, padded bench than any modern concept of a lounge.

The lounge stood on a tall dais in the centre of a cathedral-like hall.

On each side, long corridors of steep, black archways stretched into the distance. Behind each archway an alcove held two or three shimmering stained glass windows. The windows were lit by a gentle light and the faintest slivers of pattern or design shone through. Taken on their own, they were unremarkable, but collectively they were breathtaking. Anna felt as if she were sitting on the inside of an intricate Chinese carving. The room appeared to be spinning slightly too, so for a moment she wondered whether she *was* inside some sort of swaying bauble. She knew that the spinning was her own perception, so she put a hand out to steady herself. Behind the lounge stood a row of high-backed, solid wooden chairs. Two of the chairs in the middle were made from deeply carved beechwood and were a little than taller than the rest.

'Mistress. Your home.'

Anna looked from Igor to the room and back again. 'What do you mean by that?'

'It is as I once said, Mistress. This place is your home. This is where you will find your family's story.'

'But it's a fantasy. It's *only* a story.'

Again Igor was silent. He stood before the cavernous, gothic hall, seeming to let it speak for itself.

The oversized hall was a masterpiece. Utter perfection. Every intricate carving and delicate, detailed design, from floor to ceiling, immaculate and pristine. Anna found it hard to dismiss old ghost stories when sitting in a room so clearly made from their very words. She shook her head. 'Even if it wasn't just an old story, he never lived here. My family came from England, not here. You know that, Igor.' Anna smacked herself on the side of the head. 'I'm an idiot. Never mind all of this. I need to see Catalina.'

'No.' Igor shook his head. 'Mistress, she does not need to see you.'

* * *

Catalina's body lay nestled among the circle of furs and fineries. Her breathing remained steady, but from time to time her eyelids twitched.

Little Catalina ran through the field, breathless with excitement. She could see them in the distance. Her mother and father. They were helping with the harvest. Her grandmother, her Bunică, had raised her in the suburbs and had always wanted her to help with a harvest one day, but they could never afford the journey. There were harvests closer by, but they were not the right kind. Not traditional. And now here she was and there they were. In her joyous rush, Catalina tripped over her own tiny feet and fell onto the fresh cut straw. She laughed and lay back, looking at the tiny, black buckles on her shoes.

The air carried the scent of wheat. The sunlight gently warmed her face, arms and legs. She could not ever remember feeling this much contentment. She panicked for a moment and stood up. It was okay. She could still see them. She smiled. They were not going anywhere without her. All the same, she ran on, darting from stook to stook to try and find them.

In her room of contentment, Catalina smiled.

* * *

As much as it pained her, Anna could somehow sense that Igor was right. She and Catalina had grown up together. They were neighbours before either of them knew what the word was. Anna smiled as she remembered Catalina telling her the story of Anna's first word. She'd had trouble trying to say either 'mum 'or 'dad', but somehow she'd managed 'Cat'. At least that's how her parents and Catalina told it. They'd been together ever since. She'd heard of a special connection that twins shared and sometimes thought she and Catalina shared something like it. It felt that way. Right up until this moment, it had always felt that way.

She wanted not to believe Igor's words, but she couldn't deny it. She knew she was content right where she was. Catalina didn't need her. As always, it was that Anna needed Catalina, not the other way round. She buried her head in her hands. A moment later she heard Igor move. She peeked between her fingers and watched him. He was not the picture of contentment. He jumped at every creak and groan. He looked less like a hoarding castle-dweller and more like an overworked, worn-out old man. An old and broken soldier.

'I think it's time to tell me exactly what's going on, Igor,' she said.

Igor jumped. Anna took a small degree of satisfaction from it, but felt mean for doing so. 'More than about time, wouldn't you say?'

Igor looked at her and then nodded his agreement. 'Mistress. Remember the man in the painting? The one who looked akin to your father.'

Anna nodded.

'There are many Harkers. Some of them are story. This man was not.'

CHAPTER SIXTEEN

The man at the counter didn't look up when the bell over the door rang.

Harker waited and watched the man as he scribbled in the pages of a large bound volume. The pen scraped as it made its way across the paper. Behind the counter, towering stacks of bundles, packages and trunks filled the room, half blocking the light from the grubby windows.

Harker set down his oversized trunk and crossed his arms. There was still no acknowledgment of his presence, so Harker coughed once and then louder a second time.

'Can I help you, sir?' said the clerk, setting down his pen by a sturdy, glass inkwell.

'My name is Professor James Harker.'

'Yes, sir. You wish to book passage, sir?'

'Yes. To Transylvania,' said Harker, taking care to watch the clerk's face.

'Really, sir? Are you sure?' The man seemed more perturbed than surprised.

'I take it you've heard of it,' said Harker.

'Yes, sir. It has a . . . particular reputation,' he said. 'And you want to go there?'

'Yes. I have recently inherited a property there.'

'Still, sir—'

'A castle, to be exact,' said Harker.

The two men stared at each other.

Harker slid a slim bundle of notes across the broad, wooden counter.

'Well, each man knows his own mind, I always say.' The clerk pulled the notes across the counter and tucked them under the large leather volume. 'Take a seat, sir. This may take a bit of jiggling. We will see what we can do for you.'

Harker sat on his trunk and leaned back against a stack of boxes. Tipping his hat forward over his eyes, he said, 'I'll be here.'

❊ ❊ ❊

Anna interrupted Igor and said, 'Wait, one of my relatives inherited this castle?'

'Mistress, no.'

'But you just said.'

'Mistress, I did not. These were the words of Professor Harker.'

'But ...'

Igor looked, for a moment, as if he was going to speak. But he stayed silent.

Anna waited. He seemed to be gathering his thoughts and she didn't want to disrupt him or discourage him from telling her more.

At last, he said, 'Harker was a trickster and a fraud. He was many other things as well. And boasted many claims. None of them were true. He was not a professor. He was not very much of anything'. Igor paused before going on. 'Mistress, we here – the castle, the people – have been lost many times to war, to battle, to kingdoms. To many different invaders. We have been ruined and rebuilt, and rebuilt again. Only once in our history has a single man tried to claim us as his own.'

Anna was at a loss for words. She was already keenly aware of how much danger she was in. She felt as she were losing her mind. Her head swam whenever she moved. She was injured, giddy and, she suspected, feverish. And now it seemed she had been brought here to stand trial for past wrongs. At last she said, 'So, that's it'.

'Mistress, yes.'

'Okay,' she said. 'But, look, why punish me for his crimes?'

'Mistress? Punish you? No. We welcome you.'

'Sorry, what?'Anna rubbed at her aching head.

Igor ignored her comment and carried on. 'Mistress, how can any man own a thing such as this?' he said gesturing at the deep, dark architectural gem behind him. 'It is not possible.'

Igor again seemed to be struggling for the right words, so Anna again gave him time to think. She struggled to concentrate on his words. But she had to know. Her head ached and her vision blurred.

Whispered voices drifted in and out of her thoughts, and very little of it made sense. She wasn't too sure what was real anymore. She hardly cared. As long as Cat lived, it didn't matter. If she was going to die here, she had to know.

'Mistress, the castle cannot be owned. Some men have thought differently. They were wrong and they suffered for their delusions. There was no crime. There was only punishment.'

* * *

Harker rapped his walking stick against the looming castle doors. The doors seemed to swallow the sound. He knocked a few more times, but the harder he knocked the dimmer the sound became. There was a painful echo in his ears. He put down his walking stick and gave the castle doors his full attention. Their presence was commanding. Intimidating. But he was not put off.

Having planned, gambled and, in the end, swindled his way across half of Europe, Harker was not going to be stopped by a set of doors, no matter how ominous they looked. He thought for a moment. The doors reached far overhead. They threatened. As he looked up, they seemed to lean forward and cast a shadow across his face. Harker turned away and, with his back to the doors, set his monstrous trunk on the ground and sat down. The castle would open its doors and let him in or he would die waiting.

He crossed his arms and waited.

* * *

Igor stopped talking.

'Okay. So what happened?' said Anna.

'Mistress, is it not clear?'

'Nothing's clear. Come on, Igor. For once, can't you tell me the whole story?'

'Mistress, he did as he intended,' said Igor. 'He waited.'

'I don't understand,' said Anna, shaking her head and wincing at the same time.

'Mistress.' Igor shook his head. 'This is a fortress and a castle. The mighty behemoth is its own defence. A man attempts to outwait a castle? No. He waited, Mistress, he waited and waited until he was nearly starved.'

'But why didn't they let him in?'

'Mistress, they let him in. And ...' Igor looked away.

'And he died. That's it. That's the whole tale? It doesn't make any sense.'

Igor had his back to Anna. He whispered, 'This is not all.'

Anna swayed and lay back on the lounge. She couldn't hold her head up and her eyelids had become heavy again. Bile started to collect at the back of her throat. She was tired of it. It was another horror story. Another horrible death. It was the sort of night-time story she had grown up with. The sort of tale she usually loved and exactly the type of thing that had brought her here. A story she should know better than to believe. But here, in this place, she couldn't quite ignore it. But who cared what had come before? She wanted her friend. She wanted Cat. And Mihai.

She wanted to go home.

Anna made a decision. Until now she had felt manipulated at every step. Every decision, every move. She'd fought it, but hadn't won. She decided she would stay and talk to Igor. She would try and keep him happy and gather her strength. And then she would get Catalina and take them the hell away from here. She didn't care whether Catalina needed her or not. She needed Catalina. And that was enough. She had to go to her. But not yet. She had to rest first. Rest and get some goddamn strength back. She sunk backwards, her shoulder sinking into the cushions behind her. The room swam around her, encompassing her, enveloping her. She closed her eyes. Through half-lidded vision she saw that Igor had turned back to her.

Igor was watching Anna's face intently. He seemed to take her thoughtfulness for confusion. 'Mistress. Do you not see? His death. In the end, he gave his life. It bound him here. Him and his blood. Your blood.'

Anna opened her eyes fully. Igor's face was shining with a sort of intensity. A hunger.

'My blood,' said Anna, her voice hoarse and fading.

Igor nodded. 'Your blood.'

* * *

The air tasted of tin.

The villagers gathered at the edge of the empty, fresh grave. Earth piled up beside it. No one had told them to come, but they knew that they must. It was not a directive. It was the way.

Imposing clouds were building up on the horizon, boiling and trampling over one another as if they had been caught and hemmed in by the distant mountains. The sun had risen, but was already obscured by the clouds. As yet more storm clouds gathered, the sun's intensity died further away.

Pressure was building and though all of the villagers knew that a great storm was about to break, they stayed. It was their duty. The possible cost of not staying was terrifying and it was a price that no one was willing to risk.

One very young man pointed at a rapid movement up at the castle. His hand was immediately smacked back down. The men nearby gathered around him and held him still. If he struggled, they would deal with him. He was young, barely more than a child. His shoulders slumped and he stood silent. He had been told. He knew how much was at stake.

The older man had given his life for all of theirs. The only thing they could give in return was their silence. And their dignity.

It was not chance, a lottery. But a sacrifice. A deadly act of love. Decades would pass before it would happen again.

At one point, in the middle of the long and dreary night, his dying scream had been heard. The passage of time changed nothing. It neither dimmed their memory nor lessened the pain.

At last, the procession could be seen making its way down from the castle.

The villagers bowed their heads. Several of the villagers turned away, unable to look.

It was over. The cycle had begun again.

* * *

'They killed Harker? Why?'

'Mistress, no. That was not Harker's story. It was the tale of those who came before him.'

'But the villagers stood by and allowed them to kill a man. They listened to him screaming and didn't do anything. It's so horrible.' Anna shook her head, tears brimming. 'Why didn't they do anything?'

Igor was silent for a moment. He raised his head and, for once, his eyes were vivid and alive as he looked straight at her and said, 'The alternatives were worse. They had no choice. The man who held the castle embraced pain and suffering. He worshipped it. If an old man went willingly, such as this one, they were left in peace'.

A vivid memory of the horrid painting – the scene of tortured and dying men and women – flashed into Anna's mind. That painting had been left as a warning about the past. A reminder and nothing more. 'Igor?'

'Mistress.'

'Okay, just this once, answer me straight out. Did you meet that man? Did you try to stop him?'

'Yes.'

❊ ❊ ❊

The air was sharp and clear.

The villagers gathered at the edge of the newest grave. It was not empty. It had been bedded down with wildflowers. A gravestone stood ready. It bore two phrases: viteaz and strigoi vui.

Clouds were, as ever, gathering in the distance, but today they held sway.

The villagers had been told it would be the last for a long time. No one truly believed it, but they hoped. Living where they did, in the way that they did, hope was all they had ever had.

This strange young man had chosen to shorten his life. He had seen the so-called accident of the young man that went before him and had offered himself. To stop everything, once and for all. He knew what he faced and he went willingly. He gave his life for all of them and for many others not yet born.

In return they offered their gratitude and their grief. For one not their own. From this day, they made him their own.

Knowing he had accepted, so young, so willing. Many of the villagers had hoped this time would be different. But they were wrong. More than wrong. The middle of the longest night again bore witness to the scream that could not be ignored. He had known the risks, they knew, but they had hoped he would not suffer like all before him. And for what he gave, for an end to the hopeless cycle of death, each person stood vigil and listened to his suffering.

The procession could be seen making its way from the castle.

The villagers bowed their heads for the last time.

* * *

Anna tried to blink away tears. She lifted her head and said, 'No, that's not right. That's not fair. Why should one young man suffer so much? Was it the same man who died waiting? 'Anna's skin was cold and clammy; her hands trembled.

'Mistress, no. You are confused. He waited. He starved. He did not die. Not then. He was lost and alone. He sought to find a way to cease their suffering. It was his first true act of selflessness.'

'It sounds like he was tortured.'

Igor closed his eyes and nodded, almost imperceptibly.

'Starved and tortured?' He must have lost his mind. Why did he do it? Was he crazy?'

'No. For everything else that he was, this man was kind. Foolishly kind, you might think, Mistress, this relative of yours. But, in doing it, he stopped it for others. He could see the future. He understood what would happen next. He'd witnessed the death of that very young man. So young. And his accident was no accident. He could see what it meant. For whatever reason, he knew. Something had drawn him here and he knew. You see, Mistress? Do you see?' said Igor, his voice rising.

'Of course I don't see! I mean, come on. It doesn't make any sense. How would that change anything?' said Anna. 'Why would that change anything?'

'Mistress, these matters are not straightforward. This is how it was. How it is.'

'No!' Anna shook her head. It ached and her vision swam. She put out a hand to steady herself and said, 'That's not an answer. What does it even mean? Why? You need to tell me what's going on.'

'No.'

With the harshness and the cruelty in its telling, Anna refused to accept the reality of the story. 'This is ridiculous. Torture. Sacrifice. I've had enough. It's nothing more than an old wives' tale.'

'Mistress, yes. You are modern and you *know better*. I understand.'

Igor stood up and turned away, looking as though he was about to leave. 'There is more than one type of knowing. There is knowledge that can be taught and there is knowledge that can only be gained by experience. You may one day experience this and then you will know.'

Anna couldn't think straight and was struggling to understand. As much she thought it was a story, it was a story she wanted to hear finished. She tried to call him back to her. 'Please, Igor, come back.'

Igor had not moved.

'Please,' she said weakly, 'I want to understand. Explain it to me'.

'Mistress, these are only words and they are the wrong words.'

Anna spoke again, her voice barely more than a whisper, 'I'm sorry. Please help me to understand.'

Igor said, 'Mistress, I cannot teach you this'.

'Why? Are you worried about how I might react? It can't be that. Look at me. I'm lying here completely at your mercy: wounded, exhausted and ...,' she paused and lowered her voice, 'terrified. How much worse can it be? Whatever it is, just tell me. I'll accept the consequences'.

Igor turned back to her. His face was once again full of hunger and intensity. Every contorted muscle in his body stretched tight. 'You would say these words to me?'

Anna stumbled over her own confused thoughts. 'What words? What did I say?'

Igor watched Anna. Her eyes were barely open and she was drifting at the edge of sleep.

'You will learn. Mistress, this is the one thing I am certain, you will learn.'

Anna felt control of her consciousness slipping away. As she slid under, she heard Igor's hoarse whisper, 'She accepts'.

* * *

Outside the window, the rain poured.

The hail had eased off, but the rain still roared, sending thick sheets of water crashing against the stone balcony by the small bedroom.

Igor leaned against the window, the rain fiercely crashing around his face. The view comprised little more than rain. It didn't matter. It was a view he had seen thousands of times before.

Igor turned away from the window, his face peppered with raindrops. 'You invited her here. We allowed this,' he said to the empty room.

Alone, Igor appeared once more to have lost a little of his awkwardness. He was less remarkable than before. Still scarred, but more invisible. Almost as invisible as the room he now stood in. Small and commonplace. Igor had blended in with his surroundings.

'She was our idea. She is our problem. Whatever happens next is our doing. We must accept the consequences.' He began pacing the room. At every turn he spoke another sentence.

'She was delusional. We know that. 'Turn.

Igor shook his head quickly and with fury. 'She has accepted. The Mistress has accepted.' Turn.

'She was delusional. She did not understand.' Turn.

'Acceptance. We will show her the way without pain. We can ease her path.' He spun around.

'She was not right in her mind.' Igor stopped and instead of turning, slammed his fist against the jagged and barren wall. 'It is only fair!' He collapsed against the wall and said, 'It is my right'.

After a few more insensible mutterings, Igor seemed to tire. He lowered himself down onto an old, battered trunk and slumped forward, his forehead touching his knees. His broken body crumbled into the shape of despair.

'It is my right,' he whispered. 'My right.'

* * *

Igor stood in the room of seasons, looking down at Catalina. She was unmoving, sleeping, seeming to be at peace.

Igor smiled at Catalina, moving a few loose strands of hair away from her eyes. 'I will not deceive her, Mistress Catalina. I promise you.'

As he turned to go, Catalina's fingers twitched.

Without looking back, Igor said, 'It is only right'.

* * *

When Anna woke, she didn't realise where she was at first. The sheer size of the room made her think she was outside. She panicked and tried to claw her way up from the oversized lounge.

Hands shaking and drenched in sweat, she shivered from the cold. Feeling useless and lost, she slumped back down. She fought to wake up, fought to leave. But she had nothing left to fight with. She gave up and allowed herself to drift once more back to sleep.

* * *

Igor sat by Anna's side. Now and then, he wiped the sweat from her forehead. He dipped a cloth into a shallow wooden bowl full of cool, dark water. But Anna's sleep had become fitful and restless, and she jerked away from his touch. After the bowl was empty, Igor stopped his ministrations and for a time sat and quietly watched her.

The room had changed with the shifting light of daytime, each stained glass window allowing slices of colour to thread a pattern across the room. The colours brightened and dimmed as the clouds outside skittered across the wan sun. The echoing chamber moved between ornamental and oppressive as the colours wandered in and out. The patterns of dark and shimmering light seemed to soothe Igor, and his gaze eventually moved to the cavernous space ahead of him. Each colour was momentary, but moved with a slow pulsing light.

Anna woke up. When she saw Igor, she groaned. 'One of these times I will wake up and this will all have been a dream. A nightmare.' She glanced at the nearby bowl, feeling like she might have missed something important. 'What was that?'

'Water, Mistress. *Apa vie.* Restorative water.'

'Restorative water. Sure. Right.' With some care, she shook her head. 'This isn't real. *You* can't be real.'

Igor said nothing and turned away.

'I'm sorry. That was unkind.' Anna tried to sit fully upright, but found she was even weaker than before, though her aches had mostly disappeared. Desperate, and exhausted, she sat up and tried to get up from the lounge.

Igor pressed his hand against Anna's shoulder. Anna leaned back a little, but more out of fatigue than fear.

'Mistress, yes. That was unkind.'

'I know.' She shrugged and continued. 'It's this whole thing,' she said, as she attempted a gesture that encompassed the entirety of the castle. 'It's so unreal. So fanciful. I can *see* all of it,' she said, as she looked around the towering room, 'But what am I meant to say about it? And this?' She gestured at the bowl and sighed. 'What do you want from me? What do you want me to do?'

Igor said one word. 'Rest.'

Anna collapsed back into the cushions on the lounge, fast asleep.

* * *

Igor watched as Anna woke yet again. 'Mistress.'

Anna stared at him without speaking. She had no idea how long she had been asleep this time, but it felt like her thoughts were at last in some sort of order. She sat up and although her head still ached a little, her vision didn't blur and her stomach didn't churn. 'Hello, Igor. I want to go home.'

'You are home, Mistress.'

'Okay, that's enough,' she said. 'No, Igor. All the way home. To *my* home. There's been so much suffering here. I can't take it anymore.'

'You can stop the suffering, Mistress.'

'Like he did? James Harker?' She shook her head. 'Or, at least, like he thought he did. No, Igor —' Anna cut herself off and looked at him for a long moment.

Igor turned away as she stared at him.

'I want to see Cat. I want you to let both of us go.'

Igor whispered when he said, 'I cannot, Mistress. One of you must stay'.

And with a fast and terrible insight, Anna could see all of it. She'd known it on some level, but now the knowledge was bone deep. There hadn't ever been a chance of escape for her. The only way to save Catalina was to lose herself. She stared at Igor, open-mouthed. 'You planned it. Didn't you. All of it.'

'Not planned, Mistress,' said Igor shaking his head. 'Hope. I only ever hoped.'

'If I stay, you'll let her go?' she said. She stopped herself and threw her hands in the air. 'What am I saying? Pain, suffering? What else?

Would you torture me? Nope. No, no, no.'

Igor interrupted her eagerly. 'It does not have to be this way for you. I have potions for a ceremony. A ritual. It is only a ritual that the castle desires. Not suffering. I am sure. Only ritual.'

'Let me see Cat,' she said.

'Mistress?'

Anna sat up and, with care, stood up from the lounge. 'Look. If you seriously expect me to do any of this, to save the day like some sort of weird superhero, to stop the suffering ...' She paused for a moment. Stared at him, hands on hips. 'Whatever way you want to say it. I don't care. I want to see her. No. More. Arguing. I need to see her.'

She started to walk across the room, stumbled, and turned back to look at him. 'And I need to see her now.'

* * *

Igor supported Anna as she walked towards the room.

As they approached the door, Anna pulled away from his hovering hands. 'You can leave me here, Igor.'

'Mistress—'

'No, I've got to do this on my own. You're asking a lot from me. A ridiculous amount. It's too much. And I've already been through a hell of a lot. The least you can do is give me this. Or don't you trust me?' she said, tilting her head.

Igor stood in silence for a short while before he said, 'As you wish, Mistress. I will return'.

'I'll be here, Igor. I promise.' As she said it she realised she meant it. The idea of another opportunity for escape had crossed her mind, but now she was here, so close to Catalina, she knew she wouldn't try anything that might put her friend at risk. She wanted to see her safely away. To be gone and back on her way home.

Igor had watched Anna's face as she spoke, and, without hesitating, said, 'I trust you, Mistress.'

Anna allowed herself a tired smile. 'Thanks, Igor.'

He inclined his head a little, then turned and walked away.

Anna stared at the door, reluctant to go through. She realised this might be the last time she saw Catalina. She shook her head at herself. No. She couldn't let it be the last time. She'd try her best to make that not be true. She'd get Catalina out, but stay herself, and somehow, later, she'd follow. She bit her lip and pushed open the door.

This time the room seemed even more alarming in its beauty. Occasional soft catches of light played on the floor, dust motes shining in the dimming sun rays. Small ribbons of diffused colour fell into the room as the clouds broke open and closed over again. In the middle of it all lay Catalina.

Anna had forgotten exactly how beautiful Catalina looked here. Catalina belonged in this room and the sight of her erased the last of Anna's lingering doubts. Catalina's breathing was even and, from what Anna could tell, seemed pretty normal again. A gentle smile played across her friend's features. Her eyelids twitched now and then, so Anna guessed she must be dreaming. Anna sighed and slipped down next to her, wishing that she was there in the dream with her, wherever it was.

She placed her hand on Catalina's strong hand, and gently twined their fingers together. Familiar and warm, Catalina's hands had never been delicate, and the rough calloused fingers scraped against her own soft skin. Tears welled up and she let them fall. For the longest moment she sat still, letting herself to soak in every detail: the warmth of her skin; her chest rising and falling; her thick, blonde hair framing her bruised but peaceful face.

Anna closed her eyes and said, 'I'm sort of glad you're asleep, Cat. If you were awake I think you'd try and help me fix this. And I don't think we can. Not together. It's not what he wants'. Anna took in a deep breath, and as she breathed out she found that more tears fell with it. The tang as they streamed down her cheeks and over her lips was strangely satisfying. She folded down and into herself, letting go of Catalina's hand. It was too much. She couldn't say goodbye, but she needed to. Had to. She wanted to trust that Igor would let Catalina go, that she'd be okay. But though she could believe it for her friend's sake, she didn't believe for her own.

After a little while, she curled up next to Catalina on the lounge. Their heartbeats were not quite in sync, but it felt good all the same. She lay cheek-to-cheek with her and, to her own surprise, didn't drift off to sleep. Instead, she lay still and listened to the rhythm of their shared breathing. Eventually, Anna's blood pulsed in time with Catalina's.

Some moments later, and with reluctance, Anna sat up. She kissed Catalina gently on the cheek and tasted the salt of her own bitter tears. She leaned close and said, 'I'll make sure you're okay, Cat. This time it's my turn. I'll try everything. Cross my heart and hope to die. Promise I'll try and fix this'. She turned her back and looked towards the room's door.

Catalina's fingers twitched and jumped.

'Love you, Cat,' she said, her voice breaking. 'Hope I'll see you soon.'

* * *

Harker sat back in his chair. Outside, the wind cracked and whipped at the sky.

Next to Harker, an old domineering figure of a man sat in front of a dwindling fire. Behind them, the detritus of a simple dinner sat untended.

'You understand everything that I ask for. Everything?' said the old man, his face half-lit by the guttering flames. 'And you accept?'

'Yes,' said Harker.

'There is no return. Once you give yourself to the castle there is no way back,' said the older man. The

man sat emotionless and unmoving. His face was gaunt and hard, and revealed nothing. 'Only one of your blood can take this place after you. And none of your line exist here. It's possible that they may not ever do so again.'

Harker nodded. 'I accept that this is how it must be. That this is the truth as you see it.'

'This is how it is.' The other man nodded in return. 'And this is how it shall be.'

❋ ❋ ❋

Anna heard Igor as he shuffled towards the door. As he came in, she said, 'I'm still here'.

Igor nodded. 'Mistress. You have kept your promise. I will keep mine.'

'Sure. No suffering,' she said. 'Come on, Igor. There's no other way?'

Igor stood still and silent.

Even though Anna knew he wouldn't change his mind, she wanted to try. She understood now that he believed this was the only way. Reality didn't matter. The way she felt about Catalina, the castle, the story. None of it mattered. Igor was in charge and what he believed was what counted. She tried again anyway.

'Hasn't there been enough suffering, Igor?' said Anna, sitting close to Catalina. 'Look at her. Look at what happened to Mihai.' Her voice softened. 'Look at you. Surely there's been enough pain.'

'It will not do. These recent events. There was

no ritual. The castle demands more than pain or death. She demands ritual.'

Anna sat at edge of the bed and smoothed Catalina's beautiful, long, blonde hair. 'How can I know, really know, that you'll let her go?'

'You will still be here, Mistress. You will know.' Igor sat in a nearby chair and said, 'I wish to let her go. Once she wakes, I will make sure. I will see her safely away. We both will'.

'James?' tried Anna.

Igor did not flinch. He looked at Anna and said, 'No. Do not speak his name. His choice was made long ago. He made it. He has lived with it. He has no voice now'.

'You'd really ask me to do this?' said Anna, her voice cracking.

Igor hung his head low. 'I only ask what I once gave.'

Anna couldn't believe her ears. But, more, she couldn't believe what she thought she might be about to say.

Without warning, Igor was on his knees, at Anna's feet. 'I have said, Mistress. There will be no pain for you. I have found another way.' He reached up and grasped her hand.

Anna couldn't look at him.

He released her and clenched his fist hard against his chest, crookedly pointing at his broken body. 'This terrible disfigurement I have suffered, the death and pain that others have suffered, it does not need to happen to you.'

Anna looked down into Igor's pleading face. A face so full of pain that it had barely been recognisable as human when she first saw him. Right now, Anna had never seen anyone look so completely and openly human.

'It will not happen to you,' said Igor. 'I promise you.'

Anna looked at Catalina's still and peaceful face. She still wasn't sure what she was agreeing to. She still didn't trust him. But if it was down to Catalina or her, there was no decision left to make. Inside the silent desperation of her own mind, she hoped that she could leave too, once Catalina was safe. But it didn't matter. She was willing to risk it. For Catalina. And, she finally realised, for Igor. She wanted to set them free. Both of them.

Anna nodded and said, 'I accept'.

CHAPTER SEVENTEEN

'I'm not sure I really get this, Igor,' said Anna, as they came to a short, dark door in the hallway.

'Mistress, I have explained. The castle is ancient. There is much knowledge here. The ceremony of pain that bound me here is old, but not ancient. There are older rituals that speak of a different kind of sacrifice. Of willingness to serve. Some are nonsensical, some are strange. But they are not about suffering. I believe that what happened here began out of cruelty. By a man that revelled in anguish and pain. He did this in the name of the castle. It was his fiction. It is not what the castle needs.'

'But this—' Anna began.

'It is ancient, but it will work, Mistress.'

'But there's no logic to it,' she said. 'I mean, come on. There's no logic to any of this.'

'Enough!'

The intensity and volume of Igor's voice forced Anna into silence. Igor had raised his voice before, but not like this. He was masterful. And she was merely stunned.

'This is not *modern*, Mistress. It cannot be discerned. It will work. That is all you need to know.'

Anna, at a loss for anything better to say, said, 'Okay. So, what do I have to do?'

'Follow me, Mistress.' Igor opened the door. Beyond the open door lay the alchemist's room.

* * *

Anna squeezed into a humble, disordered and chaotic room. As she looked around, dozens of pairs of colours glinted back. Even in the dim light, Anna could make out a strange collection of stuffed and morbid critters.

'Um.'

'Mistress. Forgive me. I keep them here for company. They are all I have.'

Outside the castle wall, the sound of a mocking raven's caw pushed at the solid castle walls.

Anna turned to smiled at Igor before realising he was serious. The stuffed rabbits, mice, hawks and other creatures weren't gruesome and ghoulish in their arrangement. Placed with gentle and careful precision, they huddled together in a dark, sad affection.

The distant sound of ancient cawing reverberated through the sky.

When it ended, Igor made a short curt nod. He gestured Anna towards an overstuffed chair at end of the room. 'Mistress. Please. Sit.'

Anna stared at the chair. 'Uh-huh'. She scratched at her forearms before hugging her arms close. Out of ideas, Anna collapsed into the chair. She sighed and said, 'Okay. What now, Igor?'

'I will explain what happens, for I understand that you wish to know. But it matters not.'

'Yeah. No,' said Anna. 'I sort of think it does?'

Igor turned away and pulled an ornate blue bottle down from its shelf. 'It matters not,' he said, smiling. 'With this, you will not remember.'

* * *

Catalina's body lay tangled between the piles of furs and silk. Her breathing rapid, her eyelids and fingers spasmed and twitched.

Little Catalina had tripped again in the field of wheat. Her parents had left her, once again. She couldn't stand up, but someone had tried to help her. They were gone too.

Whoever had been trying to help her, she needed to find them. She remembered their breath on her face and the warmth of their hand on hers.

It felt good. She didn't know who had been holding her hand. She couldn't see them. It didn't matter. She knew *them. She wanted to be with them.*

But they'd let her hand go. She sought for it, searched for it, but they were gone. They had been gone for such a long time. Too long.

She was lost and alone without them. She needed

them.

She had to find them. Her Anna. It was Anna. She had to find her.

Anna? Where was Anna?

Catalina sat upright and, with a voice hoarse from heavy sleep and fatigue, cried out, 'Anna! Anna, where are you?'

✾ ✾ ✾

Anna walked along a dark, dank, stony hallway. Her hallway. This time though, she walked alone.

Her fingers ran over the surface of the stones. The tips of her fingers were bleeding. She smiled as she walked along. The stone scraped her fingers as she walked, but she didn't care. She wanted more and she wanted to be closer. She winced as another deep scrape was drawn, but, all the same, pushed her fingers even deeper into the stone.

Now that she had accepted her fate, she felt free to accept the castle. No guilt and no secrecy. She was doing this for them. For both of them. And now they could be together. She stopped and looked at the wall. The surface was wrong somehow, even though the wall looked like solid stone. Her vision blurred and the walls seem to shift under her gaze. Anna looked at the whorls on her fingertips and said, 'What have I accepted? What have I done?' For a moment, she was unsure again, but as she was about to move away, the wall flickered and a series of loud creaks and groans emanated from the depths of the castle. A door groaned and opened with a series of slow, jerky movements.

Beyond the doorway, Anna could see a cavernous, deep dark room. She stared into its depths, mesmerised. Anna's hands dropped to her sides, all thoughts and questions forgotten. The room called to her. It sang.

*　*　*

Catalina ran along the dark, stone-encased castle, calling Anna's name. She stumbled as she ran.

Her calls had become more frenzied the longer she searched. 'Anna! Where are you? I know you're alive,' she cried. 'I'd know if you were dead.' She stopped. 'I'd know. If you were gone. 'She slumped against the castle wall.

'Oh, Anna. I don't know. Perhaps I wouldn't know.' She sighed. 'I'm so tired.' She slipped down the wall, nearly to the floor. 'So tired,' she whispered.

Catalina shook her herself. 'No. I'd know. I'd know. 'She stood up again. 'I've got to find you.' She steadied herself against the wall, before she ran on.

*　*　*

Anna stepped into a room as dark and unmoving as the still heart of a long dead beast.

It was as Igor had described it. The room, the castle, was expecting her. She was a bit unclear about why she was here, but she knew it was noble. It was good. It was how it should be.

The walls were a piteous black. Pockmarked, rough-hewn and intricate, their surface dominated the room. Blackened red veins of colour, like marble, suffused the rock.

A servant stood before an overgrown table. Anna nodded to Igor in acknowledgment. She should have known. Of course he'd be here. It was his right.

A sound split the silence. Loud cawing rang out, and the winged beast had returned. Out of the darkness, the sky split and the raven unfurled, its wings made of storm clouds, its feathers of threatening rain. The cloud of feathers rushed, and time twisted around it as it landed. The bird cawed out again, stronger.

Igor glanced at it, but averted his gaze. He stood with his shoulders back, half-turned towards the door. His face was dark and unreadable. His stance resembled a jackal set to run.

Dozens of chairs lined the table, but only one place was set.

As Anna meandered along the length of the table, her fingers caressed the backs of all the chairs. Voices whispered to her. They gathered around her and the room seemed full, crowded. She didn't know where Catalina had gone, but for now it didn't matter. She wasn't alone. The castle would never let her be alone again. Once this was done, she would find her friend and they would be together. She wouldn't make her stay. She would let her choose. Like she had been allowed to choose.

Anna sat down, taking her rightful place at the head of the table. There was food. A great towering pile of undercooked meat. Alongside it was a carving knife. Anna's hunger gnawed at her and she salivated at the sight of the food. She laughed and picked up a haunch of meat. She ate. She ate with fervour and burning desire.

The castle was, finally, fully hers.

* * *

As Catalina turned the corner into yet another corridor, the caw of a raven rang out.
Catalina stopped. She looked to where the sound came from. A door, open, led into a blood-dark and ominous space.
The caw sounded again, louder.
She plunged through.
Catalina stopped as soon as she saw what was through the door.

* * *

Anna sat in front of a pile of dreadful, half-cooked meat. Her eyes, dark and unfocused, didn't even flicker when Catalina came into the room. Her forehead was bruised and she sat slumped at the table, gnawing at the marrow of a bone.

Catalina stared at Anna, her own face draining of colour.

'You! I gave you sanctuary,' said Igor. 'You should not be here.' Igor walked to Anna's side.

'Get away from her! What have you done to my Anna? 'Catalina ran over and violently pushed him away. Igor fell to the floor and stayed there, cowering.

'What is wrong with you, Anna?!' said Catalina. 'That's disgusting. It's barely even cooked. Put it down!'

Catalina knocked the food out of her friend's hand.

* * *

Anna blinked, three times, four. She tilted her head to look at the woman's hand on her arm. She stared until she realised it was someone she knew. She looked at the plate of food in front of her. It *was* disgusting. Her hand flew to her mouth. 'I feel sick,' said Anna. 'I think I'm going to throw up.'

'I think it might be better if you did,' said Catalina. 'You look awful. What happened to you? Why did you leave me alone like that?'

'You let me leave. You didn't even notice me go.' Anna started to cry.

'No, that's not true.' Catalina was close and trying to hold her. 'I wouldn't leave you, Anna. We have to get away from here. Now.' Catalina's voice was hoarse and she was close to tears. She pulled at

Anna's arm, trying to get her to stand up.

Anna wrenched her arm free. 'No. I can't go anywhere now. It's not safe.' Anna had begun to shake violently. She couldn't think. Thinking only moved the fog around. She couldn't clear it.

'Please, Anna,' said Catalina. 'Calm down. It's going to be okay. Trust me. We'll be okay.'

Anna tried to shake her head clear. Nothing made sense any more. She looked down. And at her feet, crouched Igor. For an instant, Anna saw a stranger in front of her. The stranger smiled at her. It enraged her. 'What have you done to us?!' She screamed at him.

Anna leaped up and looked around, her eyes searching and desperate. She grabbed at the knife.

'No! Mistress, no. No!' Igor stood and moved to stand between the two women.

Anna stared at him. She didn't know what to do, who to trust. Terrified, she clenched the knife in front of her, like a shield.

'Anna, please! Put the knife down. Put it down!'

'Mistress, please!' Igor moved closer.

Drugged and exhausted, Anna couldn't take in their pleas. She wasn't sure of anything, and all she knew was fear. And she saw a monster. A monster who had been plaguing them for days. Half-delusional, half-blind, fuelled by anger, fear and rage, she struck out at Igor.

Catalina pushed Igor aside. The blade hit Catalina full in the stomach, and Anna turned to flee.

Catalina screamed. Igor caught her as she fell.

Without looking back, Anna dropped the blade and ran.

* * *

Igor lowered Catalina's bleeding body gently to the castle's floor. 'Oh, Mistress. My Mistress.' He wiped the tears from his eyes. '*Ademeni. Sunt regrete.* It was not meant to be this way, Mistress.'

Blood bubbled up from her wound.

'I am to blame.' He kneeled down and did his best to stem the bleeding. 'I am sorry, Mistress. So sorry.'

With great care, Igor lifted Catalina's head and held her close. As he did he whispered the words, 'The castle, she is yours'.

* * *

Anna ran blindly.

She ran down nightmare corridors, up curling stairs and crashed along dark, gloomy walls. She ran to escape the memory of what she had done. Even though she wasn't exactly sure what had happened. She ran to escape it.

When she came to a stop, she found herself curled up in an alcove of the library. She had wedged herself under a shelf by the rough stones of the castle wall. Her arms, her legs, her entire body was covered in small cuts. She stared at the blood on her fingers. She wasn't sure how it had gotten there or even if it was her own. She dug her fingers into the palms of her hands. She released them and watched the semicircles fade away. She couldn't feel it. She couldn't feel anything.

As Anna leaned against the stones, she started to feel a heartbeat. She rocked back and forth to the rhythm of the castle. The pulsing sound of blood thrummed in her ears. Eventually, her rocking slowed and her panicked mind found a moment's peace.

In this brief moment of calm, Anna reach into her jacket pocket and dug out her seemingly useless phone. She reached to turn it on, but her hand stopped short.

Anna stared at her phone. She could try and call for help. Even if there was only the weakest, most hopeless connection, she could send a message. Then they would come for her. Come and help.

They would come here.

And whatever had happened to her, to Mihai, would happen to them. She blamed herself. For all of it. An image of Catalina flooded her mind. She sobbed and pushed it away. She couldn't take it. Couldn't recall what happened, and didn't want to.

Enough was enough. It had started with her and it had to end with her. She had to make it stop.

Anna smashed her phone against the castle

walls. Again and again, her blood and its shards blending with the shards of the castle stone.

She stopped. Stopped moving. Stopped feeling. Stopped fighting.

Anna sunk against the wall, her silent tears falling freely.

* * *

Some time later, Anna sat on a little crate in a quiet corner of the castle library, a twist of paper and pencils in front of her.

She gripped a pencil. As the last of her senses slipped away, and the phantoms pressed in, Anna wrote her story. She was sure she wouldn't make it out alive. But maybe her story could. She at least had to try. Try and be heard. By anyone who would listen. She had to warn them.

Warn them not to come.

The End

EPILOGUE

Anna Harker's scribbled notes were found some time after the woman and her friend, Catalina Dalca, had been reported missing. At first, it was thought to be a cruel joke.

Police eventually connected the story with the final sighting of the missing women. The pair were last seen in a remote and high altitude location in the Carpathian Mountains. They had not been heard from in months. Police interviewed locals in nearby small towns. Only one or two people recalled the women, and only as visitors passing through.

Police also tried to interview Mihai Troester, but when asked, he seemed unable or unwilling to answer. An older relative told the police that he was recovering from a climbing accident, and that he was best left alone. With no other leads to pursue, they let him be.

The women's whereabouts are still unknown.

ACKNOWLEDGEMENTS

This book exists thanks to so many of the kind people in my life. I hope I don't miss any of you, but if I do please forgive me. Your kindness was noticed and appreciated in its time. My memory, not my heart, is at fault.

To my dear husband and friend, Victor. My confidence about my ability to write is drawn from the pillars of his love, and his confidence in me. I'm so grateful that he has respect for the craft, and that he knew when I needed to give it time, space and attention.

Next my family, especially my mum and brother, Judy McIntyre and Des Wragg, for their shared love of books.

A special note for my dad, and his loving confusion at my obsession with books, and a note too for Uncle Pat and Aunty Jan, for their early love of stories. With love, too, to my stepdad Tom for his respect for my young and growing mind. May all four now rest in peace.

A big thank you to my friends Aleks Wragg, Rebecca Douglas, Stuart McKenzie, Mike Lim and Morgan

(Kristen). Each of you were there for me in the toughest moments, at different times, and also for the most joyous ones. You kept me moving. Kept me strong. You are the stuff of stars.

And for their shared word joys and many, many kindnesses, my thanks to Ambra Scarlett, JJ Heylen, Corinna Bennett, Amy Ralfs, Helen Zaltzman, Cloudhopper, Kirsty McKenzie, and, more recently, Jemima Kemp, Emily Heylen, Lauren Grantham, and dear S'OD. It's friendships like these that give oxygen to your dreams and book-ish hopes.

To my global friends, new and old. To Keith Ecklund, Shawn Leuthold and all our rusty Scrine-bird friends, for being there for my fledgling first steps, one sentence at a time. To Jay X Wolf, Milli Pichardo, Sean, Kan, B, Anna, the mysterious Breakmaster Cylinder, Lisa Smith, Thomas, Andrew Conkling, Em, Ed, Goose, Kelly, Alex and so many more of the beautiful crew in our WIPslack, for all the support, friendship and willingness to listen, especially in the early days.

A big thank you to Writers SA. It's quite something to be seen as an author when you can barely see it yourself. A little extra special nod to Dave who simply said, 'You could write a whole book, you know'. Like it wasn't the most mind-shattering thing anyone had ever said to me. A hat tip to the Fiction Feedback crew, especially the erudite Kevin O'Brien and Julie Collins (your story of a late night, bus-stop-missing read of those early chapters still makes me smile).

Another big thank you to Sumudu Narayana, my editor for the final revision. Her empathy and professionalism were extraordinary. [Ed's note from R A: This book's first version had a compile error that introduced spaces after many closing quotes. They weren't in my main final proof or in our final draft. So. Apologies to those early readers, and thanks Sumudu for such a fine manuscript.] Lastly, a big shout-out to the cover artist and magnificent local goth, my old friend, Brent Leideritz. How you could see inside my head, I'll never know. Amazing.

Indeed, all of you were amazing. Thank you, one and all.

P.S. Gnu Terry Pratchett. Because I can.

ABOUT THE AUTHOR

R A Wodecki

By day, R A Wodecki is an editor and online writer with a deep and unending love of plain English.

By night, she releases her more fantastic, weird and gothic words. If she didn't, they would just creep out on their own.

She lives with her loving husband, Victor, and their cat, Franklin, who is surely a dragon.

She owns her own sword and knows how to wield it. She's also quite fond of a castle or two.

www.ingramcontent.com/pod-product-compliance
Lightning Source LLC
Chambersburg PA
CBHW060223030726
47499CB00004B/1169